A JESSICA FAIRLING NOVEL

DECODING Jessica

AMBER DE TORFINO

Published 2024, by Bibliobean Books
PO Box 162
Franklinton, NC 27525
bibliobeanbooks.com

ISBN (paperback): 979-8-9911876-0-2 &
979-8-9911876-3-3
ISBN (e-book): 979-8-9911876-1-9
ISBN (Kindle): 979-8-9911876-2-6
Fiction/Thriller/Suspense

Written by Amber De Torfino
Cover Design by BLAC
Editing and Proofreading by Sarah Wentworth

This is a work of fiction. All characters, organizations, and events portrayed in this novel are products of the author's imagination or are used fictitiously.

For anyone who has ever tried to find themselves in the dark.

"Even a bad cup of coffee is better than no coffee at all." -

David Lynch

CHAPTER ONE

The Body

The stench of decaying flesh reaches my nostrils, instantly making me regret the decision to crouch down to get a better look at the corpse. Her cold cerulean eyes stare blankly up, as if mocking me. My own eyes trace a path down the slack features of her once beautiful face, stopping to inspect the vacant hole in her chest cavity where the heart should be. My stomach clenches as I battle to keep my meager breakfast bar and coffee in place.

Mercifully, a gentle breeze picks up, easing the sour smell. It blows strands of perfectly highlighted blond hair across her face. Instinctively, I reach out to brush them back, but think better of it at the last moment, instead fisting my latex gloved hand above the lifeless body. Exhaling what's left of the stench from my nostrils, I stand and tuck my well-worn notepad into the back pocket of my slacks. I turn to face the approaching chief of detectives, Gary Harding.

"Good morning, Chief," I say, smoothing my chestnut hair down from the wind before twisting it behind my neck and forcing it to tumble between my shoulder blades. Once he's standing next to me, I offer him the information he came for. "Based on what I can see here..." I gesture back to the cooling corpse; his slight grimace tells me he's already seen it. "I believe we're looking at the work of the same killer."

Making sure to breathe in shallow breaths, I do my best to calm my rioting stomach while watching for his reaction. The crease across his forehead deepens, his eyes slightly widen, and his nostrils flare in response.

"I was afraid that's what you would say, Detective Fairling." He sighs, smoothing his face back into the cold mask he always wears with the public.

He offers a grunt of appreciation to me before he turns and leaves the protection the yellow police tape provides. His trajectory takes him toward a large swath of press agents, eagerly waiting on the other side for a statement. Better him than me, I think.

He's a liar. His reaction to my statement told me he wasn't expecting me to say that, or maybe he was just hopeful it wasn't the same killer. Either way, I know I'm right; it's the same killer. I turn back to take one last look at the 'Jane Doe' lying on the pavement next to the Bean Scene coffee shop on 7th Ave and West 35th St. Some niggling thing inside trying to tell me I should feel something other than excitement, something other than the thrill of a good hunt, but I learned a long time ago, I'm just not wired that way.

At a young age, my adoptive sister Sarah and I learned I didn't have the same range of emotions other children did. When they would cry and throw a tantrum about going to school on the first day, I would walk off without a backward glance. This would, without fail, cause my adoptive mother to ugly cry. By ugly cry, I mean big fat tears, snot streaming, blubbering ugly cry. Sarah was always embarrassed by this excessive show of emotion, but I would just continue on to see what sort of books and toys awaited in our latest classroom. When I was punished by the teacher for not sharing these books and toys with the other children, instead of crying due to disappointing her, or fear of reprimand, I would simply stare at her with a blank expression.

As we got older, Sarah was the one who decided it was her duty to teach me how to "feel" those things, or rather how to fake that I could feel them. Every day after school, we would run off into the woods behind our childhood home, where she would set up little scenarios of our classroom with sticks and rocks. I would pretend to be the teacher, and she would pretend to be me. She did her best to teach me what faces I should make and what my body language should show when I was supposed to feel certain emotions. By the time we started fifth grade, I was able to fake most of the emotions the children around me could actually feel, and no one was the wiser. However, this age is a big turning point in any child's life; this is when you move into your teenage years. By thirteen Sarah was boy-crazed, obsessed, if you will. Every notebook she had was covered in hearts around scribbled initials, *SF & MH*, Sarah Fairling and Matthew Hartford.

Matthew Hartford was a boy who grew up in our neighborhood. He was two years older than us and the most popular boy in school. By the time we graduated high school and were supposed to be looking into college, Sarah was busy getting engaged to, none other than, Matthew Hartford. They were high school sweethearts, and as far as I could tell from what she had taught me, they were completely in love with each other.

When I was graduating from the police academy, Sarah was giving birth to her son, Aaron. She never did go to college, much to our father's dismay. Sarah knew from a very young age the thing she was meant to be was a mom. I mean, she practically raised me even though we were the same age, so she was probably relieved about having a normal child with a full range of emotions, not just anger and blind rage like I did.

That was eight years ago, eight years of being a wife, mother, sister, and daughter. It seems like it should be so unfair that she's now lying on the ground in front of a coffee shop on the corner of 7th Ave and West 35th St, staring blankly at the sky overhead while the clouds gather for an afternoon thunderstorm. If I could feel more complex emotions, I'm sure I would be feeling them all at this moment. I've watched enough crime dramas to know right now I should be kneeling on the ground next to her body, cursing the stars, screaming for justice while crying wildly. But as I already said, I'm just not wired that way.

****

Jolting awake, I sit up slowly in my bed. The early morning sun streams through the small solitary bedroom window of my apartment, causing me to blink rapidly. I do my best to adjust to having my eyes open so early on a Saturday, when I should still be asleep enjoying my one day off for the week. A loud knock on the door echoes its way through the tiny apartment, which must be what woke me. Shuffling from the bed, I throw on my flamingo pink fuzzy robe with matching slippers. I cross through the meager living room and pull the front door open without checking the peephole. An inconvenient side effect of having no emotions, I don't register when I should be afraid of things like opening the front door to an unknown visitor when living alone.

The door clangs open, leaving me standing in front of a scowling chief of detectives. His imposing uniformed frame towers over my not so imposing fuzzy pink robed frame. One look at his face tells me, if I had the ability to feel fear, that's what I would be feeling at this moment. But since I don't, I shrug my shoulders and step to the side, motioning him to come inside.

"Morning, Chief," I say to his back. He swiftly enters my cramped apartment without saying a single word, making a beeline to my small kitchen. He lets out a grunt of dissatisfaction, most likely due to the lack of coffee. "I haven't quite gotten to that yet." I strain to keep my voice in check. I don't do it to save his feelings. I do it in the hopes of keeping this visit brief, so I can go back to bed. He already appears to be frustrated this morning, and my commentary on his rudeness would only add fuel to that fire and most likely prolong his visit. Instead, I do my best to be accommodating and move things along. "If you'd like, I'd be happy to start a pot while you tell me what it is that brings you by so early on my day off." I add the last part to subtly remind him, if he didn't already know, what today is.

He grunts in my general direction and exits the kitchen, making his way back to my living room. I assume that means he does want coffee, and I go to the kitchen to make a pot. He snatches up the daily papers I have neatly collected on the corner seat of the couch and tosses them haphazardly on the coffee table. I can feel my eye twitch while watching him drop his large, booted feet heavily on top of them. The scowl returns to his face before he points a finger at me, stopping my progression.

"You could have warned me, Jessica," he all but growls out.

Interestingly, he's addressing me by my first name, letting me know he's here for a personal discussion. I watch him from the corner of my eye while scooping the ground coffee into the coffee machine. I don't respond since it's not a question. He's not wrong. I could have warned him, but I chose not to. His head falls back to stare at the ceiling, probably hoping to find some patience up there, or maybe some answers. I don't think he finds either because his face is still stern with a frown present when he looks over to where I'm making coffee in the kitchen.

"Your sister... that was your own sister?" His voice is much calmer now, even if his face isn't.

"Adoptive sister," I correct him. I press the start button on the coffee maker and walk back to the living room. The look he gives stalls me to a stop halfway across the room. "I was adopted." I tack on at the end, barely loud enough for him to hear, knowing it doesn't make any bit of difference.

Sighing heavily, he puts his feet back where they belong, on the floor. "Fairling, I have cut you a lot of slack over the years due to your..." He pauses to look around my cramped living room, eying the bookshelf as if the correct words are going to pop out of one of the many best-selling crime novels for him. "Affliction," he finally spits out. His eyes swing back to mine, and I can't help that my eyebrow climbs up my forehead in amusement at his struggle. "But you know I can't, in good conscience, keep you on this case knowing you're related to the victim."

I notice he's gone back to addressing me by my last name, meaning he's all business now. I knew this was coming; it's why I didn't scream from the rooftops that the corpse the poor, unsuspecting coffee shop employees found was my sister, Sarah. Adopted or not, she is still my family member and that causes a conflict of interest for the department.

"Completely understandable, sir," I say. I do my best to muster the smile that seems to put normal people at ease. Sarah always said my mouth's smile should also make my eyes smile, whatever that means. All I know is if I crinkle my eyes a little, like I'm squinting into the sun at the same time I smile, people relax a little more. It must work, because he breathes a sigh of relief, believing I've conceded to his request.

"Good, I'm glad we're on the same page with this," he says, before I quickly shatter his relief with a heavy dose of reality.

"However, I must insist I remain on the other cases. You know damn well I'm the most qualified detective on the squad to catch this killer due to my, as you call it, affliction." I hold up air quotes for the last word. "Aside from that, I've been on this case since the beginning, which means I know each crime scene more intimately than anyone else involved. Ultimately, my affliction makes me your best option to put an end to this." I don't bother with air quotes this time, instead probing him with an intense stare.

His face sags a little at the forced revelation, showing me how tired he is. For the better part of two years, our department has been one step behind a killer terrorizing the women of New York City with gruesome violence. Each killing is made to look as if an animal attacked the women in the middle of a city. As if we have mountain lions or bears in New York City. Cue an eye roll. This killer is clearly goading us, reveling in the fact they are a step ahead of us while we have been standing around scratching our heads.

The coffee pot emits a high-pitched beep to let me know it's finished, and I walk back to the kitchen, leaving him on my couch, most likely trying to figure out a way to convince me why I should give up this case. Fat chance of that; I quietly snort a laugh at the thought.

He thinks I want to remain on this case to further my career as a detective and now to catch my sister's killer. Truth be told, I just want to meet the monster who's given me such good chase for the last two years. In my relatively short time on the force, I've put away many killers, a lot of really bad people that have committed heinous crimes. For someone like me, it's pretty simple: I just have to think about what I'd do if I was the one who committed the murders, where I'd go, and how I'd cover it up. More times than not, we would do the same thing, but this one is different. This one switches it up every time, making them different enough that it's hard to link the murders together as having one killer. I'm of the opinion that if we were anywhere but a big city, these murders wouldn't have even been linked together. The only reason they have been is because we don't have any big game or large wildlife that lives in the middle of New York City, and a raccoon isn't taking off the arm of a full-grown adult.

I return to the living room with two steaming cups of coffee and hand him one. He takes a long, deep drink and makes appreciative noises while I take a seat in the chair opposite his place on the couch. I don't buy cheap coffee, so it's probably a welcome change from the swill that passes for coffee at the precinct. Placing my cup onto a coaster on the coffee table, I slide my gaze to his and offer a solution to our problem.

"What if we don't release a statement that this murder is thought to be related to the others? What if we say we need a little more time to process the evidence before we make that call?" His salt and peppered bushy eyebrows climb his face as he watches me over the rim of his still steaming cup. "Just for now. Obviously, once the medical examiner gets to analyze the body…" I leave the rest unsaid because we both know with certainty this murder is connected to the others. He flinches, assuming my reason for not completing that thought is my sister's murder. It's not. He gives me a guarded look, no doubt waiting for me to lose my shit. Instead, I finish my train of thought to fill the awkward silence. "They will reach the same conclusion as they did with the other four victims: this is not an animal causing these wounds. It's another brutalization made to look like an animal attack."

Sighing, he places his now empty cup directly on the coffee table, just inches shy of the coaster I've laid out for him. My eye twitches again. "Listen Fairling, I know you're not like the rest of us. Hell, for all I know, I might be the only one who knows you aren't like the rest of us. But what you're asking, it's just..." He trails off, looking out the window of my living room, at the brick wall of the neighboring apartment building. "I'll have to think about this one." He turns his soft brown eyes back to me, concern shining brightly in them. "Give me until tomorrow. Come see me in my office at the start of your shift; we can revisit this. I can't promise anything, but maybe I'll have a better idea on what we can work out."

He stands to leave, carefully watching me for any sign of emotion I might show, but finds none. I accompany him to the front door and open it. He walks out and turns to face me in the hallway with a sympathetic smile.

"Well, if I ever had any doubt that you really are different than the rest of us, this visit has put that to rest."

Before I can respond, he turns down the hallway and walks to the elevator without a backwards glance.

CHAPTER TWO

A New Threat

Sunday morning in the precinct is quieter than usual; I walk past empty desks further inside before I figure out why. A swath of detectives has congregated outside of Chief Harding's closed office door, obscuring my view of who, if anyone, is inside with him. My curiosity has me pushing through the throng of people until I finally get a glimpse of Mayor Chaplain. She's perched on the edge of her chair, scowling, and watching Chief Harding read over some document she's no doubt given him.

As if he can feel my gaze on him, his head lifts, eyes snapping to mine, and he waves me to join them. Pushing the remaining people out of the way, I squeeze past them into his office, leaving the three of us in a very silent room. Shaking his head, he passes me the paper in his hand without saying a word. Whatever's in the letter must be bad. My eyes rove over it, soaking in the contents. It contains information on not only the previous five murders, with details only the killer or an accomplice would know, but also outlines three more murders that have yet to happen. There are not enough details to stop them, of course, but enough detail to give us a glimpse of what we can expect. I place the letter on the desk and give my attention to him, waiting to hear what he has to say. He instead nods to Mayor Chaplain.

"Detective Fairling, I hear this is your case," she says, pausing to watch me. My mind churns with all the directions she could be heading after that statement; somehow, I manage to remain quiet as I wait for her to continue. "I also hear from Chief Harding that the last murder victim was awfully close to you." She narrows her small blue eyes at me, and a chill creeps up my spine from their intensity. She may be slight in stature, but she is well known to be ruthless with her power, and not many people dare to cross her; I can see why. I fully expect her next words to be something along the lines of, 'We regret to inform you that you are off this case; you can kiss your cat-and-mouse game goodbye.' But she instead surprises me with something completely unexpected. "He also tells me you are the best shot we have of putting this asshole away. So, I am willing to pull as many strings as I can to keep that relationship under wraps for as long as possible, giving you a chance to do your job, and close this case. My best guess is you'll have about two weeks until the press is able to claw, bite, or bribe their way to that knowledge. At which point, I won't have a choice but to remove you from the case." I can feel a chilling smile begin to creep across my lips. "Don't let me down, Detective," she says, eyes narrowing briefly at me. She turns to shake hands with Chief Harding and exits his office.

Pleased by the unexpected turn of events, I genuinely smile at the chief. He winks at me and then waves me out his door. My excitement is palpable; I feel like a kid on Christmas morning. I know two weeks isn't a lot of time to catch a serial killer who has evaded an entire police force for the better part of two years, but not having a wide range of emotions has a way of making one cocky.

My first step, I decide, will be revisiting the case files. Just shy of two years ago, the first victim, Lisa Louise Tinselman, was discovered face down near a dumpster in the alleyway behind a small local bookstore she frequented. Her right arm was nothing but bone from the wrist to the shoulder. Her body was discovered by a couple of sanitation workers in the early morning hours of June 23rd. The edges of the wounds resembled what flesh would look like if a large animal with sharp teeth were to take a bite of it, leading to the original theory that this was the work of an escaped predator from the nearby zoo. The murder was fresh enough that the blood on the pavement had not completely congealed, and rigor mortis had yet to set in. However, once the medical examiner had some time to inspect the wounds, he concluded that this was, in fact, not done by a large animal but rather by a person. They most likely used a serrated tool to make it look like bite wounds from a large animal in an attempt to lead us astray.

The next victim, Claire Marie Sanders, was found on the sidewalk in a local park by a pair of unfortunate early-morning joggers. That was in mid-September of the same year, and her left leg was removed at the knee. Crime scene technicians later found the missing leg in the grass just twenty feet or so from the body. Again, the wound edges appeared as if something with large teeth was doing the cutting, but after closer inspection, it was concluded by the medical examiner that, just like in the first case, this was an imitation of an animal bite.

On January 5th of the following year, behind a small grocery store, the body of Nicole Elaine Blair was discovered by a homeless woman in the early evening hours. Her throat was torn out and the wound edges matched those found on the previous two victims—the exception being her body was cleaned afterward, almost as if the killer felt some sort of remorse for the mess they made, or maybe they were concerned they left some evidence. Whatever the reasoning was, someone took the time to wash this victim down with a peroxide and water mix. The mix destroyed any evidence that may have been left behind, while also contaminating any blood samples that would be taken from the body. If that wasn't enough, her body was then fully dressed before being moved from the original murder site and placed just out of camera view behind the grocery store. This was the case that confirmed what the medical examiner was saying all along: there was absolutely no way these killings were the work of a wild or zoo animal that had somehow gotten loose and was never reported. Animals don't clean their prey, and they certainly don't dress them in jeans and pink polo shirts before dumping them behind grocery stores. The animal attack theory was finally put to rest.

On March 1st, Samantha Jane Pritchard was found, her abdomen torn open with multiple vital organs removed and scattered nearby, all left in the location where she was killed. The medical examiner confirmed this due to the ample amount of blood present under and around the body, and the uncharacteristic mess at the scene led to the belief that the killer was disturbed before they could finish whatever they were doing to her.

The latest, but by no means final victim, if the letter sent to the mayor is to be believed, is my adoptive sister, Sarah Renee Hartford. Found in the early morning hours of April 3rd, her chest cavity was cracked open by someone, or something large enough to pull it apart like a turkey on Thanksgiving Day. The heart was removed but not recovered from the scene, the theory being that the killer took it as a trophy. Sarah's body was wiped down, cleaning the majority of blood off, before she was left lying face up next to the side door of a busy downtown coffee shop.

If we go by the letter the mayor received, then we can expect three more dead bodies. I would be lying if I said I wasn't curious to see what our murderous friend had in mind for his next victims—excited even. Each new murder has been slightly more depraved than the last, telling me the killer is escalating. However, as the mayor has reminded me, the press is now on my trail, giving me about two weeks until my relation to Sarah is released. Once that happens, the public will cry out to have me removed as the lead detective on this case. That doesn't leave me very much time.

****

The following morning, I arrive at the precinct early. My plan is to go over the case files once more with the hopes of uncovering something that was missed. Pretending as if it's the first time, I study the crime scene photos closely, and comb through the medical examiner's reports. A loud growl echoes through my otherwise silent office, my stomach letting me know it's lunchtime.

I've already been over each of the case files two more times. I've even plotted out on a map the places each body was found; then, I stared at that map, willing it to show me something new until my eyes began to cross from exhaustion. Much to my frustration, I realize the case files haven't revealed anything new. I grunt at the useless documents. I need to step away for a break to eat something and calm my inner turbulence.

Reheating last night's left-over chicken and rice in the small break room microwave, I let my mind wander back to the case information, convinced there has to be something I'm missing. I go back to the basics, mentally checking off the things we are trained to look for when hunting a serial killer. No celestial events on or around the dates of the murders, no major, or minor holidays. Hell, I couldn't even find any major news events. Not to mention the most frustrating part: there's seemingly nothing to tie the victims together. A thorough check into their personal lives showed they don't share the same hairdresser, yoga class, book club, or art studio. I'm running out of possible links for them; my nostrils flare, and my anger surges.

The sound of a throat clearing nearby causes my head to snap up. Blinking slowly, I retreat from my thoughts. My eyes scan the small break room before focusing on Janice, the front desk receptionist, a very kind woman of about sixty. She's standing in the doorway, staring at something in front of me in abject horror. My eyes track down to my plate to find that, while lost in my thoughts, I have not only peeled all the chicken's meat from its bones and piled it in a large heap on the corner of my plate, but I've placed the bones in the crude shape of a body. If I squint hard enough, I can just see the overlay of the memory of my sister's body lying on the cold cement next to the coffee shop not two days ago. Add the bright red ketchup I've mindlessly smeared the bones around in, and you have a small plated horror show.

Shit, shit, shit. I do my best to offer her my kindest smile, remembering to squint my eyes the way Sarah taught me, hoping to put Janice at ease, or at the very least, keep her eyes from my plate. It must work because her eyes do leave my plate and make their way around the break room. I follow her gaze as she studies the stainless-steel refrigerator, the small black microwave with the clock that's blinked 12:12 for as long as I've worked here, all while wringing her hands in front of her. Shifting awkwardly on her feet, her stare tracks from the microwave back to the refrigerator, to the small window on the far wall. Anywhere but on me and my murder plate. Finally, her gaze does make its way up to my face and she clears her throat again.

"I'm really sorry, Jessica," she says.

Her voice comes out much softer than I expected and makes me want to flinch at the sadness riding on the words. I'm silent for a moment longer than appropriate while I wrack my brain for why she would be sorry about walking into the break room and catching me doing something a normal person would think of as grotesque. Then it hits me: she's referring to Sarah. I cringe because that means word is getting out faster than we thought it would. Which also means I don't have much time left until I get pulled from this case. My heart speeds up as the realization washes over me that I may not even have the full two weeks the mayor thought I would. Shit, shit, shit, this is no good.

I finally bring my eyes up to meet Janice's. Maybe this isn't as bad as I think; this isn't the first time she's seen me do something strange like this. Hopefully she'll gloss over this like the time she found me grinning from ear to ear while reviewing photos of a particularly gruesome crime scene. I was appreciating the way the killer remembered not only to wipe down the murder weapon but also to spray down the surfaces they may have touched with chemicals, destroying any DNA we may have recovered, and baffling everyone on the case when she found me. I explained when things are exceptionally awful and grotesque, I smile as a coping mechanism, an excuse I'd seen someone use on a courtroom TV show. She seemed to buy it because she never mentioned the incident again. Her smile begins to falter as she's waiting for me to react to the reminder that my sister is dead. Fuck, is this where I'm supposed to cry?

"Afternoon ladies." A gruff voice interrupts the awkward encounter.

Detective Carlos Osborne strolls into the break room for some coffee without making eye contact with either of us. Mercifully, he doesn't even glance at my macabre lunch setup. I use the distraction his arrival causes to start moving the bones to the side of my plate and the actual meat to the middle to be eaten.

"Afternoon, Osborne," I say, my gaze shifting to his back where he's messing with the coffee machine.

Janice must take this as a cue that I don't want this information shared because she plasters what appears to be a fake smile onto her face and turns to the fridge to retrieve her salad.

"Detective Fairling, if you need anything, I'll just be up front," she offers, giving me another kind smile before leaving the break room, followed shortly after by Detective Osborne.

I let out a sigh of relief at their departures and return my attention to my lunch. I spend the next few minutes scarfing down the chicken as quickly as possible without choking on it, hoping to avoid another awkward break room encounter.

Darkness settles outside the precinct doors. I pack the case files into my shoulder bag, stopping to rub my burning eyes, tired from staring at the same documents over and over all day.

"Fairling, I'm sorry to hear about your sister." Detective Osborne's voice startles me. I spin around to find him standing a few feet behind me, another coffee in hand, leaning against the wall. "I lost my brother when we were teenagers to a drunk driver. I understand how rough it is to lose a sibling at the hands of an asshole."

He stares off into the distance, his haunted eyes glossing over. He's lost in some horrific memory, and I do my best to smooth the anger from my face for being startled so easily. I guess I was wrong to hope Janice could keep her mouth shut about Sarah.

"Thanks, Osborne." I mutter in his direction.

Unsure of what else to do, I turn and continue packing the case files, struggling with something to say beyond that. His penetrating gaze feels like a physical touch on my back as he watches me from his perch against the wall. I turn off the desk lamp and grab my keys, slinging my bag onto my shoulder. I turn to look at him, since he's standing in my doorway blocking my exit. The look on his face seems to say, 'I see you and understand your need for distance here'. Thankful for that, I offer him a solemn nod, which he returns. He finally steps out of the doorway, allowing me to pass. Once I have the front doors of the precinct in my sight, I send up a silent prayer of thanks that male coworkers are more tolerant of my lack of outward emotions.

I thank whatever fates are watching out for me while I pass the empty reception desk at the front of the precinct that Janice has left for the day. I don't think I could successfully navigate another awkward encounter today. All I want is to pick up a to-go order from my favorite Chinese food spot, the Lemon Wok, and get home to my fuzzy robe. The fact that nothing came from all my reviewing of the case files today doesn't surprise me. I was thorough the first time I dug into each victim's life. I'm not being cocky, just honest with myself.

CHAPTER THREE
Late Night Stroll

Before I make my way to the precinct this morning, I decide to make a stop at the medical examiner's office. Inside, I find Dr. Frank Lenova, a portly man of about five foot nine inches dressed in a white lab coat, hunched over what appears to be a severely burned corpse.

I gently rap my knuckles against the glass window separating the hallway from the exam room, getting his attention. He looks up, blinking rapidly before he remembers that he's wearing a pair of high-magnification glasses, causing me to chuckle. Using his gloved hand, which unfortunately is covered in charred remnants from the corpse, he removes the glasses and places them to rest on top of his head, smearing the charred bits into his combed-over black hair. My hand raises to try to tell him, but I realize it's too late now, and let it flop back down to my side.

"Detective Fairling," he says. At least that's what I think he says; I have to read his lips due to the soundproof glass separating us. He waves for me to join him in the exam room.

Opening the door, the overwhelming smell of burnt flesh hits my nostrils and my eyes instantly begin to water. Frank points to something on the wall next to the door, I turn to find a box of face masks, and quickly slip one on.

"Good morning, Frank," I say, sidling up to his side, and look at the corpse he's working on. "I was hoping you had some time today to talk to me about the not-so animal, animal attacks?" I tear my eyes away from the remains to see he's put his glasses back on, and he's back to digging in the neck of the corpse on his table.

"For you, I'll make time." He smiles without looking up; how he can work on this particular corpse without wearing a mask is beyond me.

Frank is one of the few people who's easy for me to be around. He doesn't seem to judge anyone beyond their outer layer, which leaves me, and my inner darkness, feeling safe from prying eyes. I don't think he's like me, though; I think he's just able to disassociate himself from his work.

"I have an hour for lunch today starting at 11:30, does that work for you?" he asks, still digging in the corpse.

"That's perfect for me, Frank. Would you like the usual bourbon chicken with pork fried rice and a side of crab rangoons?" I smile, knowing that in the five years I've been working with Frank, he's never ordered anything else from the Lemon Wok, the same place I picked my dinner up from last night.

"I think that would be lovely, Jessica. I'll see you soon." He still doesn't look up from his work.

I manage to make my way through the hall and all the way to the front door before removing the mask from my face. I know it's futile to hope the smell of charred flesh isn't going to remain on me all day, but I send up a silent prayer for it, anyway. Outside, I finally suck in a full breath, but I know once that smell has permeated into your hair and the fabrics of your clothes, it's staying with you until you take a shower.

After an uneventful hour at the precinct, I place our to-go order and pick it up from the restaurant before I walk back to the medical examiner's office. I glide past the exam room, where I glimpse the body Frank was working on this morning still laying on the exam table. I walk all the way to the end of the hallway into Frank's office to find him waiting.

"Have you been able to link any of our victims?" he asks, as I hand over his food and a pair of wooden chopsticks.

The question causes me to huff a sigh of frustration before I admit defeat. "No, I haven't been able to find anything that links the women together."

"I didn't think so," he replies. My eyebrow arches and he shakes his head. I place my boxes of food down on the desk as I sit and wait for him to elaborate on why he thinks that. He looks up at me and stills his hands from mixing his food. "There's something that's been bothering me about these cases." His comment doesn't surprise me because I agree with him. I gesture for him to continue. "Each victim has what appears to be animal bites taken out of them, but each wound has different enough edges that if I were to say it was an animal bite, I would say it was a different type of animal attacking each person. If I were a killer trying to cover my tracks, I would make them all look as similar as possible, alluding to only one animal, since that would be more plausible in a large city." He continues with his food while I ponder his reasoning.

After inspecting the wounds of the first three victims, I came to a similar conclusion. If we were to go with the animal attack theory, then after the second victim, it would have been passed off as a pack of animals, but the third victim being cleaned and dressed blew that theory apart. After her, the animal attack theory was no longer entertained by anyone working on the case. Since no one has been able to confirm what sort of weapon was used, we have been dead in the water, hoping for new evidence to come from Sarah's reports. Since being wrong is one of the things I like least, I've kept my theories to myself, until now.

"Frank, have you tested the wounds on the first two victims for human saliva or any sort of DNA?" I only ask because it's Frank; I know he'll take me seriously when other medical examiners would immediately shoot me down just because I am a detective, but Frank actually respects my input.

He pauses to churn my idea around before responding. "Well, I did have a few swabs sent out to toxicology for any sort of drugs and the like, but not DNA testing, no. Why, what are you thinking?" he asks, eyeing me curiously.

"What if the wounds are not from a tool but from human teeth?"

Initially shaking his head no, he pauses to stare out his small window overlooking the parking lot. I watch his fingers drum the desk to a beat that only lives inside his head, waiting for his response.

"I know an odontologist I can confer with on this. I'll give you a call once I have an answer for you," he finally replies, standing abruptly and nearly knocking his chair over behind him. Without another word, he exits his office without a backward glance, leaving me alone to pack up my mostly empty lunch containers. I hum to myself as I take my leave and try not to get too excited that we might finally uncover something new in this case. I guess my theory wasn't so far-fetched after all.

The precinct is bustling with its usual activity for a Tuesday afternoon when I return and make my way into Chief Harding's office to let him know what I've found. After I tell him that I've actually found close to nothing new and we need to wait for toxicology to come in from the latest victim, he finally looks up from the newspaper he's reading on his desk to frown at me before he goes back to reading. I turn to leave his office, figuring that must mean we are done.

"It looks like the press is close to figuring out the identity of the last victim; I don't think I have to tell you what that means," he says, folding the paper into a neat pile on his desk. He eyes me where I stand in his doorway.

"Shit," I grind out, letting my head fall backward and

staring at his ceiling. "Frank is doing another check on the evidence from the victim's bodies to see if anything has been missed." I decide to leave out my speculation of the bites being from a human until we have some sort of confirmation. "I'm going to take the rest of the afternoon to revisit the first two crime scenes, ask around, and see if anyone can remember anything new." He mumbles his agreement to my back as I depart his office.

****

The city is unusually warm for this time of year, causing more people to use their cars, taxis, or public transport, and clogging up the streets more than normal, delaying my progression to the first crime scene. I park my car down the alley where the first victim's body was found, and I notice a camera pointing to the spot where the body was. Too little too late, I think, making my way into the shop, and up to the front counter.

"Hi, good afternoon, I'm Detective Fairling," I say, flashing my badge to the woman staffing the cash register.

"I remember." She gives me what passes for a sad smile, folding her hands on the counter in front of her. "Do you have an update on what happened to Lisa?" The look she gives me isn't hopeful; after all, this is New York City, and we probably see more unsolved crimes per year than most other cities get in five.

"We're working on it," I say, doing my best to give her a disarming smile, again with the slight squinting of my eyes. "I have a few follow-up questions for you, if you have some time."

I tap my notepad on the counter, gathering my thoughts for the interview. She watches me from the corner of her eye and steps down from the counter area, waving to a young man rearranging books on a nearby shelf. She lets him know she's stepping out for a break, and we walk across the street to an open table at a small coffee bistro.

"I saw the new security camera outside the store. That was a smart idea," I say in a sad attempt at small talk. She waves down a waiter to give our coffee order.

"Yeah, the owner thought it would make us feel safer working after hours," she scoffs, eyes rolling dramatically at the absurdity of it.

"Does it?" She releases a bark of laughter in response, and a few other patrons glance over at our table.

"A woman, not just any woman, but a regular customer that we all knew, had her arm gnawed down to the bone. Then she was left to bleed out next to the shop, and my boss thinks putting up a single security camera pointing to an alley full of garbage is going to make us feel safe again?" She shakes her head, staring at me like I'm insane for asking, and when she puts it like that, I can't help but agree with her.

"I'm sorry you feel that way," I say, regretting my question. I look down at the coffee the waiter has just delivered to our table and scan the table for sugar. Not that I like sugar or creamer in my coffee, but I just feel like I'm better at acting "normal" when I have something to keep my hands busy.

"We read in the newspaper that you think this might not be animal attacks," she says, telling me that some of the information we have not released to the general public is releasing itself.

At first, I don't respond since it's a statement and not a question, but her pointed stare tells me she's expecting me to. "I'm not really at liberty to say one way or the other. I just came by today to see if you happened to remember anything from the day before or even the day of the incident that maybe you didn't report at the time of your initial interview?" I ask, taking a sip from my now over-sugared cup of coffee. I do my best not to grimace at the taste.

She shakes her head, finally drinking her own coffee before she responds. "No, I was off the day before. I had a morning appointment that lasted well into the afternoon.

I was unfortunate enough to be scheduled to work the morning she was found, but I wasn't able to make it into the shop since the road was blocked. Didn't get paid for that day, either." Her eyes give another dramatic roll. "Look, Detective, I understand this is an ongoing investigation." She holds up air quotes around the last part. "But I need to know if I should be requesting morning-only shifts or having someone walk me home at night?"

I look away, unsure how to respond. I have no concern for my own safety, opening my front door without looking through the peephole or asking who's behind it, let alone for a stranger. I shouldn't be the person answering this for her.

"We don't have any reason to believe you would need to stop working evening or night shifts, but it might not be a bad idea to have company when walking home at night or even to call a cab." I leave it at that, not wanting to panic her, but also not wanting her added to the list of victims.

She nods a bit too quickly, her eyes glossing over a little as she does. "Thank you, Detective, thank you for being honest with me," she says, standing to shake my hand. "I have to head back to the shop. I honestly don't think Ted knows how to work the cash register, and you can forget about him answering the phone. He has headphones in his ears 24/7, so he probably wouldn't even hear it." She laughs, offering a small wave before walking across the street to the shop.

"Thank you for your time," I call out to her as she retreats into the bookstore.

My visit to the second scene goes much the same way: no one has remembered anything new, and everyone has read the news, and has developed paranoia about walking around at night. The media can be a great tool in the right situation, or so I've been told; in my experience, it's only ever been a royal pain in the ass.

As the sun sets and the temperature finally starts to drop, I return the cruiser to the precinct. Then, I do what the rest of New York City appears to be afraid to do: I walk home alone in the dark.

****

The next day begins much the same—too hot to walk the streets. Unless I want to melt on my way around, I have to check out another cruiser to make it to the remaining three crime scenes. The third crime scene, where Nicole Elaine Blair was found, is a small grocery store. The inside of the store is mostly empty; I make my way up to the counter, where, peering over, I find a clerk bent down rearranging stock.

"Good morning," I say to his back, causing him to jump as he whirls around to greet me.

"Hello! Good morning. How can I assist you today?" He plasters a smile on his face and clutches his chest from being startled.

"I'm Detective Fairling." I hold up my badge for him to check. "I'm heading up the Nicole Blair case and was wondering if..." I pause to check my notepad and make sure I'm asking for the right person. "Charles St Clair is available?"

He nods sharply, maneuvering himself around the counter to lead me into the back stock room.

"Charles, there's a detective here to see you about the dead body they found behind the store," he shouts inside the slightly opened door, shooting me a grin.

"Morning, Detective," Charles says, emerging from the doorway. He greets me with a handshake and rolls his eyes at his employee for the crass comment.

I briefly refresh his memory with the basics of the case that I have jotted down before asking if he has remembered anything new that could possibly assist with the case. He assures me he hasn't, and he has nothing unusual to report except that there's a lot less business now that the body of a young woman has been found with her throat ripped out behind his store. He should be thankful the media hasn't received the tidbit about her being bathed clean and then dressed like a macabre doll before being dumped there. After a few more questions and no new information, I depart the small grocery store, leaving Charles to his cramped stock room and snarky counter employee. My visits to the remaining two crime scenes end in much the same way, with more questions about the safety of employees after dark at the local businesses, and even more questions about the ongoing cases that I just can't answer for them.

Frustrated by my lack of progress, I deliver the cruiser back to the precinct, and again walk back to my apartment building. First, I make a detour to the Lemon Wok to pick up some dinner to go.

CHAPTER FOUR
Partners

Cole

The clock on my office wall tells me it's past seven p.m.; grading these exams is taking longer than I anticipated. Even if I leave right now and go directly home, by the time I cook something, it will be past nine. Normally, I wouldn't give a shit how late I eat; except tomorrow, I have an early meeting with the chief of detectives and the mayor at the precinct that I need to have a clear mind for. There's a Chinese food place I'll pass on my walk home that I've been meaning to try anyway, and I can finish grading papers, and go over the notes I've collected for the meeting tomorrow while I eat there. As a Professor of Forensic Psychology with a focus on criminal profiling, it's not unusual to be consulted on a high-profile case like this. Usually, it's a last-ditch effort before the FBI swoops in, resulting in the loss of the case for the local PD, which, as I understand, they hate.

The inside of the restaurant consists of a counter to place your order and two small bistro tables that claim to seat four people, but I struggle to see that with how small the tables are. I unpack my files on the small table in the corner, where I have a clear view of the front door, settling in with my soup. An appreciative hum slips past my lips on the first bite; the wontons are perfect.

A young woman in her mid-twenties with long chestnut hair cascading down her back in a low ponytail enters the restaurant, stealing my attention from the papers I'm grading. I watch her while she orders at the small counter, and I can feel her nervous energy bouncing around the small space. I continue to sip on the broth of my soup, an electric feeling causing the hairs on my arms to stand up and a shiver to make its way down my spine. I continue to watch her from the corner of my eye, sipping the broth and almost spilling it down my front when she brazenly settles into the seat across from mine at the small table.

"Hi," I manage to croak out, doing my best to not choke on the large gulp of soup.

Her wide, bright green eyes swing to mine, the surprise in them evident. The adorable smattering of freckles sprinkled across her nose stand out like beacons against the pink flush coloring her cheeks. My eyes draw to the small wispy hairs rebelliously poking out from her ponytail, framing her face, and reflecting the fluorescent overhead lighting, creating an ethereal glow.

"Hi, I'm sorry—I wasn't paying attention to my surroundings, too wrapped up in my own head tonight," she says, nervously surveying the rest of the room as if expecting someone else to be here.

The restaurant is so small that I don't even have to move my head to see that there's only us in here. The possibility she was expecting someone else in my place induces a pang of jealousy. To stop myself from scowling, I put another wonton in my mouth, and examine her for any clues that she was waiting for a date. The green flannel shirt she has tucked into her well-worn black jeans, very scuffed ankle boots, and shoulder bag bursting at the seams from the amount of paperwork she has shoved into it leads me to believe she isn't.

"I've never seen you here," she says, cocking her head to the side and giving me a questioning stare. My eyebrow tilts up in question, before she continues. "I'm in here at least two nights a week, sometimes three, if my schedule is crazy enough."

A nervous chuckle escapes her lips, drawing my eyes to

them. She sticks the side of her thumbnail between her teeth, nervously chewing on it. I force my eyes away from her mouth and back to her eyes before I respond.

"I usually only make it out to dinner once a month. I like to cook, and my schedule usually affords me the time to do so."

"Oh," she says. The owner of the restaurant brings out a plate of food to her while grinning from ear to ear. "This was a to go order..." The anxious girl in front of me squeaks out to the owner's retreating back, who pretends not to hear the protests, and continues shuffling back to the kitchen.

I manage to cover my chuckle with a cough. "I guess you're eating in," I say, and I swear her left eye just twitched.

"I guess I am," she says, squaring her shoulders and sitting up straighter in her chair. She gives me a smile that lights up her entire face, causing my outward breath to get stuck.

For the next half hour, we discuss my profession as a Professor of Forensic Psychology, which then leads into the recent murder that has been all over the news and I find myself holding back on sharing that I have a meeting tomorrow morning about consulting on them. I justify that to myself with the excuse that I'm still not sure if I'm going to participate and not because I think I don't have anything to offer them. I only agreed to go down to the station to meet with the lead detective on the case to let them decide if they think my work can be of assistance with the case.

My curriculum focuses mainly on profiling serial killers. Well, not really profiling them, but teaching people how to profile them, and teaching new agents the right questions to ask. I have taught some of the top profilers in the country and have assisted on a few cases in the past, but the bulk of my work has been writing books on the subject.

Bringing our plates up to the counter, I thank the owner with a generous tip. After all, I wouldn't have had such a nice dinner with a beautiful woman if it hadn't been for her oversight, which, judging by her mischievous smile, was, in fact, on purpose.

Outside, I offer to walk my dinner companion home, not wanting the evening to end so quickly. "May I walk you to your building? I hear that there are some wild animals loose in this city, and I'd hate to read about you in the local paper," I say, offering the most panty-dropping smile I can muster, hoping she won't deny me.

She lets out the most adorable snort, which tugs at something inside of me, and causes my heart to speed up a few beats. "Sure, I'm just five blocks this way," she says, pointing toward her apartment building. We walk in comfortable silence while I sneak glances at her from the corner of my eye, and all too soon, we are standing in front of it, awkwardly staring at each other. She finally breaks the silence, gesturing to the building beside us.

"I live here, on the twelfth floor, all the way at the end of the hall in a small one-bedroom apartment with the view of a brick wall from my living room and bedroom windows," she says, eyes darting around, face flushing red from embarrassment at the over-share. Instead of laughing at her obvious discomfort, I decide to save her from herself.

"Well, it was a pleasure having dinner with you. Your company may have just convinced me to start leaving the comforts of my kitchen more than once a month, maybe even twice a week, or possibly three," I say, my lips curling upward with pleasure at the shock on her face from remembering her earlier comments on how often she ate at the Lemon Wok. "Now I know you're safe, I can safely wish you a good night." Making an overly exaggerated bow, I tack on a wink at the end, and wonder what she might do if I kissed her right now. I just met her, but damn, if I don't want to.

"That's great... about dinner, I mean," she says. The

look on her face says she wants to add more to that, but she must think better of it.

Before I can decide if it's worth risking a slap across the face for kissing her, she turns, and all but runs inside the building. I watch her long enough to ensure she makes it onto the elevator before turning to walk the rest of the way home, cursing myself the entire way for not even getting her name.

****

A glance at my wristwatch tells me it's nine am, which means I've been in the chief's office for an hour going over the details of this case, where I learn that the so-called "animal attacks" are, in fact, serial murders. I'm not surprised to learn there's no profile for the killer they are looking for, since they aren't leaving much to be discovered. I never like to share my initial ideas until I'm absolutely certain they're correct, so I keep my thoughts of this being multiple killers to myself until I can get more info on the victim's injuries. The last thing I ever want to do is look like an amateur, especially in front of Chief Gary Harding. He has a reputation for being hard to impress and even harder to get along with.

The mayor gently touches my arm and lets me know the lead detective has arrived; I turn around and my breath catches in my throat. I watch as my last night's dinner companion stalks through the precinct like she owns it. The hostility behind the look she gives me when her eyes meet mine tells me she isn't pleased with my being here. I can't say I blame her. Out of context, it must look very odd.

"Detective Fairling." The mayor calls out to her, as she beckons the detective to join us in the cramped office with an outstretched arm. She startles at the invitation, eyes darting between the mayor's and my own.

"Good morning, Detective Fairling," I say, with a smirk as she enters the small office.

I spent the majority of last night and all of this morning kicking myself that I didn't get this woman's phone number, let alone her name. Clearly, fate had other ideas, like using her to push me into consulting on this case.

"Good morning," she says, looking at both Chief Harding and Mayor Chaplain, but completely ignoring my existence.

I frown, realizing she probably thinks I was stalking her last night, doing some sort of recon on her. Once we are out of this office and no longer have an audience, I'll have to explain how it was complete happenstance that we ended up in the same restaurant last night, some sort of kismet.

"Detective, I've received a phone call from the editor of

a large local newspaper," the mayor says, raising her arms in a surrender motion. "And before you ask, no, I'm not going to divulge which newspaper to protect my contact. But they have advised that tomorrow's front-page article, of not only their newspaper but multiple others, will release the name of the most recent victim, and concurrently, her relation to you as the lead on the case." Detective Fairling's sharp intake of breath tells me this is a surprise to her; I study her face and try to piece together what that relationship could be.

"The good news is, I think we've come up with a solution to keeping you on this case as the lead detective," Chief Harding adds, pulling my attention to him.

Everything I've learned from interacting with this man has led me to the conclusion he's a no-bullshit, gruff, all-around hard ass. The last case I consulted was under his supervision, and he had me walking on eggshells the entire time. The man in front of me right now is a stranger; the tenderness in his eyes is foreign, and even his voice has gone up an octave, or two, giving it a more tender cadence than just a few minutes ago. He holds his hand out in my direction, causing me to stand a little straighter, and file all the information I just learned away to dissect later.

"Him?" Detective Fairling asks, jabbing her thumb in

my direction, voice going up in pitch. "How is he going to help me stay on this case as the lead detective?" she practically snarls, and I smile because I love her fire.

"His name is Cole Bellamy," I say, offering her my hand to shake. Almost instinctively, she puts her very small, very sweaty hand in mine, and I gently shake it. "I'm your new partner."

The mayor's eyes twinkle with delight at my agreement to join this case. "Cole is a Professor of Forensic Psychology and has more than one best-selling book out on how to profile serial killers. He spends a lot of time in the media's attention and has a knack for public speaking. I don't think I need to tell you why that's valuable. The same editor who gave me the heads up about the article coming out tomorrow has agreed to also run an article announcing you'll remain in charge of this case with him as your partner. They will add a spin to it about how there's no one on the force with more of a reason to catch this guy than you. They will also leak that story to other editors, essentially having it printed in every newspaper on the stands."

I scowl at her presumptuousness to have already set up a story to run about me as a partner on this case before I ever agreed to join. The mayor glances down at my hand, which is still clasping Detective Fairling's, causing the detective to quickly drop it before she shocks us all with her agreement to start right away. She offers no argument, and I smile broadly at the chief and mayor. They continue their conversation while the detective and I exit the office.

CHAPTER FIVE
Coffee

My head spins, and a million thoughts pummel my brain. I lead my new "partner" from Chief Harding's office, my devastatingly handsome, horribly distracting partner. Chief Harding and I have always had an unspoken agreement, one where he ignores what I am, and I only use my darkness for good. I was under the impression that meant I would never have a partner, which has held true until right now. The distraction of having to keep my darker side locked up tight from someone's prying eyes while keeping my head in the game to catch this killer as soon as possible is damaging to my calm. I can feel something prickly just below the surface, scratching to be let out. I push the feeling back down and stomp on it a few times. I'm not going to let the addition of another person in my orbit change my plans, no matter how inconvenient the timing is.

"I promised the medical examiner lunch today," I say out loud, shaking the thoughts from my head. Frank sent a message early this morning letting me know he received the toxicology results we were waiting on. I chance a look at the man I now know as Cole Bellamy and find him watching me, probably expecting me to confront him about last night. I should absolutely ask him if he knew who I was then or if it was a surprise to him like it was to me, but I won't because it doesn't really matter. "I hope you weren't kidding about eating at the Lemon Wok two to three times a week because that's where we're picking lunch up from."

His eyes finally shift away from me, and he lets out a chuckle. "I was starting to wonder if you remembered me or not," he says. I snort out a laugh—like anyone could forget that devastating smile of his.

Frank enthusiastically waves at us when we enter the medical examiner's building. I lead Cole into the cramped office and settle into one of the seats in front of Frank's desk. I separate the food from the bags, handing each box to the corresponding person while Frank wastes no time, immediately divulging his findings.

"The lab re-ran each one of the samples, checking for any human saliva, or additional DNA from anywhere other than the victim, but the results came back inconclusive. I also went ahead and re-examined the injuries of the last victim..." he says, pausing. I look up into his beady eyes, which are now boring into mine, silently telling me he knows exactly who the last victim was to me. I wave my hand, gesturing for him to continue. "Due to the viciousness of the cuts, there's really no way to discern if the wound was made from teeth or a tool, but judging by the leverage needed to pry open a chest cavity, I'd say at least that part was done with a tool. I also took the previous victim's autopsy photos to the odontologist I told you about, but even she said it was impossible to say whether the wounds were caused by teeth or tools. The wounds are just too messy. I'm sorry, Jessica, it's looking like these ladies have told us all they are willing to tell."

"Thanks, Frank. I appreciate you looking into that theory anyway," I say, knowing it was a long shot, but I'm glad we explored the possibility.

My shoulders sag; we don't have many other avenues to explore without a fresh victim. A heavy feeling weighs down on me at the thought of needing another person to die so we can move forward. It feels like a rock in the pit of my stomach. The sensation is foreign and makes me uneasy.

"May I?" I startle at Cole's voice.

I shoot him a puzzled look. Is he really asking my permission before he questions Frank? I clear my throat and nod toward Frank.

"Please, go ahead," I say, fumbling with a crab rangoon, giving myself something else to focus on instead of the warm feeling creeping up my neck and onto my cheeks.

He stands beside me, reaching over the desk to shake Frank's hand, and I realize I never introduced them. Inwardly, I cringe, wondering what Sarah would've thought about me forgetting something as simple as a polite introduction. I shake the thought off and offer myself some grace. I am, after all, in a stressful situation, having a deadline, and now a partner making that deadline seem almost impossible to meet. My forehead creases at the thought of stress, something I have very rarely, if ever, felt the pressures of. That makes two foreign feelings on the same day; I file that away to examine later when I'm alone.

"Cole Bellamy, I'm consulting with Detective Fairling on this case. I'm a Professor of Forensic Psychology with a focus on profiling—I have a few questions about your findings that I'm hoping may shed some light on the type of person we are looking for," Cole says. Frank nods, giving him the go-ahead to ask his questions. "It appears the killer is escalating. The first two victims were quite impersonal, and then each victim gets more personal, to the point where the fourth victim was washed down and then carefully redressed. Now, a trophy has been taken from the fifth. Each murder is incredibly different, yet so similar. Do you think it's possible, in your medical opinion, we are, in fact, dealing with more than one person?"

Frank begins nodding his head, slowly at first, then quicker in his usual fashion when he's excited. "Yes, the murders are similar enough to say it could be the work of one person, but they are also different enough that we could say it's multiple people following the same instruction while adding their flare."

Multiple people, an interesting theory that is not completely out of the realm of possibility, but also a very rare possibility. I can't think of many cases where there's been a group of killers that have kept at it for this long unless we get into secret societies or cults. Even then, there are always whisperings and upset amongst the members; we haven't heard anything of the sort with these cases. I make a mental note to double-check for any religious organizations or sororities the women were part of and maybe ask their families if they've heard of any groups the women were involved in, regularly visited, or even visited at some point, religious, or not. Sarah wasn't, which would disrupt the theory that they are all linked.

Outside the medical examiner's building, I turn to face Cole, intending to ask him what makes him think there are multiple killers, but before I can, he asks me if I drink coffee. I stare at him for a moment, wondering if it would be weird to explain my long-standing love affair with the substance or if it would just make me sound insane. Deciding it would most likely make me sound like a crazy person, I instead point across the street to a small hole-in-the-wall coffee shop, so small if you blink, you would miss it altogether.

"That place has the best selection in New York City," I say.

"Sounds like a place I'd like to check out then," he says. He smiles, turning to me, offering his arm, like we are in some sort of romantic period piece drama, and I'm a lady of high rank he wishes to court. I'm not going to lie: it works for him, and I can't help the stupid grin that makes its way across my face as I loop my arm in his.

The small hole-in-the-wall shop is the only place I know of that not only carries the normal fare of cappuccinos, macchiatos, and flat whites, but also carries some obscure coffees from around the world—one of which is derived from coffee beans cats have eaten and shit out; others are less eccentric and just from exotic locations like Hawaii or Costa Rica. Stepping inside, I close my eyes and pause in the doorway, letting a small shudder run through me, and a contented sigh leave my mouth. When my eyes open, I find Jerry, the shop owner, laughing at me, and I grin at him. I've been coming to this coffee shop since I started volunteering for the department while in the academy. He knows all about my love affair with coffee and doesn't let me live it down. I give him a wink, letting him know I appreciate him letting me be.

"Jessica!" Jerry says before clapping his hands together. "Perfect timing. I just finished a fresh pot."

The excitement I feel for a fresh pot of coffee cannot be described as normal; in fact, I'm not sure normal people have any sort of excitement when it comes to a cup of black coffee. I shrug the thought away.

"Can you also add on whatever my partner would like?" Jerry's eyes widen with surprise at my request. In all the years I've been coming here, I've never brought anyone with me, let alone someone who I've called my partner. I don't really feel like explaining that mess, so I step to the side, allowing Cole to place his order.

"Hi Jerry, I'll take a cappuccino with whole milk, extra sugar, and add whipped cream, please," Cole orders with a broad smile. I turn my face toward the back of the shop to hide the look that crosses it before anyone can notice. I mean, honestly, who does that to espresso?

After collecting our coffees, we sit outside at one of the small bistro tables Jerry has set up, but no one ever stays long enough to use. Silence settles between us, and I scramble through my brain for something to say. I'm on edge, not from the silence, but from the man sitting across from me. The intensity behind his eyes as he watches me makes me feel like he's stripping back each of my well-placed shields and uncovering all the dark corners I work so hard to keep from view. I shift uncomfortably in my seat and decide to dive into my latest theory to avoid more awkward silence.

"I asked Frank to run the DNA samples from this case again to see if they could find any foreign DNA, my thought being that maybe the wounds were actually caused by human teeth and not a tool of some sort. As you heard, the tests came back inconclusive, leading me back to square one. Your theory, however, about multiple killers would change what we are looking for altogether. I assume you are referring to a cult or secret society?" I ask, hoping to distract him from watching me.

I take my first sip of the Italian coffee that's as black as night and double brewed, which Jerry makes so well, and my eyes flutter closed. A contented sigh leaves my lips when the slight tingling sensation from the caffeine makes its way up to my brain. I open my eyes to find Cole staring at me over his own cup; something dark flashes across his eyes, too quick for me to analyze. He breaks the intense eye contact and plasters a smile that could topple empires onto his face. It's taken a few of them, but now I can see that smile for what it is: a mask, the mask he shows the world when he wants to hide himself. I know that trick well.

"From a psychological point of view, it makes sense for it to be a different perpetrator each time. The M.O. is overall the same, right? Savage attacks on young singled-out females made to look like animal attacks. However, if you look deeper, each one has its own signature. One is removing the flesh from bone, another is removing a limb entirely, then they escalate to gutting and cleaning, then finally gutting, cleaning, and keeping a trophy," he says, carefully watching me as he mentions my sister's murder again.

He's probably waiting for me to open up and show him all my cracks, tell him my life's story, or whatever it is partners do. I wonder what he thinks of me when I don't. I nod my agreement and train my eyes on a yellow cab barreling down the road, again escaping the intensity of his gaze.

"That gives us a new direction for the killer or killers, but what about the victims? I haven't had much luck with linking them," I say. I hate to admit that part, but maybe the link is the killers, and not the victims at all. "Do you think it could be something as simple as convenience or ease of access to the victims that links them together?"

He looks thoughtfully down at his coffee, mulling over the question instead of jumping right into an answer, and I respect him more because of it.

"Possibly, but with this sort of violence, it feels more personal. Like the killer or killers knows the victims or has a particular link to them, to go as far as to clean them, and place them, just so. No, I think there's some sort of connection between victim and killer," he says, leaving me surprised at the relief I feel that all the footwork I've been doing to link the victims isn't for naught.

I also feel unease creeping in because that means Sarah may have known her killer, which in turn means I may know her killer. She made sure I knew everyone she did: she brought me to all her social outings and invited me to every gathering, sometimes with me kicking and screaming. She believed the more I participated in social situations, the better I could learn to imitate the people in them; of course, she was right.

"Can I ask you something?" Cole breaks into my wandering thoughts. I make eye contact and nod for him to go ahead. "What's your relationship to the last victim?"

I'm not surprised by his question, just tired of having to go through the motions of faking the emotion that comes along with the answer. In fact, I'm exhausted from the whole thing, not only the fake emotions, but I'm even tiring of the chasing. I never thought I'd get tired of the hunt. The realization makes my stomach clench.

"She was my adoptive sister," I admit, looking away from him, and I let the exhaustion show on my face. I don't think I can fake any more tears, but the exhaustion, that part is actually real. I'm fucking tired.

"Oh." He gives me a sad smile and reaches across the small table to place his hand on top of mine in a comforting act.

I stare at the connection for a moment before he slowly removes his hand. I'm surprised when I find I miss its warmth.

"Can I ask you something?" I use his words without looking at him. I decide to ask with or without his consent. "Did you know who I was last night?" I turn my eyes on him just in time to notice the grimace before he smoothes his face back to calm indifference.

"No. I didn't," is all he offers in response.

I take another moment to watch him as he watches me and decide that I believe him. I'm not sure why, maybe it's the conviction in his voice, or maybe it was his immediate reaction that he doesn't know I saw. Whatever it is, I believe him. I nod and he seems to relax a little.

Finishing the last of my coffee, I lean back in my chair to watch the passing traffic and let my mind wander while trying to take a step back from the case. I try to imagine what I would do if I were introduced to the case now instead of at the beginning two years ago. Aside from getting up to speed with the medical examiner's findings and visiting the places where the bodies were found, I suppose my next step would be to visit the victim's families. It's a step I've been avoiding because it means taking a trip home to visit my family, a trip I've been ignoring the need for since we found my sister's body almost a week ago. By now, my adoptive parents probably have everything planned for her funeral; the morgue will most likely be releasing her body this weekend, at which point our parents will hold some sort of service in her honor. I've done my best to dodge their phone calls, and for the most part, the few times I have spoken with them, I've avoided the whole topic. Whether I want to, I know it's time to go home and be not only the detective in charge of Sarah's murder investigation but also the grieving sister.

CHAPTER SIX

Plans of Home

I walk into my office on Friday morning to find Cole already perched on one of the chairs opposite my desk, his head buried in a case file. The macabre crime scene photos spread across my desk tell me he's reviewing the Samantha Pritchard case.

"I picked you up a cup of coffee on my way in," he says, not looking up from the document he's reading.

My eyes slide to the tall cup steaming from the corner of my desk. My stomach flips, causing my hand to cover it while my other one hangs my jacket on the back of my chair.

"Good morning and thank you," I say, taking my seat, and lifting the cup of sweet nectar from my desk.

I inhale the scent deeply into my lungs. The first sip of

coffee of the day is like a religious experience for me. It's an experience that must be enjoyed with your eyes closed at a leisurely pace. The warm feeling as it travels from your mouth to your stomach, the slight tingle in the base of your brain as the caffeine jump-starts the neurons, it's the closest someone like me will ever get to heaven. My eyes open to find Cole watching me, an almost hungry look on his face.

"Didn't you get yourself a cup?" I ask, checking my desk but seeing no sign of another cup having been on my desk this morning. He clears his throat and looks back down at the file he's been dissecting.

"I already drank mine. I've been here a while," he says.

My coffee was both hot and fresh. My head tilts to the side while I grapple with the thought of asking him if he stopped at the coffee shop twice this morning, and his hands tighten slightly on the paper he's reading, letting me know I should drop it before I ever even pick it up.

"Have you discovered anything new about our ladies?" I ask instead, deciding to shelve my question about the coffee for later… if I'm brave enough.

"Nothing that would add to our killer or killers' profile, no. I'm interested to know more about the victims' personal lives though. I know you've already dug into their lives on paper, but I'd like to get character information from people who were close to them. Maybe speak with their families, visit their homes, and see how they lived."

It shouldn't surprise me that his next step is the same one I was going to take, but for some reason, it does. He puts the photos and documents back in the file, then stacks it on top of the others neatly on the corner of my desk without making eye contact. It's unusual, I'm used to being the one avoiding his stare, not the other way around, and I find I miss his watchful gaze.

"My thoughts exactly; we can start with a quick visit to Lisa Tinselman's family home. It's only about an hour south of here in Trenton, New Jersey," I say, and begin gathering the files, haphazardly shoving them into my bag so we can bring them.

After a fairly intense drive, where he fails to submit to the fact that classic rock is the superior music genre, we are standing on the steps in front of Lisa's childhood home. According to her family, she lived here until three years ago before she moved in with a friend in New York City after accepting a position as a receptionist with a local law firm.

I gently knock on the front door; it swings wide and Mrs. Tinselman steps out to envelope me in a bear hug. My eyes widen, and I struggle with what to do next;

luckily, I don't have to do anything because she releases me as quickly as she grabbed me.

"Detective Fairling, I'm so sorry to hear about your sister. She was so beautiful, and so young, just like my Lisa," she all but cries before stepping forward as if she's going to embrace me again.

I take a step backward into Cole. It looks like the newspaper article was published today, just as the mayor promised. Still rattled from being manhandled so early in the day and by someone I can't exactly shoot, I look over my shoulder to my new partner for saving. The last thing I want to do is bond with her over the loss of my sister and her daughter. It would take her no time at all to figure out how different I am from her, which would cause me all sorts of problems I don't need. Thankfully, Cole picks up on my silent plea and sticks out his hand as he steps around me.

"Hi, Mrs. Tinselman, I'm Cole Bellamy. I'm working with Detective Fairling on this case. We were hoping you had time to speak with us about Lisa," he says, gently clasping her hand in a shake. I take the time she's distracted to duck my head behind his back and compose myself.

"Oh, yes, of course. Please, come in; I was just making coffee. Fred's already left for work, and this is usually when I make my grocery list," she says, her attention completely removed from me, and she shuffles back into the house, waving us in behind her. I give Cole an appreciative smile, which he returns with a look, telling me I will owe him for this later.

She motions us to sit on the couch before heading into the small kitchen in the back of the house. I sit as I inspect the abundance of framed pictures of Lisa that adorn the walls, a tribute to her short life. There are photos of her at the state fair with pigtails, appearing to be about eight years old, and another when she had braces eating ice cream with her father on what appears to be a cruise ship at about age thirteen. Then, there are some high school prom photos and professional photos of a more recent Lisa, posing in front of the office building she recently started working at. I glance over at Cole to find him watching me take all this in. He nods his head toward them.

"What do you see?" The way he asks makes me feel like I've been called on by my college professor, which shouldn't surprise me since that's, after all, what he is. Obediently, my gaze returns to the pictures, soaking them in before I answer.

"I see the life of a woman who was well loved by her family. Photos of a little girl who looks genuinely happy and photos of an adult woman who was proud of her position." I pause before I turn and ask. "What do you see?" I mimic his professor tone, which earns me a smile.

"It's not so much about what I see, but what I don't," he says, watching my face.

I look back for a third time at the pictures; this time, I get up and walk over to the wall with the most photos. Now he mentions it, there are no baby photos, no naked toddler photos, the usual embarrassing collection of photos the proudest of parents tend to display for all who enter their homes to see.

"Mrs. Tinselman, I don't see any younger photos of Lisa here. They all appear to be after age eight or so?" I ask. She looks at me, making her way back into the room with two cups, and offers one to me. Inside is a very milky, very sad-looking coffee. I take the offered cup and debate if I want to risk a taste.

"Oh, that's because we adopted Lisa at eight years old. Fred and I couldn't have children, but we wanted one so badly, so we decided to adopt. We initially thought we would adopt a baby, but when Fred and I saw a photo of Lisa, with her blond curls and freckled nose, we knew she would complete our family." She pauses to wipe her eyes, now moist with tears. "She did, she really did." A loud sob escapes her; she closes her eyes and takes a deep breath. When she opens them, she's thankfully composed herself. I never do well when people show too much emotion in front of me. "If you'd like, I can take you into Lisa's bedroom. Most of her stuff is still here, since the apartment she and Shelly rented was only supposed to be temporary."

I nod, and she stands up to lead us down a small hallway covered in more family photos into Lisa's room, where she leaves us alone. Cole and I wander around, looking at this and that, not really expecting to find too much information from a room she hasn't lived in in so long. On our way back to the living room, I spot a small half bathroom, and I peek my head in to quickly empty my coffee down the small sink drain. I don't want to offend Mrs. Tinselman by returning a full cup of untouched coffee. The foreign thought strikes me as odd: I'm not sure when I started to give a shit about things like that.

Returning to the living room, I find Cole already asking her about the adoption agency while she's digging through some old files for the paperwork. Maybe having a partner isn't such a bad thing after all; splitting up the labor is nice, especially considering this is the part of the job I struggle with most.

****

Our next stop is Claire Sanders' loft. A year and a half later, the rent for her small studio loft above a laundry mat in New York City is still being paid for by her parents. They can't bring themselves to clear out her personal items.

The inside is decorated like something out of a boho chic magazine, with fake plants, dream catchers, and throw pillows everywhere. The single-room loft is separated by a large Moroccan-style screen in the center, but for all her decorating, there isn't much showing what her life was like. There are no personal photos, certificates, or diplomas hanging; it's all just impersonal decor and I find myself wondering what it is that keeps her parents holding onto this place.

"Huh, this is interesting," Cole declares, digging through one of the desk drawers. "Looks like Claire was adopted as well. Though it appears to be from a different agency."

He holds up another certificate, much like the one that Mrs. Tinselman was kind enough to make us a copy of. He snaps a photo of the certificate and gently places it back into the drawer. We investigate the loft a little longer but don't find anything else of use before deciding to call it a day.

I let Cole drive us back to the city, and he offers to drop

me at my apartment building before delivering the car to the precinct. I agree, not because it's dark and I'm afraid to walk home alone, but because I know I need time to call my mother and make arrangements to go home for my sister's funeral.

****

After the third ring, my mother's voice comes over the line. "Jessica?"

"Hi, Mom," I say, pacing my small sparsely decorated living room, unable to sit still for this conversation.

"Oh, honey, it's so good to hear your voice. Your father and I have been so worried after what happened to Sarah and not hearing from you much. Is everything alright? Are you alright?" She barely takes a breath between words.

"Yeah, I'm alright, mom. Sorry, I haven't called; I've been busy with work." I force my voice to shake a little.

"Jessica, you're still the lead on this case? Even after what happened with Sarah?" she asks, her voice raising an octave or two. She most likely thinks the department is forcing me to stay on board and could probably never imagine I'd fight my way to stay on.

"Yeah, the chief and mayor still think I'm the best person to solve this, since I have such a close relation to the last victim." I cringe at the small gasp she lets out at the impersonal way I've just referred to my dead sister. I continue before she has a chance to comment on it. "They've assigned me a partner, a Professor of Forensic Psychology. His name is Cole; he's not just a professor, he also has a few best-selling books on how to profile serial killers. They think he might be able to offer some insight from a psychological standpoint and help us find whoever is responsible for this." I finally sit on my couch, tucking my feet underneath me before continuing. "He's really smart. I think it's a good move."

A sigh escapes me as I think exactly how smart he *really* is, how he seems to see right through me, and challenges me to think quicker than anyone ever has. Not to mention he makes me feel something I can't put my finger on, something I've never felt before, but I won't admit that part out loud. It's like when he's around, the darkness that's always pushing inside of me quiets down, and I can almost find myself forgetting it's there; that's never happened before.

The shake in my mother's voice brings me back from my musings when she asks if I'll come in for Sarah's funeral. "It's on Sunday afternoon; that's the soonest we could book it for," she adds.

I picture her sitting at the kitchen table, her gray streaked brown hair in a messy bun on top of her head, her pale pink sweatpants with the frayed ends hanging over her water boots she wears even when it's not raining. I imagine her wringing her hands with worry over whether I'm going to show up for Sarah's funeral, and it causes my stomach to roll. That heavy feeling washes over me for the second time today. Guilt, maybe?

"Yeah, Mom, I'll start making plans and let you know the details when I have them." I pause, a plan beginning to take form; not only is this a family event, but it's also the perfect time to gather more information on Sarah's life. "I'll be bringing Cole with me," I add.

I can almost hear the smile in my mother's voice when she tells me she'll get the guest room ready before reminding me to text her when we know our travel plans. Only after I've hung up does it dawn on me what the smile in her voice must mean that she thinks I'm bringing Cole along for personal reasons. Now that I have a successful career, she thinks it's time to "settle down" and start a family. Just like Sarah, she's convinced life's greatest accomplishment is starting a family. I sigh heavily, realizing this is going to be a long weekend. It's probably best to call Cole now to let him know I've volunteered him to take a trip to my very lovely, very quiet hometown of Richmond, Virginia, to be subjected to my family.

A sleep-filled husky voice answers on the second ring. "This is Cole." My stomach does that flip again, causing me to lose focus on what I was calling for.

"Hi, Cole, it's Jess… uh, Jessica… Fairling. Your partner." I smack my hand on my forehead. What the hell was that?

That same husky voice chuckles, sending a shiver down my spine. "Detective Fairling, hi." He clears his throat and, sounding a bit more like himself, asks, "To what do I owe the pleasure of this late-night phone call?" I check my watch to find it's only nine p.m.

"I, uh, wanted to give you a heads up I'm going to fly in tomorrow to my hometown to attend my sister's funeral on Sunday afternoon. I thought it might be a good idea for you to join me to speak with family members of the victim and get a sense of how she grew up."

I realize only after it's left my mouth that I just referred to my sister as "the victim" again and not by her name. That's not something a normal person would do. I hold my breath and mentally kick myself for the slip-up, waiting to see if he'll call me out on it. Instead, he offers to book a flight and hotel for himself, leaving my slip unmentioned but, I'm sure, not unnoticed.

"No, I can book flights on my business account, and we

can stay at my parents' house. I mean… if that's okay with you?" Again, I smack my forehead. What is wrong with me?

He graces me with another masculine chuckle and agrees to my plans, asking for confirmation by text message. "And Detective?"

"Yes, Cole?" My voice comes out slightly huskier than normal.

"Sleep well," he responds, before disconnecting the call.

Placing the phone down, I reflect on the conversation, wondering what is happening to me. If I wasn't certain it was impossible, I would think I'm exhibiting new emotions, and feelings organically. My brain is overwhelmed with foreign sensations and thoughts that race around in circles, eliciting a physical response such as blushing, or my stomach flopping around like a fish; it's everything Sarah taught me to fake growing up. But that can't happen. Right?

You can't just wake up one day and start feeling things. Can you?

CHAPTER SEVEN

Emotions Are Messy

Cole waves to me from the curb outside of my apartment building, and I rush out the doors with a small carry-on suitcase trailing behind me while I shield my eyes from the early morning sun.

"Good morning, Detective," he says, smiling and relieving me of my baggage.

"Good morning, Cole," I say, sliding into the backseat of the sedan, and nodding a silent hello to the driver.

Cole follows me in, forcing me to scoot over behind the driver's seat. We make the twenty-minute drive to the airport in silence, which allows me time to mull over all the signs of emotions I've recently been exhibiting. The darkness I've grown to seek comfort in is silent, hidden deep inside of me somewhere, leaving me feeling twitchy the entire drive.

Cole carries our luggage to the gate, leaving me both hands to grab us some coffee before our flight. One of the best parts about this particular airport is there's a coffee roaster inside. It's a haven for those of us that just flat-out refuse to lower our standards and drink the swill that comes out of some of the big chain coffee shops. Six dollars for a cup of mostly two percent milk and processed fake sugars just isn't my idea of money well spent.

My lips curve into a mischievous smile as I return to Cole at our gate with two very large, very dark cups of their local drip coffee. He's about to get a taste for what real coffee's like, none of that milky frou-frou shit I've been watching him drink all week. He accepts the cup I've offered him and watches suspiciously over the rim, taking his first sip. His eyes squeeze shut, and he sputters out a small cough, doing his best to not spit it out. A chuckle escapes me, and I cover my mouth, fighting not to spit my own out. Once I've swallowed the coffee, the chuckle turns into a full-blown belly laugh at the exaggerated faces he's making.

By the time I compose myself, he's staring at me again with that look from the other day: the almost hungry look; maybe I should have grabbed him a bagel, too.

After a moment of eye contact, he excuses himself to "fix" his coffee, which no doubt means ruining it with more creamer and sugar than any human should ingest in a day. I shrug while sipping my coffee and looking out the window, where a fuel truck is being unhooked from our plane, telling me it's almost time to board. A few moments later, Cole returns with a much lighter cup of coffee and a bagel. It looks like my assumption was correct: he was hungry. The attendant calls for boarding, and we enter the plane.

Fortunately, the flight is over before I can even decide on a movie to watch; sitting still on planes is not one of my strongest abilities. We stop in a small diner on the way from the airport to grab lunch, and I take the time to go over the timeline for our visit. There will be a wake this evening at the house for close friends and family, then the funeral tomorrow afternoon for everyone to attend. We plan to strategically gather information from my parents without putting them too much on edge and without divulging any other information from the case the public isn't aware of. They only know Sarah was found with her chest opened, missing her heart. They know nothing about the almost ritualistic cleaning that was done to her as well as the previous victim, Samantha Pritchard, and I stress to him we need to keep it that way. By midafternoon, we arrive at the home where Sarah and I spent our childhood. It's a modest two-story house, sitting on ten acres of land that my adoptive parents use to farm some vegetables in the nicer weather and house some small livestock along with chickens.

I step out of the cab and see my mother running out the front door toward us. I drop my luggage and brace for impact, knowing exactly where this is going. She flings herself into my arms, squeezing until I feel like my eyes may actually pop out, the same way she has always done when I'm away from her for more than twenty-four hours.

"Hi, Mom." I finally manage to get out once she lets up enough. She tries to hide the fact she's crying from me by quickly wiping tears away from her face, and she smiles in Cole's direction.

"Good afternoon, Mrs. Fairling," he says, reaching out to shake her hand. Instead, he is met with the same bearlike hug I received. His eyes go wide while he looks over her shoulder at me to help him. I won't; he's on his own with her.

"Yeah, sorry, I forgot to mention that she's a hugger, and you better call her Leanne; she's offended by formalities," I say, shrugging. I grab my luggage and head to the front door, leaving him staring after me, still in my mother's tight embrace.

The smell of cinnamon greets me as I step inside. It doesn't matter what time of year it is; my mother's always baking something, and her favorite ingredient to add to her baking is cinnamon. It could be cookies, cake, or just bread she's making, but you can always bet there will be cinnamon inside. She insists cinnamon is the smell of a home full of love. I close my eyes and take a deep breath, letting the scent of my mother's baking fill my lungs. I only open them again when I hear my father calling out to her.

"LeeLee, what time are we expecting Jess to arrive? I'd like to get..." he trails off when he rounds the corner, all but running into me.

"Hi, Dad," I say, offering him a sad smile, taking in his scruffy appearance.

My father has always been a meticulous groomer, with his hair always neatly cut, beard trimmed, and nails short and buffed. The man staring back at me, appearing fifteen pounds lighter than I remember, has shaggy, unkempt hair with a beard that rivals someone who has spent an entire season living in the wilderness without a mirror; he doesn't look like my father at all. I set my luggage on the floor and step into him for a hug, squeezing him as tightly as my mother did me. He returns the hug, letting out a small sob into my hair, and it causes my chest to feel tight.

"Jess, we are so happy to see you," he says, letting me go to wipe the tears from his face. He peers around me to where Cole and my mother are now entering the house, giving them a watery smile.

"Dad, this is my partner, Cole Bellamy." I step to the side, allowing them to shake hands. "Cole, this is my dad, Joe Fairling."

"Nice to meet you, Mr. Fairling, I'm very sorry for your loss." Cole offers a small smile and my mother waves that away.

"No, we don't want to be sorry for the loss of Sarah. Instead, this is to be a celebration of her life. She was so much more than a victim." My mother beams at my father, who returns a smile that is only half as bright. "Sarah wouldn't have wanted people to cry over her."

She nods her head at my father for reassurance, and he nods back. I also nod because I know Sarah would never want people crying over or mourning the loss of her. She would most definitely prefer a celebration that included tequila and dancing to a sad, sober wake in her name.

After a small tour of the first floor, I lead Cole upstairs to the guest bedroom where he'll be staying while pointing out the other rooms along the way of the classic antebellum home I grew up in. I show him the small library, the bathroom, my old room, Sarah's old room, and finally, at the end of the hallway, the room he's staying in. True to her word, my mother has set the guest room up nicely with new linens on the bed, towels for the shower, and even lit, yeah, you guessed it, a cinnamon-scented candle. Leaving him to unpack his bag, I intend to make my way to my childhood bedroom. Instead, I find myself standing in the middle of Sarah's. An odd sensation creeps over me, along with the overwhelming urge to lie down on her bed. I shake my head, attempting to clear the static that's taken residence inside of it, leaving me confused and itching to do… I don't know what. Sarah hadn't lived in this room for over eight years, but still, my mother insisted on keeping both our rooms as they were in case we ever wanted to move back in.

All her track medals remain hanging on a cork board attached to the wall, her bookshelf full of high school textbooks, untouched for years, and her pink writing desk, with the unicorns we painted on the drawers when we were eleven, still sits in the corner. A single tear falls down my cheek, causing me to take a sharp breath. I wipe the wetness from my cheek and stare at the foreign substance of the tear as it dries on my thumb. My next breath gets stuck as I fight the burning sensation behind my eyes, making me slightly dizzy from lack of oxygen. The urge to run out of the room hits me like a steamroller, causing me to turn for a quick escape, but I'm stopped by a brick wall. Except it's not really a wall: it's a warm, firm chest. The realization that it's Cole's warm, firm chest causes me to let out a yip and step farther into the room.

"I'm so sorry, I didn't know you were in here, too," I say, eyes darting around the room, trying to look anywhere except at him.

"Sorry, Detective, I was coming to find you to see if you wanted to go over some questions before I posed them to your family when I saw you standing in here. I only just arrived at the doorway when…" He makes a gesture at his chest, then back to me. My face flushes, and my stomach flips again; I don't know that I like this feeling thing. I inhale deeply, finally meeting his eyes.

"Jessica… you can call me Jessica or just Jess… if you want." I offer him a weak smile, then gesture for him to take a seat in the chair at the pink unicorn desk, while I sit cross-legged on the floor next to the bed.

I decide this is the best place for us to have the discussion, hoping the feeling of sadness I'm having being in Sarah's old room will keep whatever feelings I'm having when in his vicinity at bay. He lets me know the questions he plans to ask my parents, family, and Sarah's friends at the wake tonight, and funeral, tomorrow. Then, the conversation comfortably shifts to stories from my childhood, as the sun sets. He's migrated to the floor next to me and I lay with my back flat on the floor and my feet on the bed.

"Once, when we were twelve, our dad promised if we both got straight A's on our report cards, he would take us out for all the ice cream we could eat, then let us play in the park until the sun went down. So, of course, we worked our asses off and got all A's. Sarah and I, the gluttonous little children we were, both ate two of the largest ice cream cones we could get, then decided the merry-go-round was where we wanted to start at the park. So, we took turns spinning each other as fast as we could until she threw up while still spinning, plastering our dad's pant legs with half-digested ice cream."

I almost don't get the last part out because I'm giggling so hard that I roll over on my side with laughter, clutching my stomach. I can barely breathe from laughing so hard, which, of course, causes me to laugh even harder. Then, a wave of sadness hits me, causing my laugh to morph into a gut-wrenching sob, the sound only appearing once before I struggle through silently while gasping for air. I squeeze my eyes shut as tight as I can, which is probably why I'm so startled when Cole's strong arms lift me from the floor and settle me into his lap as he gently brushes the hair from across my forehead. I go completely still and slowly open my eyes to find myself staring up at his face, which is filled with concern for my little breakdown. The silent sobs mercifully stop. I watch him as his hand slips down from my hair across my cheek and settles just over the tender spot below my ear, making me shiver.

"Jess, Cole, guests are starting to arrive, and we thought you might like to come down to say hello," my mother says, walking into the room.

Her eyes widen almost comically at the realization of what she's looking at, and a broad smile spreads across her face. She says nothing but makes a clucking sound, much like a mother hen, and then leaves the room. My attention swings back to Cole, who's still staring at me while one arm is snaked around my waist, keeping me dangerously close to his body.

"I guess that's our cue to start our interrogation," I say, wiping at the remaining tear tracks on my cheeks, and I wonder what the hell just happened to me. He clears his throat before he finally looks away.

"That's probably a good idea. Getting started with the close family and friends," he agrees. Another minute passes, and he brings his eyes back to mine before letting out a laugh.

"What's so funny?" I ask, unsure what there is to laugh at.

"Jessica, I can't get up if you're still in my lap," he says, but the tension I feel in his arm still wrapped around my waist tells me that maybe he doesn't want me to get up, either. I slowly extract myself from his grip, my face feeling like I just stuck it far too close to a volcanic eruption.

"Sorry," I offer, unable to meet his stare. I quickly head out of the room toward the staircase.

CHAPTER EIGHT
Butterflies

Downstairs is a flurry of activity. Cousins, aunts, uncles, and close friends swarm around the house, eating, drinking, chatting, and reminiscing. Cole and I are met with a few curious stares, but no one speaks up or asks about our relationship. That's probably for the best since I'm not sure how they would feel knowing our intentions. I decide to introduce Cole as my friend to a few of them while he asks them some broad questions about Sarah's life, and we manage to grab a few bites to eat while wandering around.

We wave the remainder of the guests off as the grandfather clock in the foyer chimes midnight. I plop down heavily on the front porch swing, careful not to spill the coffee my mother brewed before she and my father quietly retreated to bed an hour ago, leaving Cole and I to close the house up after everyone departs. From my seat on the front porch swing, I watch Cole staring down the street, watching a car carrying the last guests disappear. The perfect sloping of the bridge of his nose and sharp contour of his cheeks ignites the warm, flushed feeling from earlier in the night to return to my less contoured and slightly rounder cheeks. I really need to figure out what's going on with me and how to stop it. Against my better judgment, I pat the space next to me on the front porch swing, inviting him to sit. He looks at me, his eyebrows raising in surprise, but takes me up on the offer. Settling next to me on the swing, he begins rocking us gently, and I tuck my sore feet under my legs, getting comfortable.

"I think you're handling all of this really well, Jess," he says, smiling down at me because he's that much taller; even when sitting, he's about a head taller than me.

I struggle with how to respond to that, my gaze wandering over to a streetlight flickering down the road. I mean, for a normal person, yeah, sure, I'm handling this all really well. But I am not a normal person. Yet somehow, I'm having normal feelings. So, is that really handling it well? I briefly consider telling him that I am, in fact, not a normal person, telling him that I don't have normal feelings and emotions, that somehow this is a glitch. I want to tell him that I am glitching out and I just want to go back to not having feelings, not rolling around in tears on my dead sister's bedroom floor, but I can't. I can't just tell him that secret. Keeping that between Sarah, Chief Harding, and myself is the only way I've made it this far in my job.

Would the NYPD really want to know they have a psychopath on the force chasing down other psychopaths? Probably not. How do you convince the world you aren't like the other psychopaths and don't want to kill people or gnaw the flesh off their appendages? No, I can't tell him. I can't tell anybody.

I refocus my eyes, realizing I've spaced out and now waited too long to respond. I sigh heavily and let the tired feeling I've been pushing away since Sarah's death wash over me. I let the exhaustion sink into my bones. I rest my head on his shoulder, and my eyes flutter closed to rest them, just for a moment. I might be able to truly relax a little, knowing nothing is expected of me right now, sitting here with him. He doesn't even really know me or what I am. Maybe that's why I'm comfortable enough to fall asleep with my head still resting on his shoulder, sitting on the front porch of my childhood home.

The sun warms my cheek and my eyes snap open to a

familiar yet unfamiliar view, my childhood bedroom. The more awake I become, the more of yesterday evening I remember. Laughing on Sarah's old bedroom floor, crying on her old bedroom floor, and sitting on the front porch swing with Cole all flash through my mind. I must've fallen asleep out there after everyone left, and he must've carried me inside. The thought of him holding me like a small child with my head cradled against his firm chest has my face heating up and my heart rate climbing. So, is this what it feels like to have a crush on someone? Sarah always said it was an enjoyable feeling, like butterflies floating around in your gut. I can honestly say there's nothing enjoyable about this feeling. It feels like I have food poisoning.

Groaning, I sit up on my very cramped childhood bed, and squint toward the window, cursing its sheer curtain. Gently extracting myself from the tiny bed, I collect the simple baby blue dress from the closet. The color was Sarah's favorite, and it's the color my mother insisted close family wear to the funeral to honor her. With my toiletry bag, dress, and towel in hand, I walk to the bathroom for a shower. I push the door open and run face-first into a warm, smooth wall of flesh. Cole's chest… again. Laughing at my luck, I quickly back out of the cramped space, distancing myself from a half-naked Cole.

"I'm sorry, I keep getting so up close and personal with your chest," I say, doing my best to avoid eye contact.

He's standing in the doorway wearing nothing but a towel, water still dripping down his very toned arms and chest. I audibly swallow while my eyes track a droplet of water making its way down his bare chest before disappearing under the towel tied around his waist. My face burns; at this point, I'm certain it's multiple shades of red. My heart beats frantically in my ears, letting me know it's at least working. My useless brain will not afford me any words to break the awkward silence. Instead, I struggle not to look into his eyes, and stare at a spot behind him on the counter.

"Good morning, Jess," he says, breaking the silence and somehow giving me the strength to finally look up at his face, where I find a very masculine smirk. "How did you sleep?" I can't say for certain, but I swear his voice is an octave lower than normal.

"I, uh, I slept really well," I admit, doing my best to remember when the last time I did sleep that well was. "Thank you for putting me to bed." I look away from that smirk before I begin to squirm like a worm on a hook. "I didn't realize I was that exhausted, or I would have just taken myself to bed." His hand finds my shoulder and gives it a gentle squeeze, the move surprisingly calming.

"It's no problem at all. I know you're going through a lot right now and you've been pushing hard at work trying to solve these cases. I'm just glad I can help you in any way."

The sincerity in his voice calms my mind even more, making this exchange less awkward, even while standing in the hallway of my parents' house with a very attractive half- naked man. And... it's back, the awkward feeling along with the flaming heat on my cheeks.

"I'll let you finish up in here," I manage to squeak out. Not able to stand here any longer without doing something to further embarrass myself, I turn to walk back to my room, but he grabs my hand and gently pulls me back toward the bathroom.

"I'm finished, I was just about to exit when you..." His lips curl into a broad smile and my stomach tightens. "Became reacquainted with my chest."

He brushes past me, exiting the bathroom on his way to the end of the hall to his room. I, like a creepy stalker, stand in the middle of my parents' hallway, watching the gentle swaying of his hips wrapped tightly in a blue towel with little yellow daisies on it. I shake my head at myself —bad Jessica, bad bad bad, and yet, I watch the entire time until he closes the door behind him, not once glancing back at me.

Once showered, dressed, and certain I'm not getting my hair any straighter with the flat iron, I head downstairs where I can already hear family members gathering. My father greets me at the bottom of the staircase, holding a steaming cup of black coffee in my direction. Grateful, I give his arm a gentle squeeze before he disappears into the crowd, and I down my cup of coffee, mentally preparing myself for today. The thought of saying goodbye to my sister so publicly sends a shudder down my spine. Normally, this is when I would start wondering if I'm supposed to squeeze out the tears before I reach the podium or after I've started my speech. Do I carry a tissue around and gently wipe my eyes periodically so they appear red and bloodshot? How long do I pause between my words? Oddly, I don't find myself wondering about any of that today.

Instead, I'm wondering if the eulogy I wrote on a small note card one week ago, the evening after Sarah's body was found lifeless staring up at the sky, is what I would honestly say to her if I had one last chance. Given my recent emotional breakthrough or whatever we're calling what's happened to me, I'm not sure the pitiful goodbye I carefully extracted from an internet search of popular eulogies is going to cut it. A smile creeps across my lips as I think of what Sarah would say about me having these feelings, how much she would delight in the awkwardness of it all.

I feel Cole before I can see him as he makes his way through the living room and to my side, nursing his own cup of coffee. His is a much lighter shade than mine, considering mine is black, and his probably contains half the contents of a carton of creamer and an entire bag of sugar. Somehow, with everything going on, Cole standing beside me manages to chase away the fog that's taken residence in my brain, pushing all my doubts and worries to the side, leaving me blessedly level-headed for what's to come.

My father ushers us into the limo they've rented so immediate family can arrive together. Everyone else follows behind in their vehicles to the cemetery, where we will say goodbye one last time to Sarah before she's laid to rest. I begin the process of extracting my mother's hand from mine as we arrive and help her out of the car. Thankfully, the rain has held off today, and we cross the grounds to gather around the casket. Sarah's eight-year-old son Aaron speaks first, and his heart-wrenching goodbye to his mother doesn't leave a single dry eye, me included. The feeling of crying from sadness is an altogether new one, and as selfish as it may sound, I'm glad other people around are also crying. It lets me know

I'm not doing it wrong.

My mind wanders to the other victims—none of them mothers, in fact, none of them even had husbands, only one was engaged to be married—none of them like Sarah. Something cold slithers inside me, causing the ever-present darkness there to shift, and I make a solemn vow to it that this killer *will* have to answer with their life. Someone will answer for leaving a motherless child on this Earth, for taking my sister away. From not only Aaron, but from us all. A cold resolution settles between my shoulder blades, and I feel a gentle hand pushing my lower back. Blinking away my murderous thoughts, I see my father with his hand gently nudging me up. It's my time to speak about my dead sister.

CHAPTER NINE
Take Your Time

Cole

I grab my toothbrush and turn toward the bathroom door, but the handle turns before I can get a hold of it. I take a step back to avoid being smacked in the face with the door when a very groggy Jessica runs face-first into my naked chest, and I teeter slightly backward from the impact. I brace myself with a hand on the counter next to me and her wide eyes settle on my chest as she tries hard not to meet my eyes.

"I'm sorry, I keep getting so up close and personal with your chest," she says, nervously biting her bottom lip.

I go very still, watching her eyes follow a rogue water drop that makes its way down my chest and into the towel I have wrapped around my hips. Her face flushes a brilliant red, making her freckles stand out across her nose, and I would give anything in that moment to know what she's thinking.

"Good morning, Jess," I say, a smirk easing its way across my lips. Her eyes finally make their way up to mine. "How did you sleep?" I ask.

"I, uh, I slept really well. Thank you for putting me to bed," she stumbles out. Her eyes focus on the counter behind me, and I watch as she composes herself. "I didn't realize I was that exhausted, or I would have just taken myself to bed."

That would have been a shame; I enjoyed taking care of her after she nodded off on my shoulder. Her features were pixie-like, and all the lines of worry that cover them during the waking hours were relaxed and smooth. I reach out, gently squeezing her shoulder, using a lot of willpower to keep from hugging her tightly to my chest in a crushing hug. If I've learned anything over the last few days about Detective Jessica Fairling, it's that, much like a wild animal, you have to approach her slowly, or she gets spooked.

"It's no problem at all. I know you're going through a lot right now and you've been pushing hard at work trying to solve these cases. I'm just glad I can help you, in any way." I say, watching her face flush red again.

"I'll let you finish up in here," she says and tries to turn to leave. I grab her hand before I can think better of it.

"I'm finished, I was just about to exit when you..." I struggle with my thoughts, what I want to say, and what I should say warring in my mind. Instead, I offer a wicked grin. "Became reacquainted with my chest."

Before I tell her just how much I like her against my chest and really spook her, I shuffle past her. I leave the cramped bathroom and slowly walk down the hallway to my room to get ready for the service. I feel her eyes on me the entire time, but I don't dare turn around to let her know. If I want to get closer to her, I need to let her come to me in her own time; I just hope I can wait that long.

****

Later than planned, we rush to the airport to catch our Monday morning flight home. Her parents' tearful goodbyes, understandably taking a bit longer, tell me Jess doesn't come around too often. We rush through the small airport, and I can clearly see that she's struggling with her emotions. Her face is flushed, her jaw is ticking, and she's clenching her teeth over and over. In the security line, she zones out, not noticing the line has moved. She leaves a huge gap between us and the metal detectors, which are now empty and waiting for us to pass through. I place my hand on her cheek to gently bring her back from her rampant thoughts.

"Where did you go just now, Jess?"

"I... well, I guess I was thinking about my sister," she admits. Her eyes dart around to take in her surroundings. "I was thinking about how awful it must have been to have me as a sister. How Sarah didn't get to choose to have me, in fact, she had no say in the matter. She probably spent the first seven years of her life thinking she would be an only child, just to have me come along. Quite possibly the worst sister anyone could get stuck with." She pauses and angrily wipes away the tears that start to fall. "She got stuck with me, but never once complained about it. She was always kind to me, always watched out for me, and always had my back no matter what..." she trails off, eyes shifting to stare at the ground before us. I lift her chin with my knuckles, forcing eye contact.

"That's how family is," I say. I use my thumb to gently wipe away a tear that's descending her cheek. "I'm sure she loved you no matter what."

"I don't think you understand." She huffs a frustrated breath, her angry eyes slicing through me. "I was awful to her." She turns around, practically running through the remainder of the security line. I let her go, knowing she needs a moment to collect herself.

On the plane, she chooses a middle seat between two other passengers, clearly telling me to back off. I pass her on my way to the back of the plane and she fidgets with her seatbelt, avoiding having to look at me. I want nothing more than to rip her out of that seat and hug her to my chest until her petite body is wracked with tears and emotions, letting her purge all that pent up sadness she's refusing to let go. Fuck, I hate that she thinks she has to hold on to that shit.

In the short time we are in the air, I try to get comfortable enough to take a nap, and fail miserably. Once we land, she jumps out of her seat like it's on fire, and hurries off the plane as fast as the other passengers will allow. I'm surprised she doesn't pull out her badge and force them to move. Halfway across the airport, where the taxi lanes are, I'm finally able to catch up.

"Jessica. Are you alright?"

"Me? Oh yeah, I'm good, just have a lot to catch up on, you know, on the cases," she says, slowing enough to switch her handful of jacket and small carry-on luggage to her left hand.

I watch her pull out her phone, opening an app for a cab, and frown; she's shut me out. I pushed too hard, and her wild animal instinct kicked in, sending her into fight-or-flight mode. I guess I'm lucky she chose flight and isn't currently battling me in the middle of the airport. Although I'm certain the fire she would bring to that battle would be glorious, I'll give her the space she needs; I can be patient while she figures this all out.

"Alright, well, I'm around if you need me," I offer. I stop walking to watch her exit the airport and get into a cab outside.

I wait until her cab is out of sight before I exit the airport to call my own. It's time for me to pay a visit to Chief Harding. I'm going to suggest he convince Jess to take more time off to process everything. She's clearly running on fumes and in desperate need of a break. She can't keep compartmentalizing everything instead of dealing with it. My professional opinion, which I will tell him when I arrive, is she take another week off. Maybe then I can convince her to speak with someone about everything. I have the driver take me to the precinct, hoping to catch him before he leaves for the evening.

"Cole!" Chief Harding calls out as I stride into the station. Perfect. I slightly turn to reroute my path to his office.

"Chief Harding, good to see you," I say, extending my hand to shake his.

"Have a seat." He gestures to one of the empty chairs in front of his desk. I perch on the edge, trying not to get comfortable in case he isn't friendly about my suggestion. I am, after all, going to be overstepping what I've been brought in for.

"How was the service for Detective Fairling's sister?" He steeples his hands on the desk in front of him, giving me the perfect opportunity to bring up her mental state.

"It was a nice service. Of course, the family is beside themselves with grief, but still managed to hold a lovely wake for her in their home beforehand." I feel my heart speed up at the memory of Jess's petite frame cradled against me on her sister's childhood bedroom floor. I quickly swallow the memory down and focus on his response.

"Good to hear." He nods while giving me a scrutinizing stare; my heart speeds up more. Logically, I know he can't read my mind, but the look he's giving me says otherwise. I shift a little uncomfortably in thc chair. "How's she doing?" he finally asks. I let out a surprised chuckle, mostly at my own paranoia, but also that he would even ask. Of course, she's not good. Who would be in her position?

"Well, that's actually why I'm here. I think it would be a good idea for her to take a little bit more time to herself. Maybe another week, so she can process everything." I watch for his reaction, but he offers nothing. That's what years of working as a detective will get you, a perfect poker face.

He finally lets out a sigh and settles farther back into the seat, his eyes silently telling me he's not buying that Jess needs more time. I decide to give him a little more to convince him the idea is a sound one.

"While sitting in her sister's childhood room, surrounded by her memory, Detective Fairling had a slight breakdown." His eyes widen and his jaw clenches; finally, a reaction.

"She had a what?" he asks, leaning forward in his chair. He's still giving me a look that tells me he's skeptical.

"Nothing serious, no need for medical intervention, but she's exhausted from trying to hold herself together. I think she needs a break and I'm sure I can talk her into speaking to someone about everything going on. Even if it's only a few sessions, I think she needs to discuss this with someone before she explodes," I say, finally sitting farther back in my chair, settling in for a long debate. He glares at me until finally nodding his agreement.

"Okay, I'll give her a few more days off for bereavement," he concedes, still looking slightly confused by the revelation his top detective isn't a robot.

It's no wonder she's trying to overcompensate and keep everything bottled up inside. I sigh. I have my victory and I'm going to leave it at that. Standing up, I reach out to shake his hand, when his cellphone rings. We both look down at the caller ID to see Jess's name pop up on the screen; he motions for me to sit back down before answering.

"Detective Fairling, how was your sister's service?" he asks. Pausing to listen to her, he gives me a look I can't decipher. I hear her on the other end of the call but can't make out what she's saying. "Jessica, you can't come back tomorrow, it's too soon. Normally, a person in your situation would take some time off after something like this. I think it's best if you return next Tuesday. This amount of time shows people you're hurting over the loss of a family member you were close to, but you're also committed to solving these cases," he says, looking over to me.

I nod my encouragement to him, reminding him it's the right thing to do, even if it was a weird way for him to phrase it. I hear her voice speed up and get slightly louder; I can just make out the tail end of what she's saying come through the receiver. "I can't just sit at home while they're out there!" I knew she wouldn't like this idea. I can already tell she's a stubborn one. I smirk; she's most definitely a stubborn one.

"Take some time at home; I don't want to hear from

you again until I see you next week," he barks into the phone, then pauses for a moment, looking over at me before he adds. "I don't want to hear from anyone you are covertly working when you should be grieving, understand?" he pauses, listening to whatever she's saying, and nods to let me know she's agreed. "Good, now get some rest. I suggest catching up on some you time. Whatever it is that makes you relax, makes you feel good, just do that." Letting out a large sigh, he rubs a hand over his eyes while placing his phone on the desk.

"I can hear it in her voice," he says, sounding surprised.

I just nod, not saying any of the callous things I want to in this moment. How can he be so surprised about this? I walk to the doorway before I turn back to look at him.

"It's the right thing for her, even if she doesn't know it right now," I assure him.

He gives me a nod before he begins shuffling through the paperwork on his desk, dismissing me.

CHAPTER TEN

Me Time

My mother squeezes tighter as I attempt to pry myself from the vise grip that is her hug while standing on the front porch of my parent's house. I'm plagued by a slight headache accompanied by puffy eyes, compliments of all the crying I've done this weekend. I have to wonder how anyone gets anything done with this array of feelings always spiraling out of control inside them. I'm frustrated, and if I'm totally honest with myself, I feel helpless. I can't remember a time in my life when I felt helpless, probably because I can't remember a time when I ever felt anything other than the general discomfort about the fact that I don't feel anything like everyone else. I've always just been an emotional void. That was nice; it was quiet in my brain, and there was much less crying. How do I get that back?

Later than we would like, thanks to my parents' warranted but inconvenient, tearful goodbyes taking longer than planned, Cole and I are walking to our gate in the small airport of my hometown. Standing in the security line, waiting for my turn, I'm overtaken by a memory so vivid I would swear I was reliving it.

Sarah has a hold of my hand and is dragging me through this same airport to our gate. The plane is scheduled for take-off in less than fifteen minutes.

"Come on, Jess, we're going to miss the flight! I can't miss the flight for my own wedding!" she begs, trying to convince me of the urgency, face red with clear frustration.

Our final destination is Cancun, after two lay-overs and three planes. Even knowing it's because of me and seeing that her cheeks are flushed red, and her jaw is clenching in frustration, I can't seem to bring myself to care. In typical fashion, I have no anxiety or fear. Who cares if I miss a flight? Who cares if I miss her wedding? It's just another social interaction I'm being forced to pretend in.

Watching myself in the memory gives me an unsettled feeling, and I begin to hate the person who is, in fact, me from my past. I hate the detached, bored look that sits across my face, making me look like a stranger compared to what I see in the mirror today. I feel a warm hand on my cheek, causing me to blink back from the memory.

Cole stands in front of me, cradling my face in his palms.

"Where did you go to just now, Jess?" His calm voice washes over me and chases away the memory. His concern for me shines in his eyes.

"I…uh, well, I guess I was thinking about my sister." I look away from those kind eyes, wanting to seethe in my self-hatred a little while longer. "I was thinking about how awful it must have been to have me as a sister. How Sarah didn't get to choose to have me. In fact, she had no say in the matter. She probably spent the first seven years of her life thinking she would be an only child, just to have me come along. Quite possibly the worst sister anyone could get stuck with." I frantically wipe at the tears now streaming down my face, the flames of anger at myself flaring even hotter. "She got stuck with me, but never once complained about it. She was always kind to me, always watched out for me, and always had my back no matter what…" I trail off, staring intently at a crack in the tile beneath my left foot, wishing it would open up and swallow me whole.

I try to cling to the anger and push the sadness back behind one of the many walls I've been working on constructing in my own mind. Cole has other ideas; he slides his knuckles under my chin and gently lifts my face until I'm forced to stare into his emerald eyes.

"That's how family is," he says with a smile, expecting it to just make sense to me, like something so complicated can be explained in just a simple sentence. He wipes a tear that trails down my cheek. "I'm sure she loved you, no matter what." The knife in my chest twists, and I flinch at the immediate pain his words cause because he's right. Sarah did love me no matter how horrid I was to her; no matter how much I didn't deserve her love, she loved me anyway.

"I don't think you understand," I huff out. I look up into his eyes and somehow manage to swallow the bile threatening to rise in my throat. "I was awful to her," I hiss. Pulling my chin from his grip, I continue through the line, finish security checks, and briskly walk toward our gate, where we are mercifully ushered onto the plane.

Being late has its advantages when you're politely trying to avoid continuing a conversation you don't want to have with your travel companion. I make my way down the small center aisle of the plane and find there are no open seats next to one another left—a small mercy. I quickly sit between two other passengers, making sure to spend a bit longer buckling my seatbelt than necessary—a blatant attempt to avoid Cole's piercing stare when he walks past my aisle to his seat five rows behind. It's a brief reprieve because I already know this conversation has been filed away, to be continued at a later time, in his sharp mind. Another time where he will do his damnedest to convince me not to hate myself without knowing all the facts. I'm not ready to tell him why I have every right to hate myself. I know, in the end, once I tell him all those reasons, not only will I hate myself, but he will, too.

I'm halfway across the airport, having jumped up and shoved my way off the plane as quickly as someone with such a small stature can before he finally manages to catch up with me.

"Jessica. Are you alright?" he asks, practically panting from running after me.

"Me? Oh yeah, I'm good. I just have a lot to catch up on, you know, on the cases," I lie.

The guilt I feel for acting like a petulant child begins nudging the back of my brain, threatening to topple down the wall I crammed all of my sadness behind to make room for my hatred and anger. I slow my mad dash toward the door, shifting my jacket and carry-on luggage to my left hand. I fumble with the app on my phone to order a cab home and do my best not to look into his eyes. The same eyes that'll surely crumble all the patchwork I've been slathering over the cracks in that wall.

I send up a silent prayer that he will, just this once, let me be a liar, so I don't have to have a mental breakdown in the middle of a busy New York airport on a Monday afternoon. He frowns, but doesn't push the matter any further. Instead, he reminds me I can call him if I need him while he gestures toward the door, giving me my escape. I nod my appreciation at this tentative truce and rush out the doors to the cab waiting for me.

****

Some people call ice cream dessert, but apparently tonight I'll be calling it dinner. I release a long sigh and settle into the acceptance of my life choice. It's not enough that I have to feel my feelings but, apparently, I also have to eat them. I throw the now empty container into the trash and decide now is a good time to call Chief Harding to let him know how the service went and check in to see if anything happened while we were gone.

"Detective Fairling, how was your sister's service?" His gruff voice greets me, oddly settling my nerves a bit.

"Hi, Chief Harding, it was… both sad and cathartic," I say. My eyes begin to well up with tears at the memory of how sad it was. Oh, great, here we go again. Ice cream, puppies playing in a meadow, kittens catching yarn… I repeat these happy thoughts in my mind, trying to curb the waterworks while I attempt to push the conversation forward. "I was calling to see if anything new happened while I was away so that I'm prepared when I come back tomorrow morning," I say, finding my way into the living room to curl up on the couch, waterworks officially curbed.

"Jessica, you can't come back tomorrow. It's too soon. Normally, a person in your situation would take some time off after something like this. I think it's best if you return next Tuesday. This amount of time shows people you're hurting over the loss of a family member you were close to, but you're also committed to solving these cases," he orders.

His response causes a tendril of anger to wiggle its way into my heart, but I do my best to stomp on it. He's thought this over; he's actually sat down to come up with a time frame for me to pretend to have feelings and help me cover up that I have none. The problem is, I no longer have to pretend; I now have those feelings. In fact, this is such a bad idea now to have time alone with my feelings. I don't want that at all.

"But the killer is still out there. What if there's another murder? What if they're committing it right now?" I attempt to appeal to the detective in him. I stand from the couch and begin pacing my small living room. "I can't just sit at home while they're out there."

I do my best to keep the emotion from my voice when, really, I just want to scream at the top of my lungs. I want to scream that I can't be left alone with my feelings. I want to scream that they have to pay for what they've done to my sister and the other women, and I need to be the one who catches them. It has to be now and not later.

"Take some time at home; I don't want to hear from you again until I see you next week," he pauses, and I hold my breath, hoping maybe he's reconsidering, or he'll give me a covert mission to investigate the case during my so-called grieving time. "I don't want to hear from anyone that you are covertly working when you should be grieving, understand?"

Shit. "Yes, sir. I understand." I grit my teeth in frustration while he tells me to do whatever makes me relax before he ends the call.

Throwing my cellphone on the couch, I grab the closest pillow and scream into it. I scream until tears flood down my cheeks. I scream until my throat is raw, and all I feel inside is an empty void. A void threatening to pull me into it, offering the sweetest oblivion of nothingness. I curl myself into a ball on the couch and let that void pull me into one of the deepest periods of sleep I can ever remember having.

A loud knocking causes me to roll over and almost off

the couch. Shit, my neck hurts. I climb to my feet, gently rolling my head from side to side to stretch it out. In yesterday's clothes, with puffy eyes, I make my way to the door, remembering to peer out the peephole, and see nothing. What the hell? I step out of my apartment to check the hallway but find it empty; maybe I dreamt the knocking. Turning to go back inside, I see an envelope taped to the door with my name typed on it. I grab it and check down the hallway one more time; still seeing no one, I lock my door shut. I throw the envelope on the kitchen counter, deciding I'd much rather find out what's inside with a cup of strong, dark coffee in my hand.

Settling into one of the chairs at the counter nursing a fresh cup of dark coffee, I slowly open the envelope while my heart pounds loudly in my ears. Inside is a typed letter.

Jessica Fairling,

I think it's time we meet. Hollow Cove Marina, tonight at 11 pm.

Come alone.

Reading the letter again, a shudder works its way down my spine. I wonder if this could be the killer. It wouldn't be that far-fetched for them to contact me directly since I am the lead detective on the case. I'm well aware that the proper protocol is for me to call this into the precinct and let the chief know, but he's benched me for the week. I'm absolutely certain if I call him about this letter, I'll end up watching from the sidelines while he sends some other detectives to Hollow Cove to find whoever's responsible for the death of Sarah and arrest them. This sorry excuse for a human being deserves far worse than the inside of a cell and a "fair trial." Whoever caused my adoptive father to fall into such a dark place, causing him to let his normally meticulously groomed appearance go, and dark black circles creep in underneath his normally bright green eyes, won't get that privilege. Not if I have anything to say about it. No, I don't think I'll be following protocol here. This is going to be my little secret.

I mentally make a list of distractions I can busy myself with before tonight's meeting, and I finish drinking the remainder of my coffee. It seems impossible, but somehow, I need to find things to occupy myself for the next twelve hours.

By dinnertime, I had cleaned my apartment, washed every piece of laundry I own, and rearranged my bookshelves four times, finally settling on alphabetical by author. I realize this must be anxiety. I have no idea how people deal with this stuff day in and day out. Feelings, ick.

I sit quietly on my couch, inhaling deeply, then slowly

exhaling with my eyes closed and my head back. I let a sense of calm wash over me, and I do my best to think of absolutely nothing. I suppose some would call it meditation. However, my calm is completely destroyed by the ringing of my phone. I snatch it from the table next to me and see it's Cole calling. I debate whether I should answer the call at all. I can't afford to be distracted, and I know well enough that he's a huge distraction. I can barely put coherent thoughts together in his general vicinity, and he certainly doesn't let me hold on to my self-loathing or anger, that I need in order to make tonight work for me. After the third ring, I decide it's better to answer his call than it is to put him off. If I don't answer, he might stop by to check in on me, and I definitely can't afford an in-person Cole distraction.

"Hi, Cole," I answer in the calmest voice I can muster. I can't let him hear the anxiety currently rolling around inside me or else he'll know something is up.

"Hey, Jess. How are you holding up?" he asks. It's such a generic question, but with him, he actually is curious. He truly cares about how I feel, and how I answer him will depend on his next move.

"I'm doing alright," I say, not wanting to commit to feeling good, or bad.

If I'm too good, then he'll think something's wrong

with me, and that will raise red flags. If I'm too bad, then he'll want to come over and comfort me. While the thought of Cole coming to my apartment to comfort me is a genuinely intriguing thought, I can't let that happen, either. In just a few hours, I'll be face to face with whoever killed my sister. Finally, face to face with the person, or even persons, who killed all these women because if there is one thing I know for sure, it's these murders are connected.

"Chief has me taking some time off. He suggested I take a little at-home time to get some rest and recuperate," I say as nonchalantly as I can manage. I don't want to let him know I don't agree with it. I need him to think this is something I'm agreeing to, not internally fighting.

"Yeah, I met with him," he says. He clears his throat before continuing. "I suggested you take some more time off."

I shoot up from the couch, anger rolling over me like a wave. What the fuck? Cole suggested I take time off. He's the one who suggested I rest and recuperate, not Chief Harding. Not only am I overwhelmed with anger, but I also feel the hit of betrayal like a punch to the gut. It feels like everyone got together to discuss my mental state without ever consulting me; they just decided what's best for me without my input at all. I close my eyes and take in a cleansing breath. I lower myself back down to the couch; I need to calm down because I have to play this off. If I want any chance of getting out to Hollow Cove without him or the chief involved, then I have to convince him I'm fine with the time off.

"Thank you, Cole. Truly, thank you for looking out for me," I say to him, but my mind is screaming, fuck you, Cole, fuck you for getting involved at all.

He goes on to tell me nothing new has been discovered in our time away, but everyone is still diligently working on what info we have. Hearing that causes my shoulders to slowly relax and my jaw to loosen little by little. If I'm honest with myself, that gives me a feeling of relief. I know it's utterly selfish, I know I should want nothing more than progress to happen whether I'm there. I'm well aware I should want anyone to put an end to this sooner rather than later, but I've decided I have to be honest with myself if no one else. So, I let myself feel jealous. I allow the feeling of envy that there are other people, other detectives rifling around in my case files, reading about my killer, and attempting to solve my case. Yes, this is my case; after all, I'm the one who received the letter on their front door, confirming I'm the cat to their mouse.

CHAPTER ELEVEN

Hollow Cove

With Cole finally convinced I'm spending the evening at home with a book, I can start readying for the meeting with my mystery pursuer. I dress in all black: black jeans, a black sweater, and black boots, and I feel like I'm dressed to go and rob a bank. I chuckle at the absurdity while slipping my .38 Special into my ankle holster before sliding my jeans leg back over it. Okay, now I feel like I'm ready. It's still over an hour until the meeting, but I figure there's no harm in showing up early to get the lay of the area and note all the exits—that kind of stuff.

I call for a cab and anxiously fidget in the back seat the entire drive. At the last minute, I decide to have the driver drop me in front of a pizza place a few blocks away, instead of at the marina itself. It's better if no one else is around when I arrive; the last thing I want to do is spook whoever I'm meeting. I watch the cab's taillights disappear and start to walk toward Hollow Cove Marina. My phone vibrates, letting me know I've arrived at my destination.

The small marina has a single road serving as the entrance and exit—smart choice for them to select this place. The late hour means the marina office is long closed, as well as the restaurant. The overhead streetlights peppering the small road are dim, giving it an overall eerie feeling, and setting me on edge. I have a moment of doubt where I wonder what the hell is wrong with me, and my brain goes over all the reasons why I shouldn't be here. I conclude that even with a .38 Special tucked in my pant leg, this is a really stupid idea. I feel my palms start to sweat and become acutely aware that I can hear my heartbeat in my ears, which is now blocking out the sound of my surroundings.

I remind myself that if I don't do this tonight, they might never try to make further contact and just disappear. I can't let that happen; I have to do this now, for Sarah, for all the victims. I straighten my spine and hold my head up as I round the corner. There's an elderly man, hunched over, standing next to a bench overlooking the tiny marina. My steps slow to a stop, and I briefly scan the area for someone else. This can't be right. This guy has to be here for something else, which means he has to get the hell out of here. This man has to leave. I can't risk that he'll witness whatever happens here. It puts his life at risk. Panic settles in, making me consider turning around and walking back to the pizza place to call a cab to take me back to my apartment. I could pretend I never got the letter; it's not like it was handed to me and no one else knows I'm here. The thought causes the panic to tighten its grip on my chest and my breathing to speed up. No one knows I'm here. If the killer is, in fact, killers, like our latest theory suggests, then I'm outnumbered. Sure, I have a gun, but I only have one clip. Fuck, this was a stupid idea.

The old man starts waving me over. I blink a few times, bringing my thoughts back to the present and clearing the haze of panic from my head. I check behind me to ensure he isn't waving to someone else, but there's no one there, which means he's who I'm meeting. I turn back to him, and he's still waving at me to sit next to where he's now sitting on the bench facing the boats. My legs slowly carry me to the bench, and I uneasily sit on the edge. I wait for him to realize I'm not who he thought I was and hurry himself away to somewhere safer. Instead, he smiles somberly at me, then looks out over the boats in the marina. I don't take my eyes off him. I study him, looking for any clue as to whether this could be the man responsible for the death of my sister and the other women. He stands shorter than me, five feet five inches, with hunched shoulders, a head of gray hair, and large gold-framed glasses, which make his eyes look much larger than they are, like a bug. He pulls his beige windbreaker around his shoulders, then makes eye contact with me. His eyes are sad.

"Hello, Jessica," he says, nodding to me. I startle at his use of my first name. "I know it's a lot to ask of you to come here, to trust in a stranger while you are in the middle of hunting as you are." He takes his glasses off to wipe at a smudge on the left lens with his shirtsleeve. "I've asked you here because I think I can help you." He places his glasses back on his face, then stares right at me; it feels like he's seeing right to my core. It seems like a lot of people have been making me feel that way lately. His stare causes me to shift uneasily on the bench's edge.

"Jessica, I know what you are," he says, and I draw back on the bench, bumping into the arm of it to back away from him. My mind struggles to keep up with the thoughts flitting across it at breakneck speed. How could he know what I am? He said, 'I know what you are', not who you are. What exactly does that mean? Does he know I'm a detective? Does he know I'm Sarah's sister? I want to ask all these questions out loud, but something inside my mind niggles at me, telling me I know exactly what he means. How does this stranger know anything about me?

"Your parents, your biological parents, were part of an experiment. It was a psychological experiment carried out by a group of people who went too far," he pauses, staring out over the boats again. His eyes gloss over as if he's lost deep in some horrific memory.

He sits for a minute, with a haunted look on his face, and I let him. I let what he's said sink in, rolling it around in my brain, trying to make sense of it. I still have so many questions, but I won't ask them. In training, they teach us to let the witness speak first; they know what they need to tell you, just let them have the time to do so. So, that's what I do. I sit patiently, waiting for him to return from whatever memory haunts him and tell me what he needs to say.

"I can't give you much more information," he finally says, returning eye contact to me and sighing. "I can't tell you much more without giving myself up and putting myself in danger. I'm sorry, but I won't do that." He straightens his jacket cuffs, pulling them down past his shirt cuffs, and forces himself to sit straighter. "What I can tell you is soon you will start to get witnesses, people who have fragments of memories that can help you with this case. Trust me when I say they aren't delusional. Trust me when I tell you that you need to take them seriously. It's not their fault. The group doesn't know about you, and I suspect you are smart enough to keep it that way. Once this is over, I'll find you. I can fix you."

His beady eyes bore into mine. He thinks I still can't feel things. I let out a breath and struggle to keep my face neutral. I'll let him think I still don't feel things, let him think he needs to fix me, then he can come back to me after everything is done and I'll put him down, too. Justice for all. I nod my head in agreement, letting him think that's what I want.

"You will need to dig into your biological parents' lives to learn more information. You must be careful. As I said, they still don't know about you. You flew under their radar, somehow. My advice is to never let them find out, or you might end up like your father," he says.

Now it's my turn to stare out over the boats. I never cared who my biological father was or what events led to his suicide. Why should I? He gave his only child up, then killed himself. The old man stands, and, in turn, I stand. He shuffles to the back of the bench and turns to face me.

"Good luck Jessica," he says, letting out a heavy sigh.

"This isn't an easy task, but if anyone's equipped to put an end to this, it's you."

I watch him shuffle his way down the only exit road from the marina. Once he's out of sight, I sit heavily on the bench, take in a deep breath, and wonder what the fuck that meant. I release the deep breath and look up to the stars. I even contemplate asking them for help. I chuckle at myself for ever considering they would help someone like me.

****

An obnoxious ringing rips through the quiet of my bedroom. I grunt and roll across the bed to answer the phone without looking at the caller ID. "Hello?" I do my best to sound like I've been awake. Judging by the sunlight filtering in through my tiny bedroom window, it's late.

"Good morning," Cole's masculine voice greets me on the other end of the phone line. He's no doubt calling to check on my mental state.

"Hi, Cole." I pry my eyes open to stare at the water stains that cover the ceiling over my bed.

My tiny shoe box apartment has discolored paint peeling off the walls in most places and nothing but the view of a brick wall from all three tiny windows in the whole place. It easily costs me twice what it's actually worth, with its staining down the walls from countless leaks that the landlord has let go over the years and its heater that only works whenever it feels like it.

"Jess? What do you think?" Cole's voice brings me out of my musings.

"Oh, sorry, what was that?"

"I asked if you want to grab lunch. There isn't much going on here, and I wanted to see how you're doing." He sounds pensive, almost like it would hurt his feelings if I said no.

"Sure, we can get some lunch. How's our favorite Chinese food place sound?" I ask, trying to put a smile in my voice. It's hard to do when staring at a stained ceiling, in an apartment that's literally crumbling around you.

"Great, see you in an hour," he says, ending the call. I sigh heavily, wondering if he knows a realtor.

An hour later, I walk into the Lemon Wok and find Cole at our usual table, not hard when there's only two in the whole place. I hang my bag on the back of my chair and settle into the seat across from his.

"How are you doing?" he asks, reaching across the table and placing his large hands over my much smaller ones, making them disappear.

I take a moment to let my eyes scan the empty restaurant in an attempt to cool the simmering anger still burning from being stuck at home for a week on his recommendation. Finally, they settle back on Cole: his kind smile and attentive eyes, always watching me, always learning me.

"I'm doing okay. In fact, time off has been good for me," I say, knowing he wants to hear that I'm grateful to be home, to be left alone to sort through all the emotions I'm feeling. While I give that to him, it's actually far from the truth.

What I really want is to be out hunting for these fuckers, hunting down every last one of them. My frustration clouds my thoughts and I withdraw my hands from Cole's, leaning back in my chair. He smiles, his calculating eyes watching my every movement, stripping me bare.

"You know it's okay for you not to be okay, right?" He looks up at me through his lashes and rubs the back of his neck. "This is a really hard thing you're going through. Not only having the stress of being the lead detective on a serial killer case, but also your sister's case."

"Killers," I add, under my breath.

Cole's eyebrows shoot up. "What?"

Shit, I cringe. Granted, it was his theory this wasn't one person. He just can't know that I can now confirm that based on what the old man in the marina told me last night, because I don't plan on telling him about that meeting. I quickly do my best to change the subject; I need to buy myself more time to find another way to confirm that.

"After all this soul searching, I've had time to do, I think I'm going to take some of my 'me time' to head to DC. I've never really wanted to learn anything about my biological parents before, but after losing Sarah..." I trail off, the backs of my eyes stinging with tears that I have to fight not to fall. "Well, I guess I'm curious now."

He sits up straighter in his chair. "I think that's a great idea. In fact, I'd love to join you." He looks so honest, so pure of intention. "If you'd like me to, of course." He tacks on, looking a little embarrassed at the admission. I know if I said no, he would understand, but I have to be honest with myself. I'd really enjoy his company.

"Okay," I say, and offer him a smile.

After lunch, we walk hand in hand to my apartment building, the silence comfortable and his touch comforting. Standing outside the building, I drop his hand and turn to him. His eyes flicker with some emotion I can't read, and the weight of unsaid words hangs heavily between us. Well, it hangs heavily from me, anyway. I'm never sure what he's thinking, but I wholeheartedly believe he's a mind reader and knows what I'm thinking at all times.

"Do you know a local realtor?" I blurt out, causing his mouth to open and close quickly, reminding me of a fish. I bet that whatever he was thinking I'd say, that wasn't it. Maybe he isn't a mind reader after all.

"I um, yeah, I do. The realtor who helped me with my most recent apartment was decent," he says, finally recovering from my abrupt change of subject and lets out a chuckle. "Are you looking to move?"

I must sound like a crazy person, working a case as big as this, losing my sister, and now deciding to finally dig into the details of my biological parents.

"Yeah, my lease is almost up, and I don't want to stick it out another year in this place." I point up toward the building. "The roof leaks." I smile weakly, knowing damn well my lease is good for another six months. He nods as if my white lie makes sense, even though I know I still sound crazy. He texts over the contact details to his realtor, nonetheless.

"Sometimes a drastic change and a fresh start are exactly what you need." He lays his hand on my shoulder and gives it a comforting squeeze. "Let me know when you want to head to DC so I can give the chief a heads up that I'll be out of town."

I agree to let him know my plans, then head back

inside to my leaking, peeling, shoe box of an apartment. I have a realtor to call.

CHAPTER TWELVE

Burns on the Way Down

My neck protests as I crane it, looking up to the top floor of the modern glass apartment building I'm standing in front of. Through the floor-to-ceiling glass doors, I see a security guard behind a desk, checking the IDs of the people who enter, offering an extra level of security. I stand outside, admiring the building and waiting for my realtor. What a difference five blocks can make.

My realtor, a petite, platinum-blond woman, saunters up next to me, clutching a folder in her hand. She flashes me a bright smile, showing perfectly straight white teeth, and reaches out to shake my hand. I arch an eyebrow and take her in from the heels of her sensible black pumps, perfectly pressed pantsuit to the curl of her hair spiraling out of the bun on her head. This woman has clearly taken more time securing her hair than I have in my entire morning routine. I look down at my faded black jeans and unremarkable blue T-shirt. I never figured I'd feel under-dressed apartment hunting. Wait, I feel... under-dressed. Is this another anxiety thing? Do people wander around all day worried about what other people look like? Are they wondering if they should have worn a nicer pair of pants or a brighter shade of lipstick? Internally, I groan at the revelation and come to the conclusion feelings really do suck. She shakes my hand with her perfectly manicured pink fingernails, causing me to sigh yet again, catching sight of my un-manicured naked fingernails, which I quickly shove in my pockets.

"The unit is located on the 23rd floor; it's as close to the top as you can get without having a penthouse," she says. She practically glows. I wonder if it's rude to ask about her skincare routine. "We just have to sign in with the doorman and he'll open the elevator for us. It's a very secure building."

She leads us to the desk with the doorman, and we hand over our IDs to sign-in. Reaching the 23rd floor, she leads us to the apartment, almost at the end of the hallway. I pause just inside the door, gawking at the white marble kitchen counter in a kitchen that's larger than my current apartment's living room. My gaze travels farther in and catches on the floor-to-ceiling windows that overlook the city and a nearby park. I smile to myself, admiring the light bamboo floors and large built-in bookshelf, complete with LED lighting in the main living area. I venture farther inside and find the bedroom also has floor-to-ceiling windows, a walk-in closet attached to an en-suite bathroom, and a full-sized soaking tub held up with clawed feet. I do my best to smooth my face back to neutral, wiping the stupid grin off it from imagining myself soaking while reading one of my crime novels. Then, I turn to 'Rebeca, but you can call me Becky' and find her smiling, standing in the doorway. She knows she's already got me; I note the folder she's still holding onto and can only assume the rental agreement is inside. I'm sure the paperwork's been filled in with my information since I called her last night to explain my current situation. Nevertheless, I find myself returning her smile. Fuck it.

"I'll take it," I proclaim. Her smile somehow grows even larger, and she wastes no time leading us over to the kitchen counter for me to sign.

Back in my soon-to-be ex-apartment, after packing most of what little personal belongings I have, I decide to give myself a break and come back to the books later. Sitting down on the couch with a cup of hot tea, yes, it's odd. I know, it's not coffee, I get the overwhelming urge to call Cole. I want to call him and tell him about my new apartment, tell him about my day, and how I feel. That feels dangerous, so instead, I decide to call my mom.

"Hi, Jessica!" She all but yells into the phone after the second ring.

"Hi, Mom," I say, smiling at her enthusiasm.

"Let me get your father on the line as well."

There is some shuffling while I hear her cover the mouthpiece of the phone and yell for my father.

"Hi, honey," my father's gruff voice greets over the line.

"Hi, Dad," I say, looking over at all the packed boxes occupying my living room. "I got a new apartment today," I tell them. "It's only a few blocks away, but it's bigger, newer, and much safer." I smile at the memory of floor-to-ceiling windows with all the natural light pouring in over the light wood floors and the clawfoot tub.

"Oh, honey, that's wonderful," my mother croons. "Isn't that wonderful, Joe?" she prompts my father.

"Yeah, yes, that's great, honey. We are so proud of you," my father's hollow voice responds to her prodding.

The thought of his unkempt hair with his untrimmed beard flashes in my memory, and I'm hit with a massive wave of guilt. My sister's killers are still out there, and here I am playing house.

"I, um, I just thought I'd give you guys a heads up that I'll have a new address soon. I'll send you an e-mail with the new one once I get everything settled. I love you guys. I've gotta run, busy morning and all."

I don't really have to go. Honestly, I just can't bear to hear the sadness in my father's voice. The sadness that won't ever go away, but might ease up if only I can catch the people responsible for taking away his daughter.

"Okay, honey. We love you very much. Good luck with the move, Jess." My mother responds while my father mumbles his goodbyes, as if on autopilot.

****

The dripping of water from a new slow leak in the bathroom sink forces me out of bed on Friday morning. Cole and I leave for DC today, and I remind myself that when we return, all my stuff will be in the new apartment. Then, I won't ever have to come back here. I pack my toiletries into a bag before I shut the water valve under the sink off. I don't need this place flooding before I can get out of it. My stomach flips at the thought of a long weekend in DC with him. In the interest of saving money after upgrading to my new lavish apartment, we opted to share a hotel room with two double beds. If I'm honest with myself, which I have to be, I'm more excited about being in such close quarters with my work partner than I am about finding anything about my biological parents. I wonder what that says about me: the lead detective on a serial killer case finds she's more boy-crazed than catching killers crazed. I drag my hand over my face; it's going to be a long weekend.

This time, I opt to meet Cole at the airport instead of sharing a cab with him, giving me a little extra time to compartmentalize the myriad of emotions swimming around inside of me. Before I go to the gate, I, of course, decide to make a stop at the coffee roaster inside the airport. Walking up to the counter, I catch sight of Cole sitting in front of our gate, wearing a pair of well-worn blue jeans that easily show me which pocket he keeps his keys in. The white T-shirt he's chosen accentuates his tanned arms and is just snug enough around his chest to show he's no slouch in the gym. Someone clears their throat, dragging my attention from him, and I look up to find the barista behind the counter with a goofy grin plastered on her face watching me.

"He's quite a looker, isn't he?" she asks, winking at me conspiratorially. I offer her an awkward smile, not exactly sure how to respond to that. "Don't worry, I had the same look on my face when he walked up this morning to order those coffees." She nods toward the two coffee cups beside him on a small table. "The only reason I didn't give him my number is because of what he said when he ordered the second coffee," she pauses for effect, and I raise an eyebrow, coaxing her to continue. "The one that's black as night and twice as strong as the usual, he said 'she likes it to burn on the way down.'" She chuckles while brushing her hair back from her forehead. "Any chick who orders that kind of coffee is not one I want to cross if you get me."

She shrugs, watching me eye Cole again, and this time a genuine smile creeps its way across my face. I tear my eyes off him to take a look at the barista. She's cute enough, with a short bob of red hair, a pale complexion, and a dusting of freckles across her nose, which is pierced with a small hoop. I can't help but chuckle. I think I feel whatever the opposite of jealousy is. Is that even an emotion?

"Smart move," I agree, winking at her. She has more sense than I'd have given her credit for. I smile at her before turning on my heel and walking over to Cole.

He looks up from his phone as I approach, offering me one of his real smiles, and hands me the coffee in question. The one I've been assured will burn on the way down. I sit in the chair next to him and take that first sip. The sip that makes your eyes close while it tingles all the right spots on the way down, firing my neurons up, and I know, I just know, the look he's giving me. The one where he looks as if he would like nothing more than to eat me alive. The coffee somehow tastes better, knowing that his look is for me, even if I don't fully understand it yet. I open my eyes to the coffee counter, where I catch the barista watching me, and laughing to herself. She smiles, then gives her full attention to the espresso machine, as if her life depends on its cleanliness.

"Do you know her?" Cole asks, breaking my stare down with the barista.

"Nope, sure don't," I say, smiling.

We stand when the airline attendant calls out to begin boarding our plane, and we shuffle our way on board. This time, we're seated next to each other, and I take the short time on our flight to review the information I've located on my father. It isn't much. He must have been pretty high on security clearance lists for his position. The majority of what I could find was information about his death or, rather, his suicide. At age thirty-one, my father shot himself in the head with his .45 caliber pistol after downing a bottle of bourbon in a hotel room. Due to his security clearance, it only made a short blurb in the papers. The housekeeping staff of the high-class hotel where he decided to commit the atrocity had the misfortune of finding him the following morning. I wasn't able to locate much more information on him, as most of his records were sealed, including his home address. Not that the address would help much since this happened twenty years ago and has likely changed hands more than once since then. I was, however, able to locate a newspaper article about his funeral with the names of a few attendees I managed to look up. Cole, of course, believing I want nothing more than to connect to my dead father's memory, is on board for finding these people with me. I know it's going to get a bit awkward when I start questioning them about secret genetic experiments.

We enjoy our dinner in a small, darker-than-necessary hole-in-the-wall restaurant, and watch one of the funeral attendees, Robert Mitchell. He's a slightly older, slightly rounder version of the man in the photos from the newspaper article I found. He stands in front of the bar talking with, who I can only imagine, based on their suits and ties, a few work colleagues. He appears all business, wearing a pale green button-up shirt under a charcoal gray suit, no tie to note, but gold cuff links shining in the dim bars lighting. I momentarily wonder if this is what my father would look like now if he hadn't killed himself. I never cared much about learning much about my biological parents; they gave me up, and the Fairling's took me in. There was never a reason for me to wonder why or who they actually were. Sure, I know what happened to them, but I know nothing about what kind of people they were. Until now, until they have something to do with the murder of my adoptive sister. I shake the thought from my head while I take a sip of my bourbon, mulling over my choice of drink this evening. Maybe I'm a bit more like my biological father than I think.

Eventually, Robert's work colleagues empty out, leaving him alone and still drinking. I pat Cole on the arm and get up to make my way to the bar. Luckily, Cole understands this is a conversation I want to start on my own, so he hangs back at our small table, waiting for me.

"Hello there," I say, offering a smile to Robert and taking a seat on the bar stool next to where he's leaning.

He startles, which doesn't say much considering how much I've watched him drink this evening. At this point, I'm sure a gentle breeze from the door opening would be enough to startle him.

"Oh, hello," he replies, turning his attention to me, then down to the empty glass I have brought to the bar. Squinting his eyes, he takes me in from head to toe. "You look… familiar?" He slurs, planting himself firmly onto the stool next to mine.

"Do I?" I ask. Perfect, I guess I did inherit more than my choice of alcohol from my father. Well, this makes introductions easier. "Maybe you knew my father," I suggest, flagging down the bartender for a refill of my drink. "His name was Thomas Carson." I make eye contact just in time to watch Robert flinch at the memories that name brings up.

"Thomas didn't have a child," he scoffs, his alcohol-flushed face scrunching with doubt.

"Well, he and my mother were estranged," I add. The bartender hands me another bourbon. "I guess it's just taken me this long to want to find out who he was." I smile innocently, sipping the bourbon. "Did you know my father well?"

"I did..." He nods and looks down at his hands, cradling what's left of his own drink. "Thomas was my partner." This I already knew from the newspaper article. "I guess I thought I knew him well." He takes a long swig from his drink, finishing it before he lets out a sigh. "We went to college, graduated, and worked in the same division together. To think he somehow had a child in that time without me knowing..." he trails off, looking down at the bottom of his empty glass.

"Well, don't take offense," I say, patting his arm gently. "My mother insisted he kept the information private. She was a young businesswoman, not wanting to ruin her reputation being unwed and with child." The lie rolls easily off my tongue. For all I know, it's the truth. I keep my hand on Robert's arm and gently squeeze it. "Is there anything you can tell me about my father that would help me get to know him better?"

His glassy eyes make contact with my much clearer ones. "Well, I have a small box of his belongings at my house. He didn't have any immediate family." His eyes go wide as he realizes who he's speaking to. "I mean, that I knew of," he quickly adds on, shaking his head in apology. I smile and nod for him to continue. "I'd be happy to give it over to you. I don't live far from here."

Robert tries to stand on his own, almost face-planting into the bar on his way back down to sitting on the bar stool, and I wave Cole over.

"That's very kind of you, Robert; we can accompany you home in a cab. Make sure you make it there safely," I say, nodding to Cole. He pulls out his cell phone to order a cab for us while Robert rattles off his address. His house isn't far from here, but at this point, I don't trust him standing on his own, let alone walking, and I certainly don't want to carry him.

CHAPTER THIRTEEN

I Think I Need More Bourbon

Cole watches me pace the small hotel room from his seat on the bed. A shoe box, the object of my anxiety, sits next to him.

"I don't know if I'm ready for this," I say, wringing my hands in front of me.

"It's a lot," he agrees. I slow my frantic pacing to listen to what he has to say. "This is a person who you've had no connection to your entire life, for all intents and purposes, a stranger." I nod; even though he was my biological parent, I still never knew anything about him. "It's a huge step to try to learn who this man was that gave you up for adoption, then took his own life. And, to do this with everything else that's going on right now in your life?" Sitting up straight, he places his hands on his knees. "Well, you're an amazingly strong person."

He finally makes eye contact with me and offers me a smile. Not the award-winning toothy smile he gives everyone to show how disarming he is, but his real smile. The smile I get to see more of as we spend more time together, the one that lights the room with a different kind of fire. I look away from that smile; not only does that smile light the room, but it also lights a fire in me.

"I think I need more bourbon." I laugh, taking a seat on the bed and leaving the box between us.

He stands and gently brushes a lock of rogue hair that's fallen over my forehead behind my ear before offering to go downstairs to the hotel bar and grab us a bottle. I gaze into his concerned eyes and can do nothing other than nod. I definitely need more bourbon; I think while watching him walk out the door. I use the time he's gone to calm my nerves. The box next to me mocks me the entire time. I have no idea what it contains, and that makes me uneasy. I'm still staring at the box, willing it to whisper its secrets to me, when Cole returns with a bottle and two plastic cups in hand. He fills the cups and repositions himself on the other side of the box as before.

Taking a large drink of bourbon, I take in a deep breath and finally crack the lid. Inside, I find a few newspaper clippings along with some older photos of my father. The meager contents hold no great clue to any psychological experiments he's participated in, no confession letter of genetic experiments, or anything useful really. I'm not sure what I was expecting, but I feel a large rock of disappointment settle in my gut. The newspaper clippings are about his brief college sports career, and most of the photos are of him with classmates, but there's one photo with a woman who has my eyes. This must be my mother; I think, taking in the familiar slope of her nose and round cheeks. The two people staring back at me through time captured in this photo, the creators of my life, are the same two creators who gave me away.

Anger snakes its way in, and my grip tightens on the photo, bending it slightly. I welcome it; anger is an emotion I understand and am comfortable with. These two people just left me for someone else to raise, for someone else to feed and clothe while they both...well, died. Just like that, the small sprout of anger I was cultivating in the hope it would grow into a massive tree dies, too. It was almost like they knew what was coming for them: my mother was murdered, and my father took his own life shortly after. The timing can't be a coincidence. Maybe they weren't giving me up so much as saving me, but from what? I shake my head, dislodging the thoughts, and find Cole watching me.

"Penny for your thoughts?" he quietly asks. I chuckle

before I take another healthy sip of bourbon.

"Is that your clever way of asking me 'how does that make you feel'?" I cock my eyebrow in amusement.

"Yeah, I guess it is." He chuckles and takes a sip of his own bourbon.

"Well, I guess at first it made me angry, seeing a box of memories that don't include me, his own child. Almost like he didn't give a shit about the seven years my mother raised me." I take another drink to fortify my nerves. "Then…" I scoot across the bed and settle my back against the headboard, stretching my legs in front of me on the mattress. "Then, I have to wonder if that wasn't it at all. I have to wonder if they knew what would happen to them, and that's why they gave me up. Maybe he left me alone with my mother for our safety. Then, when things went sideways… maybe they knew someone was after my mother." I take another sip of bourbon, feeling my head start to float a little. "My biological mother was murdered." I make eye contact with Cole, who's now scooting up to lean against the headboard as I am.

"I know. I read your adoption file," he admits, grimacing and not making eye contact with me.

I can't say I'm shocked; Cole's a thorough guy. I have no doubt he's researched all he can find about the person he's working with.

"Penny for *your* thoughts?" I use his question on him, earning me a smile.

"Well..." he says hesitantly, "I was intrigued; your mother's murder was only six months after you were given up for adoption. I was even more surprised to learn before that you were home schooled while kept mostly by a nanny. Do you remember much of your mother?"

"Honestly, no. I don't even remember what she looked like, and seeing that photo of her and my father doesn't spark any sort of memories for me," I admit. It felt like looking at two strangers.

I look into his kind, concerned, beautifully green eyes. Had I noticed his eyes were that green before? Like the damp, green moss on the forest floor, shining in the sunlight. The bizarreness of that line of thinking snaps me back to reality, and I huff out a small laugh and take another long drink.

"Well, that's not too surprising." He shrugs, having no idea what a weird turn my thoughts have taken. "Being given up for adoption would have been a pretty traumatic experience for a child at that age, so not remembering anything before that experience isn't out of the norm." He places a hand on my arm for comfort, which, in his defense, does exactly that: it makes me feel better. "It's okay to feel angry, Jess," he says, affirming my feelings, which makes me feel even better than his hand on my arm. "It's okay to feel betrayed by them; that's normal human behavior."

I catch sight of those beautiful green eyes again and thoughts of closing the distance between us race through my mind. I imagine how soft his lips would feel and how warm his mouth would be against mine. He tilts his head slightly to the side, eyes heating with the same fire I can feel behind mine, and I go for it.

My mouth crashes into his; it's a far cry from the graceful fantasy that played out in my mind moments ago. My teeth bang into his, causing him to tense and me to wince, thinking maybe I've hurt him, but he leans into the kiss, returning the intensity. He nips and bites at my bottom lip, and I climb over his legs to straddle him against the headboard of the small double bed. I feel the flame we've been dancing around finally ignite into a full-blown inferno and I beg for it to burn me to the ground.

Almost as abruptly as it began, he grabs my arms and pulls me back from him. For a moment, we just stare into each other's eyes, taking in the hunger residing just below the surface. He audibly swallows, then shutters the look behind his eyes.

"Jess..." he grits out in a strained voice, sounding like he's in physical pain. "We've had a lot to drink tonight."

His statement causes us both to look over at the empty bottle of bourbon on the nightstand. "As much as I want this to happen..." He clears his throat but never finishes the thought, essentially never telling me no.

I sit up slowly, leaning back onto his legs while pulling his hands from my shoulders to hold them between us and try to clear the lustful thoughts from my head. Once my mental clarity returns, I nod my agreement. He's right. This can't be something that happens without full disclosure; it's something that needs to be slowly explored with both parties fully invested and knowing the stakes. This means, at some point soon, I'm going to have to let him in on my secret—the secret that could burn my whole world to the ground: that I'm a recovering psychopath.

****

A vise grip tightens around my skull and a loud thumping noise has me attempting to bury my head under my pillow. Except when I grope under my head for it, I realize I'm not lying on a pillow. I force my strained eyes to open, squinting against the light streaming in through the unclosed curtains. I turn my face toward the mattress, finding very quickly I'm not lying on a mattress; I'm lying on a body. The events of last night flood my memory, causing my cheeks to burn and my heart to speed up as I realize whose body it is I'm draped on top of. My eyes make their way up to Cole's still sleeping face, I fight the urge to run my finger down his cheek and across those soft, slightly pouting lips while he sleeps.

The thumping noise returns with a vengeance, causing me to suck in a breath and squeeze my eyes shut. Why hasn't the racket woken him up yet? More neurons fire, waking me further to realize it's because the horrid noise is inside my head. My eyes dart over to the nightstand, where an empty bottle of bourbon taunts me, and I let out a small groan; Cole pulls me tighter against his chest.

"Mmm... good morning," he says into my hair. I freeze, uncertain what to do.

"Good morning," I say, squeezing my eyes shut again, wishing his warm arms could somehow quell the pounding in my skull. He gently kisses the top of my head, causing my breath to stutter as he pulls back enough to look into my eyes.

"Don't worry," he says, smiling at my discomfort. "I packed a bottle of ibuprofen." I let out a sigh of relief. My savior, in more ways than one.

A bottle of water and four pills later, I manage to take a scalding hot shower and make my way downstairs to the hotel's restaurant, where there's mercifully fresh coffee.

Cole sips his own cup from where he sits across the table from me.

If I thought the events of last night would change the way he acts around me, I would have been completely wrong. In his typical fashion, he remains unwavering in kindness, his gentle manner of handling me and making me feel as if I'm somehow special. Ugh, I feel like I should have felt as a teenager: pining over her first crush, learning what hormones actually feel like. Instead, as a teenager, I just accrued a long list of "one and dones," you know the kind, one night with them, then done with them, completely ghosted.

At one point in my early twenties, Sarah convinced me I needed to keep one around, if not for me, for our parents' sake. So, that's what I did with Daniel Stratenberg II. Daniel was in law school to become a criminal defense attorney, just like his father. He was a shoo-in for his father's firm, and by the time he hit thirty, he would be a fully vested partner. I'm not sure if it speaks to his character or the general character of defense attorneys, but he was a fast-talking, double-dealing type of man. Being the apt pupil I was in the police academy and having to fake emotions based on my surroundings my entire life, I was very well-versed in reading other people. I knew all of his tells: a slight upward left glance when he lied, and a small tick of the jaw when he wasn't sharing information. The problem was, I didn't care. He was just arm candy for me, and he thought the same of me; what better arm candy than a police detective for an up-and-coming lawyer? Two years into our relationship, he found a better piece of arm candy. One who he very quickly, after our split, married and knocked up with a little Stratenberg, a baby boy to follow in his crooked path.

In a city as large as New York, it's easy to part ways and never have to cross paths with someone again. With over eight million people, Daniel Stratenberg II just disappeared. Luckily for me, after the split, my family assumed I was heartbroken, so they didn't push for me to rush into another relationship; instead, they left me to my own devices, and everyone focused on Sarah and her newborn son. There is nothing like a newborn baby to take the heat off of your own personal affairs.

I watch Cole from across the table, intently reading over the breakfast menu. He's nothing like Daniel. He doesn't lie or hide things from me, even when he knows I won't like them, like telling the chief to give me time off to grieve without consulting me first or looking into my past. As far as I can tell, he's a very good man, which leaves me wondering how he's still on the market. He glances up from the menu to notice me staring at him and laughs.

"I was just trying to decide if I wanted hash browns or grits with my breakfast. You know, life's important questions," he says, grinning a boyish grin and making me bark out a laugh.

CHAPTER FOURTEEN
Memories of a Past Life

Cole maneuvers the rental car into a parking space along the sidewalk on the small suburban street containing my home in Bowling Green, Virginia. I take in the house my biological mother hid us in for the early part of my life, a modest, single-story, beige-colored wooden thing. It sits halfway down a dead-end road with a tall off-white fence circling the property, providing privacy from the road. Faint memories of playing in an overgrown yard flit across my mind, and the feeling of being lost in an endless jungle brings a slight curve to my lips. The property, in reality, isn't very large, probably under half an acre, but my memories continue to skew that truth, telling me it was much larger back then. It's odd. I can remember this house, but not the woman who gave birth to me.

Parked halfway down the street, we sit in silence, giving me time to absorb the house that was once my home. I watch for any movement on the property. I did a fair bit of research on the house before making this trip, learning my aunt still owns it, but has never rented or lived in it. She's kept it for some reason or another, maybe for the connection it has to her sister. Maybe she just hasn't gotten around to selling it for a decent price. Either way, she lives two cities away and the property should be vacant.

A blacked-out town car creeps its way down the street before turning into the driveway of the house. Three large men in black business suits, looking much like mafia henchmen from movies, exit the vehicle and scan the area as they walk up the narrow pathway to the front door. On instinct, I duck down to shield myself from their view, and Cole mimics the motion while giving me a confused look. We hunker down near the center console, staring at each other in silence. After what feels like a lifetime, but is probably only a minute or two, he lifts his head and peers out of the windshield.

"They've gone inside," he grumbles.

He opens the driver's side door, quietly closes it behind him, and walks to the trunk of our vehicle. I follow after him, keeping my movements as silent as I can. My senses are on high alert from the unexpected visitors. I'm overwhelmed by the urge to tell Cole everything about the strange meeting I had with the old man at the marina and about what I've learned with my biological parents being involved in some top-secret experiment. I just can't find the words. Instead, I reach over and clutch his hand. He only hesitates a moment before he returns the gesture, giving me the confidence he's still here with me.

"Who are those men?" he asks, watching the house from our spot behind the car.

I shrug in response, not knowing who they are or how to explain why I have the overwhelming urge to hide from them. The front door of the house swings open and I duck down behind the car, pulling Cole with me, gesturing for him to keep quiet. We remain crouched, hidden from view, while their car makes its way down the street. The panic from the very real possibility that they might look in the rear-view mirror and see two people crouching behind a vehicle weighs heavily on me. I finally take in a full breath when the vehicle turns and the sound of the engine fades away. We both stand and brush off the dirt we collected from our crouched position. I feel his eyes on me but refuse to acknowledge them, not knowing how to respond.

"Want to tell me why we're hiding from men in suits

that you *don't know,* but who clearly have a key to your deceased mother's house?" Cole asks in a slightly sarcastic manner while watching me from the side of his eye.

"I don't know who those men are, or how they have a key to the house. I told you what I know," I answer with a sigh, knowing he won't believe me. Not that I can blame him; I wouldn't believe me, either.

I start walking across the street toward the house while trying to quell my guilt. I remind myself that I'm not exactly lying; I'm just not exactly giving him all the information. We approach the faded yellow door of the house and I check the handle. It's locked. I curse under my breath, not feeling hopeful the scary-looking men in suits left a key under the doormat.

For the past twenty years since my mother was murdered, this house has been empty, but it appears to have been maintained. Judging by the fact it's still standing and doesn't have any condemned stickers on the outside, someone's clearly taking care of the lawn, pressure cleaning the driveway and front sidewalk. From the outside, it appears to be someone's residence. With any luck, there could be a lockbox with a key hidden somewhere that we can break into.

A loud crashing sound from the back of the house derails my train of thought. I rush through the open side gate to the back porch, where I see Cole's feet disappear through a small open window. Before I can call out to make sure he's okay, the back door opens, and he greets me, grinning like a crazy person who just broke into a house. He opens his hands wide to present the open doorway.

"Since we're clearly not the only strangers who want access to this place, I figured I'd find us an easy way in," he says, stepping aside so I can pass through the narrow doorway. I can't help but laugh.

Inside the small kitchen, I find a few cooking pans lying on the floor, which must have been the noise I heard from outside. He picks them up and stacks them on top of the counter in what I assume is how he found them before his entrance. Further inside the house is a small room with a few sparse decorations, a small couch with crocheted pillows on each end, and an old tube-style TV sitting on a dark wood stand.

A short hallway branches off to the bedrooms, and I make my way to the one that's clearly the master. I check the closet first because that's where most people store important things. I shuffle through blankets, clothes, and linens that fill it but find it void of anything else. The dust I've stirred up causes me to have a coughing fit, forcing me to back my way out of the closet. I shut the doors while using the sleeve of my shirt to cover my nose and mouth and get my breathing under control. Apparently, whoever takes care of the outside of the house doesn't do the inside.

Standing in the middle of the room, I study each item of furniture, trying my best to dredge up a memory of it, a memory of anything inside this house, but I come up blank. I begin to pace the room, trailing my hands through the dust that's accumulated on top of the furniture, leaving a clean line along each one. I stop short at the end of the bed and look down at a small circular rug in the center of the room; the rug is completely out of place. Everything in the house seems vintage, early seventies-style furniture and decor, but this rug is, well, it's new. How do I know it's new? It hasn't accumulated any dust yet. I bend down and push it to the side, exposing a floorboard that doesn't look secure. I gently step on the edge of it, watching it shift under my weight. I pull my keys from my pocket and use the edge of one to pry up the board. Under it, I find a shoe box, like the one Robert gave me that was my father's.

Inside, I find a stack of photos; shuffling through them, I find photos of my mother and father together. Eventually, I make my way to a photo of a younger version of me, wearing pigtails in my hair and overalls.

The photo was taken at a carnival, where I'm enjoying a large hot dog covered in ketchup, grinning ear to ear. The rest of the photo seems normal enough, but it's what I see in the background that gives me pause. A younger version of the old man I met at Hollow Cove Marina smiles back at me and my heart stutters in my chest.

It's all true…

A sinking feeling pulls at my gut; deep down inside, there was a small part of me hoping he was lying, just fucking with me. The backs of my eyes begin to sting, and I feel tears pool into the bottoms of them. I quickly pull the picture from the pile and shove it into my back pocket. Swiftly shuffling through the remaining photos, I don't uncover much else, just a few more photos of my parents in front of what looks like a college campus, smiling and clearly in love. The stinging behind my eyes returns and I put the photos back in the box while I wrestle down the feeling of sadness that's threatening to overwhelm my senses. Under the photos, I find an envelope and pull it out. It has the insignia from the White House embossed on the corner, and I don't have to open it to know what it contains.

I feel Cole's presence when he enters the room, even before he's standing at my side, looking down at the envelope in my hand. I already know the information that's going to be inside, but the question is, do I want him to know? Can I trust he isn't going to grab it and run back to the chief, revealing this is all connected to me?

I turn and look into his eyes. Like every other time I've gazed into them, I find the same concern and tenderness. He gives me a watered-down version of a smile, the smile he only gives to me when his guard is down, and no one else is watching. It's the smile that, at full force, makes my insides flip and my heart pound in my ears. It's that smile that makes me realize I need Cole for this; I need him to know everything, to understand it all, to understand me. If that's going to happen, it's time for me to come clean and hope he still gives me that smile when he knows the truth. I tuck the envelope under my arm and turn to face him.

"Cole, I have a lot I need to tell you," I say. Glancing around my mother's old room, a shiver works its way up my spine; the need to get out of here pushes at me like a physical force. "This just isn't the place to do it."

"Okay, let's get out of here then," he says.

I give him a sad smile; in turn, he lets his smile peek out, the one that causes my breath to hitch and stomach to flutter. For the first time, I look away from that smile, guilt crashing into me like a wave. He can't give me that smile yet, not until he knows the truth.

I collect the box from the floor, shove the envelope back in below the photos, and tuck the floorboard into place. Cole positions the rug over the floorboard, and we make our way in silence to the back door of the house. He closes the kitchen window as it was before he snuck through it and secures the back door once we are outside. We head down the side of the house toward the street, but before we make it fully out of the backyard, I catch sight of the black town car. I grab Cole's sleeve, pulling him back against the side of the house behind me. Crouching to peer around the corner of the house through a small bush, I can make out the same three men we saw earlier hurrying up the walkway to the house. My stomach drops. I don't know who these men are or what exactly they're doing here, but some instinct tells me I don't want to confront them to find out.

Checking my ankle holster, I confirm my gun's securely in place before motioning to Cole that we need to head through the overgrown backyard. He gives me a stern look but nods and does as I suggest. We duck into the backyard, crouching behind a large rosebush. I take a moment to be thankful that, this time of year, the bush is overgrown and in full bloom to hide us from view. From our vantage point, we see large shadows moving through the house's kitchen. Someone opens the back door, and I see the barrel of a gun before seeing the head of the man who's checking outside.

"Okay, Jess, what the fuck is going on?" Cole's eyes bulge as he whispers frantically to me.

I put my fingers to my mouth, motioning him to be quiet, then point to a large tree trunk behind the rose bushes. We duck walk our way further into the overgrown yard that was once my childhood playground. I can barely make out the muffled voices as we push ourselves up against the tree trunk that's wide enough to conceal both of us at once if we stand sideways, facing opposite directions.

"No, sir, I don't see any movement out here; they must have gone another direction." The man with the gun speaks into a radio as he squints out into the yard. "Yes, sir, I'm out here right now." He responds to a voice over the radio I can't make out. "Yes, sir, I secured the kitchen window lock," he says, grunting. "Yes, I know what you saw on the front door camera; I saw it too, but they aren't out here."

He pauses with a frustrated look on his face, turns on his heel, and goes back inside the back door. I send up a silent thank you for the laziness of the average person. All he had to do was take a few steps into the yard, and we would be out of luck. Cole and I share a relieved look before I scan the yard for any breaks in the fence surrounding it while I contemplate how much of a pain it's going to be to scale an eight-foot wooden fence. Luck is on our side, and I spot a few rotted-out planks in the far corner of the yard, well hidden by an overgrown shade tree. I grab Cole's arm, guiding him behind me to the corner where I pull a few boards away to open a hole large enough for us to squeeze through and into a neighbor's yard, who thankfully appears to be at work. Slipping out from the side of the house, we silently make our way over to the next block and briskly walk the rest of the neighborhood to a twenty-four-hour diner a few blocks away.

CHAPTER FIFTEEN

Monster Secrets

The best part about 24-hour diners is that breakfast is always an option.

Cole and I share the same side of a booth in the back of the diner. I tell myself it's so we can both watch the door, but really, I'm just soaking up what could be the last time he'll ever want to be this close to me. I'm selfishly collecting these moments, locking them deep inside for later, for something to hold on to after I set off the nuclear bomb that's going to ruin whatever chance we had to be something.

Our waitress delivers a few menus to the table with hot coffee, reminding me of another reason I love diners—all you can drink coffee. She takes our orders before disappearing into the nearby kitchen, where a digital wall clock flips over to six o'clock. Based on the time of year, sunset will take place in approximately an hour and a half, giving us the cover of darkness we need to covertly collect the rental car and giving me just about an hour to spill my entire life story to Cole. If I'm lucky, and he hasn't run screaming from the diner before I can do my damnedest to convince him I'm the *good* kind of psychopath, I still have to beg his forgiveness for not being upfront with him in the first place.

The first sip of coffee leaves a bitter, burnt taste on my tongue, but I can still feel it working its magic as it makes its way to my brain. Cole is not as forgiving of the flavor. He pushes his cup to the edge of the table, a look of offense covering his face.

"I think you've officially turned me into a coffee snob," he states.

I do my best to smile through the anxiety churning around inside me while we wait for the waitress to deliver our orders. The adrenaline rush, coupled with not eating lunch today, has made me hungrier than I thought. I practically inhale the food, barely stopping to thank the waitress as she tops off my coffee. After I finish, I push my plate aside, instantly regretting eating so fast because that was my respite from the impending conversation, and now it's gone. Steeling my spine, I swallow down my nervousness and take one last sip of the coffee, knowing the momentary delay does nothing to help me. My eyes lock on Cole's; he must see the fear behind them because he takes my hands in his and offers a disarming smile. Nodding his head, he lets me know he's ready to hear what I have to say while I silently struggle with where to even begin. He lifts the envelope out of the box, sitting on the bench between us, as if he can read my mind.

"This is probably a good place to start. I'm guessing it'll explain who those men were," he suggests.

"Okay," I agree.

My hands shake as I take the envelope from his and pull the documents out, placing them on the table in front of us. They contain two fully mapped-out genomes. One for my mother and one for my father, not exactly what I expected. I glance at Cole and can see from the look of pure awe on his face that he wasn't either. As far as the general public knows, hell, as far as I knew, we have only in the last four years discovered how to map out a person's full genome. These are at least twenty years old. The next page is information pertaining to the specific genes believed to control emotions and feelings, or, as an entire faction of science would call it today, the psychopath genes. The only reason I even know that is because someone has scribbled notes over top of the markings telling me so. My breath catches in my throat as the very real possibly that I could have been a part of these experiments hits me. Could this be why my parents sent me away and why they both died shortly after?

The documents below are more notes on my parents. There is a note on how my father's response to the repression of his genes and my mother's response were different. They aren't too clear, but from what I understand, it seems to say my father took to the gene editing, but my mother didn't. There are some additional pages containing dates and names, a list of people with my father's name on the top, but no other information. Could these possibly be other subjects?

My head spins with this information, causing my brain to become a spiraling mess of chaos. I lean back in the booth and suck in a deep breath in an attempt to quiet my head. If the government letterheads, envelopes, and stamps are legitimate, then this goes much deeper than a rogue group of scientists. This changes everything about the case and makes my end goal seem like a now impossible task.

"Cole," I say, my voice cracking and coming out more like a whisper. I clear my throat before trying again. "Cole, remember how you said I'm taking my sister's death really well?" This time, my voice comes out even, and he nods that he remembers. "And I told you that it's not really normal?" I twist my hands in my lap, squeezing my fingers together until the bite of pain grounds me in reality. He nods again. "Well, that's because normal for me is not having emotions." My exhalation comes out uneven and I focus all my attention on my hands. "I am… or rather, I was, a psychopath. I never had feelings up until the week of Sarah's death. I went my entire life faking them. I faked smiles, tears, I faked all of it, and she taught me how."

A single tear tracks its way down my cheek, the feeling still foreign enough that it causes me to pause while I wipe it away. "I didn't feel a damned thing until the week she died and I met you." My eyes finally raise to look into his. The blank expression I find looking back causes my insides to twist into knots. I continue my confession, despite it. "The first time I saw you in the Lemon Wok, I thought I had food poisoning. My heart raced too fast, my cheeks burned and my stomach did flips." I squeeze my eyes shut, not wanting to see the disgust I fear is about to cover his face once my admission sinks in and he comes to his senses about me. My voice drops down to a whisper. "The reason I'm so good at catching the monsters is because I am a monster."

Another tear slips free; I've always known it, but apparently knowing it and speaking it aloud are two very different things. Sitting perfectly still, my eyes shut tight, I don't bother to wipe the tears from my cheeks. I fail to see the point in it since I know more will follow once he walks out of the diner and leaves me to my fate. I can't feel him next to me in the booth any longer; I can't even hear his breathing. Icy fingers of panic squeeze my chest and, without my consent, they convince my eyes to fly open to make sure he hasn't left already.

My heart sputters in my chest when I find him inches from my face, his hands slowly coming up to wipe the tears from my cheeks. He meets my eyes with his own for a brief moment before he pulls my face forward and brutally kisses me. The kiss is in no way suited for the public location we're in. It's the sort of kiss that sends a shot of warmth coursing through my blood, heating it to a raging boil as it promises to deliver on every delicious dark thought I've ever had about him. He whispers my name when he pulls his lips from mine, and I'm only able to offer him a shiver while I adjust to the lack of his heat that was, only moments ago, consuming my entire being.

"You are not a monster," he says. The conviction in his eyes is something I've never seen the likes of. "You are *not* a monster," he says again, voice dropping to a whisper while he gently squeezes my cheeks, pushing his forehead against mine.

My greedy heart soaks up the sentiment he offers, locking it up safely within the darkness to be protected from the fires I'm setting whenever I open my mouth because it knows I'm not done burning just yet.

"Thank you, Cole, but you don't know everything yet."

I take out the photo I shoved in my back pocket earlier, the one of me at the carnival with the younger version of the now old man in the background. Pointing him out to Cole, I tell him about my meeting at the marina. I confess I didn't tell him because I was sure he'd tell the chief, who would give the case to another detective. I stoke the fire even more with the admission that the reason I wanted to stay on this case was because of the excitement I felt when I learned these killers weren't going to stop until someone brought them to a violent end, which meant letting more innocent people die just so I could continue my sick chase. I hold nothing back, telling him everything I've been keeping from him. What's the point in holding onto any of it now? When I've finally confessed each of my dark sins, I wipe the tears that have escaped and do my best to push all the feelings back behind one of those carefully constructed walls I've come to rely on so heavily in the last week. I push them back alongside all the terrible things I've spent a lifetime thinking about or doing, things I never gave a second thought about actually having to reconcile with. He clears his throat, bringing my thoughts back on track and making me flinch.

"That's changed though, hasn't it?" he asks. His eyes bore into mine, searching for something. I would give it to him, if I only knew what it was. "You now care about finding who did this to Sarah and the other women to stop it from happening again. You also care about bringing justice to the people who took them all away from their families, the people who took Sarah from you, from your family, your nephew."

I don't even have to think about my response. I begin nodding because he's right. I do care about all of those things. Every day, I wake up caring about those things while they drive me to the brink of insanity with how helpless this case makes me feel. Every night, I barely sleep because of the fear I won't be able to stop them before they find their next victim. Something has shifted inside me, leaving me with a fierce determination to bring peace to those families, to my own family, to my brother-in-law Matthew and nephew Aaron. It has filled me with determination to wipe the haunted look from my father's eyes and save at least some of the man he was before Sarah died. I don't just want to help them; I want to avenge them; I want to be the iron fist of justice for them.

"That's why you aren't a monster. Even when you didn't feel emotions, you never strayed from doing the right thing. You went above and beyond just so you *could* do the right thing. You used the fact you could think like a killer to catch killers and because of that, you were able to catch the killers others couldn't. You used it as a gift, not a curse," he says, smiling at his defense of my life's work. I stare at him with eyes too wide, shocked not only by the fact he hasn't run screaming into the street at my confession but that he's also defending me against myself. "It's normal to feel guilty about keeping such a large secret from the people you care about. Judging by the way your parents treat you and the way you react to them; I'm assuming Sarah is the only one who knew." The softness returns to his eyes when he asks me about her.

"Sarah and Chief Harding," I say, offering up more of my secrets.

Surprise dances across his face at my admission. "Okay, so Sarah and Chief Harding. That explains so much..." he says, voice trailing off at the end. I imagine the puzzle pieces of my life gently fitting together inside his mind. "Jess, you are doing amazing. There's nothing wrong with you, or the way you're handling any of this. The feeling of wanting to hold the cards close to your chest is also normal. This case means something to you, something more now that you can feel it in a whole different way. Of course, you want to find closure for those women's families, and most importantly, you want closure for your own family."

I lean my head back and work to digest everything he's said to me; the fact that everything I'm feeling is normal. For the first time in my life, I'm normal; my feelings are normal, and I'm no longer completely different from everyone around me. I feel a smile cross my lips; so, this is what I've been missing. I don't have to worry if my smile is wide enough, if my tears will come at the right time, or whether my facial expressions will show whatever a normal person expects to see in them because I'm finally normal.

CHAPTER SIXTEEN
A Different Kind of Darkness

"I may have a theory about why you were that way and why you aren't now." Cole says, bringing my thoughts to a halt. I can't help the incredulous look I give him.

"Really? That's a thing? Someone can just recover from it?" I ask. The idea sounds so far-fetched I have to wonder if he's grasping at straws to make me feel better.

"Well, no, not just anybody," he says, thoughtfully scratching the day-old stubble on his chin. My attention is now drawn to it. I notice it makes him look slightly older and more distinguished, and I can't say I hate it. "I suppose it would have to be someone in your unique circumstance." My attention snaps back to what he's saying. He sits up straight, turning his body and slightly grazing my knee with his. "Scientists have been working on a way to edit genes since the nineteen-eighties, but it wasn't public knowledge until the early nineties this science was even possible. It looks like, based on the information we've learned about your parents, secret human trials began well before then. Gene editing can be used to eradicate genetic predispositions to diseases, such as sickle cell anemia or HIV, but it can also be used to edit the genes that control something as simple as hair or eye color, making designer babies possible. Of course, there's a huge morality question there. A lot of people don't think humans have the right to play God. To think that there are people who would allow so much suffering when we have the ability at our fingertips to stop some of it." He pauses, and something dark flashes behind his eyes. He furrows his eyebrows before looking back at me.

"Anyway, the thing I'm getting at is these genetic changes made to your parents theoretically could be passed down to their offspring, quite a bit of the gene expression we have is inherited from our parents. There's been a lot of discussion in the psychology community about whether being a psychopath is a case of nature, meaning it's in our genetics, or nurture, meaning it's in how we're raised and our environment." He leans back in the booth, regarding me with a look I would imagine rivals that of a scientist looking at a lab mouse, and a shiver works its way through me. "I guess you just proved it's a healthy mix of both."

"Okay, I can follow that logic, but how did I just wake up one day with emotions?" I ask, looking away from his stare, unnerved by the feelings it's giving me. His eyes soften while he shakes his head, making me feel less like a lab mouse and more like a human again.

"Trauma. I think it was trauma, more specifically, the loss of Sarah. She was the only person who knew the real you and was your emotional caretaker for most of your life. She made sure you felt as normal as possible in your situation; she included you in everything and taught you the skills you needed to be successful in life. According to you, she was the one who molded you into who you are and was your moral compass. The loss of her must have caused the expression of the repressed genes, allowing you to feel emotions." Trauma, something I've never had to think about, is now the reason I can feel emotions like a normal person.

My eyes dart around the diner, settling on a young woman around my age sitting four booths in front of us. She wipes a small child's face, cleaning the formula he's spilled while guzzling it down like he'll never get another sip. My eyes swing to the booth across from hers, where an older man sits alone, reading a newspaper while sipping coffee and picking at a slice of what appears to be cherry pie with a spoon. My mind wanders around all the reasons he would be here alone, none of them happy.

I glance at the booth near the front doors, where a young couple sits with their heads down, whispering and giggling conspiratorially with each other. I openly stare for a minute, taking in the gentle crease of the man's brow as he tells the woman what appears to be a joke. I watch his eyes light up, and she covers her mouth to keep her laugh contained. I watch how he scoots his chair closer to hers while her eyes are closed in laughter, thinking she won't notice. Longing rolls through me, a harsh reminder I've wasted twenty-six years of my life not having this, not having any of the emotions and feelings most people don't even give a second thought.

My gaze eventually returns to the man sitting next to me. He's returned to reading the notes about my parents, learning not only about them but also about me. No matter what happens moving forward, I'm certain of one thing: we have to take these people down, not only for the victims and the families of the victims but for me. For the years of my life I can't get back, the years I've lived as an emotionless monster, missing out on so many things. Something unfurls inside me, something that's been wrapped around inside since this all began, clutching tight—a darkness I recognize as my own, a piece of myself that's been tucked away waiting. The feeling is almost overwhelming, causing me to suck in a breath of air, and I vow that we will be the ones who put an end to this. The darkness and I, together, we will end this.

The sun sets outside, and a different kind of darkness falls. It prompts us to pay our check and walk back to where the rental car waits. The silence we share during this walk is not as uncomfortable as the one we shared on the way to the diner. Cole grabs my hand, pulling me to a stop a block from where the car is.

"I think it's probably better if you stay back," he suggests. Judging by the way he winced after he said it, I know he's aware I don't like what he's said. He's correct. I don't like it at all, but I can see the logic in it. I'm not totally unreasonable.

By now, the newspaper articles have circulated and not only reveal I was Sarah's adopted sister, but they also paint a nice little backstory about my life. The story of a young girl of seven put up for adoption by parents who worked for the government and died tragic deaths at an early age. Even without all my dirty details, the story is a scandal in itself. The papers herald me as a hero, sticking up for my fellow women or whatever nonsense they're feeding to the public at the mayor's urging. I know full well that makes me target number one for these assholes, so I reluctantly agree to remain back here while Cole retrieves the car alone. I relieve him of the box; it's probably best if he's empty-handed, in case he has to run again. I only have to wait a few minutes before he pulls the rental car in front of me and leans over the seat to push the door open.

"Was anyone there?" I ask, climbing in the car. I buckle the seatbelt and place the box on the floorboards between my feet.

"Honestly, I crept through a few of the neighbors' backyards, so when I walked up to the car, it looked like I lived in one of the houses and was just leaving. Before I got in the car, I took a quick glance at the house and saw the front porch light was on. I don't remember seeing it on earlier today," he says, easing us away from the curb. I scour my memories for the porch light.

"No, you're right; it wasn't, but it could be on a timer." I shrug, relieved that it went as smoothly as it did. I lean my head back on the headrest as we take off toward New York City, exhausted from everything.

A bump in the road has my eyes springing open, and I reach for my ankle holster.

"Whoa, hold on there, cowboy, it was just a pothole." Cole laughs from the driver's seat.

His wider-than-usual eyes nervously watch my hand

that's still resting on my gun. I grumble in agreement and look at my watch, finding it's half past midnight. We should be very close to getting home. Stifling a yawn, I crack my neck while I curse how stiff my back is from sleeping in this seat.

After spending what feels like forever arguing that I'm more than capable of walking myself up to my own apartment, Cole finally concedes and lets me out of the car in front of my new apartment building. It's not like he was holding me hostage or anything, but he did present a pretty convincing argument about how we did just get chased by men with guns not too long ago. I'm glad he gave in when he did because I was starting to have a hard time remembering exactly why letting him up to my apartment to spend the night with me was a bad idea. Against what my body wants, my brain and I somehow convinced him the security in the building is good enough that I can walk the fifty feet to the elevator and be safely in my apartment before he even leaves the street. He finally caved with the caveat that he's waiting outside at the curb until I text him to let him know I'm inside safely, which I do as soon as I lock the door behind me. I admire my new apartment that's been set up by the moving company in my absence.

Placing the shoebox on the kitchen counter, I notice a

small envelope with my name printed on the front, and my stomach drops, causing me to go over all the possibilities of where this letter came from. No one knows where I live except Cole; I haven't even had a chance to tell my parents yet. I carefully open the envelope to find another typed message.

Jessica,

I see you took my advice and went to your childhood home. By this time, I'm sure you have put the pieces together that I knew your mother. After they experimented on her and decided she was of no use to them, she discovered she was pregnant with you. She took some time off work to hide her pregnancy. Because of the experiments, your father didn't want anyone to know he was your father, so they kept separate for your safety, not because he didn't want to be your father. As I remember, he was very excited by the thought of it. Anyway, they decided it was best for your mother to move out of state. When she did, I secretly helped her with you up until her death. She was a good woman with a kind soul; they both were good people and never would have put you in harm's way.

The gene expression experiments were not the only experiments that went on. There was another much worse experiment, an experiment I later found out would allow them to turn the subjects into killers. This was after I recused myself from the collective, refusing to be part of the things they were doing. The second experiment allowed them to trigger a person to kill by using the same brainwashing techniques the military uses to torture prisoners and terrorists. They were brainwashed to kill like animals.

A chill runs down my spine. To kill like animals, like how Sarah was killed.

Your mother learned about this and immediately decided to place you in a foster home. She was afraid she was one of those experiments. She never would have thought her own stubborn genes would save her from that fate and instead leave her to a much worse one. As it turned out, your father was not so lucky. They programmed his brain to view your mother as a threat and attack her on sight. He was then sent to her and, unable to fight it, did what he was programmed to do. The experiments were based on the theory that the genetic alterations would make it so the subjects wouldn't feel remorse, making them the perfect killing machines. You can imagine now why the government allowed and even funded these experiments.

However, something went wrong. Based on what your father did next, I can only assume the gene suppression failed, and he remembered everything, causing him so much grief he took his own life. I'm sorry you have to endure this, Jessica. I wish there were a way for me to erase it all or go back and stop it, but I can't.

Now, you are probably the only person with the ability to take them down, since you're living proof of the experiments they've done. A scientist would only have to map your genetics and compare them to those in the files of your parents, which, coupled with the documents I left for you under your mother's floorboards, would be enough to prove it.

I will leave this letter taped to your door like the last one. I won't chance another meeting for your safety. I do hope one day you can forgive me for the part I played in this mess. I meant what I said, once this is all over, I will seek you out and if you want it, I'll do everything I can to reverse it for you.

Very sincerely,

Victor

A sigh of relief puffs its way out. The movers must have found the envelope on my old apartment door and brought it with them when they delivered my belongings. My shoulders sag; he doesn't know where I live, after all. I grab my cell phone to call Cole and tell him about the letter, but change my mind at the last minute. There's nothing either of us can do about it at this hour, and it'll just cause him to worry. I think better of it and instead plug my phone into its charger, leaving it on the kitchen counter.

I take my time changing into pajamas before crawling into bed, my mind racing with the new knowledge that my biological father killed my biological mother. All the years of wondering why the case went cold, I never once considered it wasn't actually cold, just swept under the rug. I climb under the covers and do my best to convince myself it's the right move to not call Cole to come back over and stay the rest of the night.

CHAPTER SEVENTEEN
My Monster

Cole

My jaw clenches while watching Jessica flash a brilliant smile to the security guard sitting behind a desk in the lobby of her new apartment building. From where I sit in the car parked outside, I watch her scan her ID card to call the elevator. I'm well aware I'm being overprotective, overly cautious, and generally overbearing by waiting out here until she confirms she's made it upstairs to her apartment. The rational part of me knows she's a fully trained, armed detective, and I'm an untrained, unarmed college professor. The irrational masculine side of me that wants to protect her from everything that'll ever go bump in the night won out this time. I impatiently tap my thumb along the steering wheel, shifting in the driver's seat, trying to alleviate some of the pressure building within my spine from the last six hours of sitting in the same position. Finally, my phone lights up, and a text message flashes across the lock screen, telling me she's made it safely to her apartment. I reluctantly pull away from the curb and make the short drive to my own apartment.

I pace my way from the kitchen, through the living room, until I reach the threshold of the bedroom door and back again. I curse my overly anxious brain for not letting me sleep. I can't stop going over everything Jess told me tonight, or rather last night, since it's well past midnight. How she bared her soul to me, letting me into the deepest, darkest parts of her, all the while thinking they'd push me away when it did nothing but pull me in closer. It fit more pieces to the puzzle that is Jessica Fairling neatly into place. Finally, her relationship with Chief Harding makes sense, but I need him to answer the one question I have left. I need him to tell me why he'd allow someone in her state to remain on his force. I want to know what his end goal is with her.

The pacing is getting me nowhere, and it's not like I can go see him now; it's well past three a.m. Instead, I start searching online for what I can find on the group of scientists from the early nineties I remember hearing about. If what I remember is correct, they fought to get approval for genetic testing and experimentation on death row inmates. They, of course, had absolutely no public support from the scientific community or the psychology community, but that doesn't mean they couldn't have had silent benefactors for their research. I gather as much information as I can, which ends up being an infuriatingly small amount. Finally giving up, I sprawl myself across the couch with the hope that sleep will be kind enough to take me under.

Not enough hours of fitful sleep later, I send Jess a text to check how she's doing. I refuse to treat her any differently than I would if I didn't know her deepest, darkest secret, but fuck if her secret isn't dark. The reality is, I don't think anyone or anything could push me away from her. In fact, the more layers I peel back and the more darkness she shows me, the more I want to just burrow inside to make myself a home. If she's the abyss, then I'll be damned if I don't want to step inside and never see the light of day again.

She hasn't responded to my text; she's probably still sleeping after our eventful weekend. I decide instead to go over to the precinct, knowing even though it's Sunday morning, assuming Chief Harding will be there. The man's a workaholic; I honestly don't think there is a day off for him. I smirk at my correct guess when I enter the station and see his broad shoulders through the doorway of the break room, hunched over, making himself a cup of coffee.

"Morning, Chief." I casually lean against the door frame behind him.

He turns to face me, taking a drink from his well-worn coffee-stained NYPD mug. He lifts it in a makeshift salute in lieu of a verbal greeting while swallowing down more of the coffee. I fall in step behind him, making our way back through the bullpen and over to his office. I shut the door behind us, and he raises his eyebrow, taking his seat behind his desk. He gestures to one of the chairs in front of his desk and I take it, pausing to observe the man sitting across from me.

Exhaustion radiates from the depth of his eyes, his forehead scored from the weight of the responsibility he's carried over the years, proudly displaying the burden he's willingly chosen to bear. The wrinkles outline each of his hardened eyes, a testament to the countless hours spent poring over case files, scrutinizing evidence, and being responsible for an entire station of detectives doing the same. I let loose a sigh, knowing I'm about to make those lines deeper by adding further burdens to his plate.

"Why did you let her stay on the force?" I ask. He knows exactly who and what I'm referring to; there's no sense in stating the obvious. "Even knowing what she was, knowing what she was capable of becoming, you still let her stay. Why?" It's his turn to let out a sigh, his shoulders slumping forward as if a large burden was lifted from them.

"Because she can be the monster the rest of us can't," he says, letting his eyes bore into mine, begging me to see what he does. "Unlike you or me, she won't hesitate to pull the trigger. She won't let anyone else die to save her conscience. Some people might see that as a problem or as a reason to keep her from doing this sort of job, but not me; I see it as a bonus. That's what makes her special and what makes her belong right here, doing exactly this." He taps his finger on his desk to drive his point home.

I stare back at him, not necessarily agreeing but also ready to point out the glaring problem with his thinking, then it dawns on me. She hasn't told him yet. He still thinks she has no emotions, that she's still a "monster" as she puts it. Fuck.

"Let me tell you a story about a time that changed my life forever, a time when I would have given anything in this world to be like her," he offers. I nod, beckoning him to tell me his story.

"It was December 5th, 2003, down a typical New York

City alleyway. The alley was cluttered with trash bags, overflowing dumpsters, and graffiti-covered walls, when my life was irrevocably changed. The entire experience was made even less enjoyable by a heavy dusting of snow covering the streets from that morning; the only good thing from that God-forsaken snow was it stifled the overpowering smell of garbage. By the time my partner, Marcus, and I were called out, the snow had piled high enough against the walls, leaving only a narrow, twisting path through the middle of the alley. He walked slightly ahead of me, weaving his way through to the end of the alley, and signaled toward the dumpster crammed under a fire escape ladder, where we could see fresh footprints. He went up the ladder first, and I followed close on his heels, with our service weapons drawn as we made our way to the platform above. The guy we were after, a real piece of work named Max, was wanted for a laundry list of shit having to do with human trafficking—kidnapping, extortion, money laundering, just to name a few." He holds up a finger for each offense listed off before closing that hand into a fist on top of his desk.

"Once the NYPD caught wind of this guy, two years previous, we started to monitor his whereabouts and began collecting what evidence we could to build a case. The problem was, as soon as we had enough for one, he went underground. That was six months before. Now, we had received a fresh tip from an informant that he was back, apparently hanging around the same beat Marcus and I patrolled. Lucky us," he says before letting out a humorless laugh.

"Marcus took point, going ahead of me around a corner, and I hear him shout, 'Freeze shit bag, you have nowhere to go!' When I made it around the corner, I saw Marcus pointing his gun at Max. I, being the cocky rookie I was, decide to try to reason with Max. I tell him it's two against one, he needs to just give it up, and no one has to get hurt. I figured he's got nowhere to go now; he has no other choice but to give it up, right?" He shakes his head.

"I should have known better than to be cocky. Max was no better than an animal and animals do desperate shit when they're cornered. A bullet ripped from the shotgun Max was holding, hitting Marcus in the gut and deafening me in the process. The shock of my partner and best friend getting shot caused me to hesitate. My hesitation gave Max the chance to run to the end of the platform where a second escape ladder was, but the short fat fuck couldn't reach it. In the time it took for me to register what was happening, Max was already pointing a shotgun at me and pulling the trigger. I must be the luckiest fucker around because all it did was click. It jammed… the fucking thing jammed." His eyes refocus, and he swallows loudly.

"I pointed my gun at Max's head, ready to shoot him, but paused when I felt Marcus grab my leg. I shouldn't have looked, but I couldn't help myself. I looked down at my partner, at the shiny intestines showing through the cannon-sized hole in his gut. It was then I realized that Max wasn't going anywhere, but Marcus was. He never would have made it to the hospital, or even to the ambulance that would have arrived in less than ten minutes. Hell, Marcus wasn't even going to make it down the fire escape ladders to the ground. So, I did what any good partner would do. I bent down, pulled off my jacket, and stuffed it in the gaping hole in his gut, leaving Max on the platform to wait. I called dispatch for medical backup, knowing they'll never make it in time, and I begged my partner to stay with me. I begged him to hold on, even though inside I knew it was too late. I knew no one survives a shotgun blast at close range to their gut, but it's not easy to watch your best friend of ten years bleed out in front of you when there's not a damned thing you can do but hold his intestines together." He pauses and I patiently wait for him to fight his way back from the cobwebs of his memories.

"Marcus began to violently shake, either from the cold or from the blood loss. And, like a coward, I closed my eyes as tight as I could close them. I couldn't watch him take his last breath. I waited until the shuddering stopped and his body stilled before I opened them again to confirm he was, in fact, gone." He lets out a sigh, takes a sip of coffee, and shifts himself in his chair, causing it to squeak loudly before he continues.

"When I looked back to the corner where I left Max cowering, I saw only his broken shotgun. I made it to the edge of the platform just in time to catch Max's back as he turned around the corner of the alleyway, escaping my view. He must have jumped from the second-floor platform. I called back up to let them know to send all available units in Max's direction before I made it across the platform to the ladder. Skipping half the steps on the way down, I jumped the last few and landed heavy enough on the dumpster that the top collapsed. I managed to roll off before it did, twisting my ankle badly enough to require a brace. I took off after Max, but by the time I made it around the corner he had turned onto, not even one minute before, there was no sign of him. The fucker just vanished." His haunted eyes turn away from mine and I can see the pain etch its way across his face. He swallows thickly.

"If I could have been like her..." He pauses to take a shaky breath. "If I could have been Jessica in that moment, I would have killed Max while Marcus was alive to see it. I could have given him that before he left this earth, instead of letting my emotions distract me." His eyes find their way back to mine. "That's why I let her on my force; that's why I protect her and guide her the best way I know how. She may be one of the monsters, but I would much rather have a monster on my side than have one on Max's side."

After that story, I'm surprised he stayed on the force at all.

"Shortly after that, I was moved up to chief of detectives. I almost didn't take the position. Hell, I'm not even sure why I did." He fidgets with his coffee mug. "Not long after I became chief, I found Jessica, or she found me. From the first time I met her, I knew there was something different about her. Maybe my head was still fucked up from what happened with Marcus, or maybe it wasn't, and that's just my excuse. Whatever it was, I gladly took her under my wing and gave her some of the most heinous crimes that have sent other detectives into an early retirement. She not only came out the other side of those cases victorious, but also asked for more," he says, eyes shining with pride for her.

I can only nod while I process everything he's said, the final piece of the puzzle sliding into place. Judging by the reverence in his voice, I can see he really does care for her. I just have to wonder how he's going to feel now she isn't his monster anymore; now, she's no longer the emotionless machine he's relied on so frequently to take out the Maxs of the world for him. I won't be the one to give him that news; that has to be up to her. It's her secret to share.

I leave the station, turning toward her apartment building, concern quickening my pace. She hasn't returned my texts, and I hate how helpless I feel not knowing if she's okay. I'm painfully aware I left her less than nine hours ago, but damn if I can't keep my anxiety in check. I know exactly how to woo her into seeing me this morning, and I head to see Jerry at the coffee shop. This way, when she's pissed off about me showing up on her doorstep, I stand a chance of forgiveness.

I smile at the daytime security guard whose name tag reads 'Jeremy' and hand him my ID to let me up to Jess's floor. He frowns as he apologizes, telling me I'm not on the guest list. I do everything I can to hold on to the growl of frustration that tries to leave my throat but fail. Eyes wide, he offers to call her apartment and let her know she has company. Afraid of how my voice might sound, I nod my agreement to him. I don't need to frighten the kid who's trying to help me, even though I called her and got no answer on my walk over from the coffee shop. He calls her phone and grins at me when he receives an answer. The scowl I offer him in return makes his smile to disappear. I grind my jaw in frustration at the possibility she's avoiding me.

"Tell her I have coffee," I say, holding the two steaming cups in my hands to show him. Jeremy relays my message and pulls the phone from his ear with a cringe. I hear her high-pitched approval to send me up come through. I smirk at Jeremy as I breeze past him onto the waiting elevator and up to her floor.

Her apartment door swings wide open before I have a chance to knock, and I'm greeted with a sight that all but takes my breath away. Wearing an oversized band T-shirt, cut-up light-washed jeans, and barefoot with her hair in a messy bun piled on top of her head, is Jessica. It's not so much what she's wearing that makes my breath hitch, but the look of pure want on her face.

"Come to Momma," she says, reaching out to pluck the cup from my hand. I'm instantly envious of the molten liquid inside as she gulps it down like it's not scalding hot. My thoughts turn dark when she steps aside, allowing me to enter her new apartment.

CHAPTER EIGHTEEN

Thinking Backwards

A moment of pure panic jolts me upright from bed before I remember that I slept in my new apartment last night. Easing the panic, I fall back onto the bed with relief. After that rush of adrenaline, I know there's no chance I'm getting back to sleep, so I instead drag myself to the kitchen to hunt for coffee supplies. On my way past the counter, I grab my phone to check the time; it's quarter past eleven, and I have five missed calls. I groan and pretend I didn't see those on the screen yet, trying to steal another few precious minutes before I have to start my day. Precious minutes before I have to face Cole, now that he's had time to go over what I've told him about myself and inevitably decide I'm the same as all the other monsters before he shuts me out.

The phone rings and I almost jump out of my skin.

"Shit," I yelp, dropping the coffee filters that I just unearthed to answer it. "Hello, this is Detective Fairling," I say, balancing the phone on my shoulder to tear open the next box, still not finding my coffee tin.

"Good morning, Detective. It's Jeremy from the front desk. There's a gentleman here named Cole Bellamy requesting to come up," he says, higher in pitch than usual. I hear Cole in the background, but can't quite make out what he's saying. Jeremy relays it. "He says he has coffee for you."

"Please send him up!" My reply comes out a little too desperate, and I cringe at myself, abandoning the boxes on the counter. Jeremy offers a forced laugh before agreeing to allow Cole up and ending the call.

I struggle into an old pair of jeans and a baggy band shirt on top of a pile inside the first box I wrestled open. I quickly brush my teeth before opening the door to find Cole with a cup of coffee in each hand. I push the door wider and relieve him of one of the cups.

"Come to Momma," I croon into the coffee before taking a deep drink of the delicious elixir of life and saunter to the couch with my morning prize.

Cole locks the door and walks to one of the chairs across from the couch. Before he has a chance to sit, I point him toward the kitchen counter, where the note from last night lays. He cocks an eyebrow in silent question, but walks over to read it without me having to explain. After he's read the note, he takes the chair in front of me and silently gathers his thoughts.

"After I got home last night, I couldn't sleep, so I did some research," he says. I fight to keep my face neutral despite the flood of interest that overtakes me. "Like I mentioned in the diner, I've heard rumors of a rogue group of scientists from the early nineties that were set on experimenting with genetics. I remember them fighting for approval to carry out these experiments on certain death row inmates. They had a list they circulated, exposing each inmate's crimes and psychological evaluations without consent, trying to persuade others in the community to back them by using those details. Of course, their requests were immediately shut down in both the psychology and scientific communities. I couldn't remember what happened to them. They made noise for a few years, with every request getting shot down, then just seemed to disappear." He pauses to take a sip of coffee, and I absorb what he's saying. "I couldn't find any definitive information on them, just some people on a message board discussing similar ideals." A hopeful glimmer shines in his eye, and he sits straighter in his seat. "Do you have any way to contact the man who left you this note?" I shake my head no and look up at the ceiling with frustration.

"I can't even do as he suggested and take this information to anyone to compare my genetics with my biological parents because, apparently, I just got better," I raise my arms, then let them flop down beside me on the couch, trying to release some of the frustration that's pulling my muscles tight. He watches me momentarily before looking into his coffee cup as if it will give him the answers. "Is there a way to turn me back into a psychopath?" I cringe the moment the words leave my mouth, not even sure why I let them in the first place. His eyes widen almost comically before piercing me with an unfriendly glare.

"Come again?" he asks. A tendril of anger I've never heard from him creeps into his voice, and I fidget in my seat on the couch.

"I mean, obviously, it would only be temporary," I clarify, regretting saying anything out loud in the first place. "I need to be able to focus on my… our case." I sit forward and place both feet flat on the floor, resting my forearms on my thighs. "I just can't with all these emotions running rampant." I rub the heels of my hands into my closed eyes so hard that I see stars. I hear him get up from his seat, then feel the couch dip with his weight as he sits beside me.

"Jess, I know this has to be difficult for you," he says, his voice back to the kind timber I've grown to know so well. Thankfully, there's no trace of the anger left, and I feel his hand gently touch my back. "There is no 'on and off switch' for human emotions… at least not one that's ethical," he pauses, and rubs a gentle circle on my back. "Nor should there be." I sit up straight and his hand falls from my back. I instantly miss its warmth.

"How am I supposed to solve this case, then?" I ask, and my eyes focus on the carpet under my toes, ignoring the emotions threatening to roll over me like a steamroller. "I can't think like them when I'm not like them." I let a little more frustration than I mean seep into my voice, making me sound like a petulant child.

Cole is silent for so long that I have to turn to look at him to be sure he's still sitting next to me and hasn't disappeared into thin air. He's gives me a look I haven't seen from him before, a look I can only describe as hurt before shaking his head and shuttering it away.

"I can give you the phone number of a therapist I know. She can't turn your emotions off, but she can help you deal with them." He looks away from me and pulls his phone from his pocket, searching for the contact. I place my hand on his wrist, and he goes still.

"I don't want to talk to anyone about this that isn't you." I stare at his wrist where my hand lays. "I want you to help me deal with the emotions I'm feeling, not some stranger. I trust you." I lift my eyes to his, silently pleading for him to understand.

His eyes immediately soften, and he places his other hand on top of mine. Smiling a tentative smile, he nods. "Okay. But you have to promise me that you'll stop thinking like that. Promise me you don't really want to go back to not having emotions."

We sit in silence for a moment, and I take in what he's asking me to do. It's not a hard decision because, in reality, I know I don't want to go back. I know I wouldn't trade what I now have for anything in the world; I'm not even sure why I asked him that. Instead of pouring out more of my broken soul, I just return his nod and offer a simple agreement not to do it again.

"I need your words, Jessica," he says, watching me closely. The command in his voice causes me to sit up straighter.

"I... I promise I won't say anything like that again," I agree. My eyes make their way to meet his. He tilts his head to the side, waiting for me to continue, clearly not satisfied with my response. "I promise that's not really how I feel. I'm just... frustrated." The admission causes his features to finally soften, and relief vibrates off him. I lean my head on his shoulder. "What now?" I ask. He sighs, leaning back into the couch and taking me with him as he does.

"You continue with your sabbatical while I go back to the case files and start from the beginning. There has to be something we missed before we knew all of this new information," he answers.

I hum my agreement. He has a good point; we weren't looking at this the same way a week ago. Now we're armed with new intimate knowledge of the people responsible for this. Instead of working the case forward, now we are going to be working the case backward. We know the why and the how, we just need to figure out the who of it all.

****

My swollen eyes strain to open from yet another fitful night's sleep. I'm starting to wonder if I'll ever have a good night's rest again. I roll over to see the sun hasn't even fully risen. Dragging myself out of bed, I shuffle my way to the kitchen with plans to make a strong cup of coffee only to discover the empty tin I unpacked last night after Cole left. I must have used it all before we left for our trip to DC and never replaced it. This is every coffee addict's nightmare: an empty coffee tin on a morning after a night of poor sleep.

My brain struggles to accept forgoing my early morning coffee when a blog suggesting taking a morning run pops up in my memory. It said that not only is running supposed to wake you up as well as a cup of coffee would, but it's also believed to give you time to compartmentalize your anxious thoughts, which I have many of now. I let out a groan, tipping my head back to stare at the ceiling. I haven't run any distance since I absolutely had to in training about eight years ago. I drag myself back into the bedroom to wrestle my way into my workout gear and promise myself the run will end at the coffee shop.

"This is what hell must be like," I complain to literally no one. I stand in my empty bedroom, struggling to get into a t-backed top with a built-in sports bra and embarrassingly working up a sweat. When I finally do manage to get into the thing, I step in front of the mirror to tame my now awful mess of hair and let out a squeak. "Are you fucking kidding me?" I groan at my reflection in the mirror and curse at my inside-out top. "You know what? Fuck it." Not bothering with the brush, I violently pull my hair into a messy bun, grab my baggy shirt from yesterday, and put it on over the inside-out tank top. No one needs to know about this little disaster.

For what feels like the millionth time this morning, I curse myself for allowing the lack of coffee in my kitchen and exit my apartment. Not before I make one last lazy attempt to delay the inevitable, I choose to take the elevator down to the first floor instead of the stairs. I use the time to check my messages on my phone. There's a text from Cole waiting for me from either very late or very early, depending on what sort of person you are, I suppose. He wants me to meet him for coffee before he goes to the precinct. I text him back and let him know I'll meet him at Jerry's, just as the elevator dings to let me know I'm out of avoidance time.

The elevator doors slide open, and I'm greeted with the intense glare of the sun that shines straight through the lobby windows and directly into my still-tired eyes. The groan that escapes me earns a strange look from the security guard that I don't recognize behind the desk. I plaster a fake smile on my face and wave to him on my way out the doors.

CHAPTER NINETEEN

Cacophony

I desperately shield my poor, delicate, un-caffeinated eyeballs from the blinding light and promise them I'll purchase some dark sunglasses. If I'm going to start doing this regularly, then I'll definitely need some eye protection. Outside the building, I pop my headphones in and make an immediate right to take the long way to the coffee shop to give this running thing a genuine try. I start at a brisk walk before I work into a slow jog and curse myself for not having the foresight to stretch my muscles before leaving my apartment. My quads are already screaming at me. I ignore them, instead focusing on my breath, blocking out other thoughts, and working to even it out, just like they taught us in the academy. My emotions were locked away and non-existent back then.

I've taken to thinking about that time like I was on

autopilot, just going through the motions of daily life, barely scratching the surface. Had I known what life could be like with those emotions and feelings, messy or not, would I have chosen to have them? I'm certainly not the same person I was when all this began, not even close. The answer to that question is, without a doubt, very different today than it would have been almost a month ago, before I stood over Sarah's lifeless body outside of that coffee shop.

As much as I've struggled with them, having my emotions crop up out of nowhere, as inconvenient and frightening as it has been, I realize now I wouldn't trade it for anything. Yeah, I know that just the other morning I asked Cole if there was a way to turn them back off, but I don't believe for a second that I would have actually gone through with it. For the first time, I'm actually experiencing my life instead of just watching it like a stranger from the outside, like a monster in the closet watching you sleep. I have no idea how I survived so long without feeling anything, just as a husk of a human being.

My thoughts shatter when my shoe slides between two pieces of uneven concrete, causing my left ankle to roll to the side. I windmill my arms, trying not to faceplant into the sidewalk. A warm hand circles my bicep, steadying me, and I catch my uneven breath, trying not to hyperventilate. Pulling my left earphone out, I turn to thank my savior only to realize it's Cole's hand that's circling my arm while he stands smiling down at me.

"I didn't know you were a runner," he says.

His stare lingers on the baggy shirt he saw me in yesterday and pauses when he makes it down to my hot pink workout shorts that only barely peek out below the shirt. Finally, his eyes make their way to my running shoes, which are so new they may as well still have the tags hanging off them.

My face slightly flushes, and I look away before quietly admitting. "I just started again today."

"We should make time to train together. I was on the track team in college and try to get out to any 5Ks my schedule allows me to." His smile tells me he knows this isn't something I do often, or at all, and he is, in fact, teasing me.

"Of course you do," I say, shaking my head smiling. There's no way to look as good as he does without doing something insane like that.

He lets out an amused laugh before asking if I, of all people, am ready to have coffee.

"After the morning I've had, I'm more than ready for coffee," I say, carefully taking a step over the uneven pavement.

I enter the coffee shop and nod to Jerry before placing my order. Behind me, Cole orders some perverted version of a coffee with more creamer and sugar than should be legal. We make the leisurely stroll back to my apartment, both enjoying our coffees and commenting on the crispness of the air afforded us by the shade of the buildings since the sun hasn't yet reached its apex. To be honest, I'm mostly enjoying the fact the sun isn't glaring into my poor eyeballs, and while we are on the topic of my eyeballs, they are currently enjoying the view, as Cole saunters slightly ahead of me. He turns to face me while walking backward, commenting on something I didn't pay attention to, and catches the fact that my eyes are much lower than his face. He clears his throat, and I avert my eyes to anywhere but his, desperately trying to control the burning sensation across my cheeks.

"Enjoying the morning view, Jessica?" he asks with a dark smirk.

Oh my God, he just had to go ahead and make it a thing. He sidesteps, so he's right in front of me before abruptly stopping, causing me to run right into his chest. I barely have enough time to hold my coffee to the side and save it from spilling all over me.

"What the heck, Cole?" I say, laughing before trying to

take a step backward. His arm snakes around my waist, stopping any progression I may have made.

He leans down and his lips brush the shell of my ear, his voice tantalizingly low. "I like how you flush when I catch you looking at me."

Before I can recover from him being that close, he's gone, having taken a step back and turned forward. Once I can breathe evenly again, a stupid grin splits my face, and I have to jog to catch up to him. Damn his long legs.

Waving at Jeremy, I slide my card into the reader to call down the elevator. Inside, I lean against the cool metal wall, my mind blessedly calm after the morning run. I guess the internet does know a few things after all.

"As much as I love having early morning coffee with you and as much as I really, really love seeing you in those hot pink workout shorts," he says, giving a very lascivious look down to my shorts, coupled with a grin that turns my insides liquid. "I actually had a case related reason to talk to you about this morning."

My eyes open wide and I push off the elevator wall to stand rigidly straight. I take in a shallow breath, then another, my head swimming from the lack of oxygen. My panicked eyes swing to him, and he pulls me tightly to his chest, stroking my wild hair down while making quiet shushing noises.

"Shh, it's okay. It's okay." He whispers into my hair, gently rubbing soothing circles across my shoulder. "It's okay that you took a moment for yourself, Jessica. It's more than okay. It's very good."

He uses my shoulders to hold me slightly away from his chest, checking to see how far into a mental break I am. I inhale a deep breath through my nose, then exhale it slowly from my mouth. I repeat that a few more times until I can finally offer him a watery smile with a nod, not trusting my voice. By the time the elevator delivers us to the twelfth floor, my breathing is mostly normal again and we make our way down the hallway to my apartment.

He locks the door behind us and goes to the kitchen, where he grabs two bottles of water. He opens mine and makes sure I'm okay sitting on the couch. I drink the entirc bottle, not realizing how thirsty I was. Restlessness rolls over me in waves and causes me to stand. I pace my living room, chewing on the side of my thumbnail, another nervous habit I've managed to pick up now that I have emotions.

Cole takes a seat in the chair across from the couch and watches me, patiently waiting for me to give him my attention. Instead of forcing the issue, he watches me pace, and he watches me chew like a puppy on a teething bone. Well, shit, that's embarrassing. I tuck both arms down by my sides like I'm in a straitjacket, which I clearly need to be in today.

There's been a cacophony of thoughts and emotions in my head since my feelings decided to poke through that day at the Lemon Wok. My brain's been like the inside of a tornado ever since, everything whirling around and wreaking havoc on my insides, twisting them all up in knots. For the first time this morning, that all slowed down, and I was finally able to take a full breath. I was finally able to just exist in the moment and not worry about everything else whirling around inside me; then, it all crashed back in. I flop down on the couch, let out a huff of frustration, and raise my eyes to Cole's. He's now sitting with his left ankle resting on his right knee, hands evenly spaced beside him on the chair arms. His calm eyes watch the storm in front of him, in the perfect stance I would imagine of a psychologist watching his patient.

"Penny for your thoughts?" I ask, wondering what sort of picture I paint for him. His head tilts to the side and a mischievous smile creeps across his face.

"Of all the things going on in that beautiful head of yours and you're worried what I'm thinking about you?"

I glance down to the floor, then back up at him, gently biting my lip in thought. As silly as it is, yes, I am worried. I'm worried whether whatever I feel and whatever I think is normal. That I'm even doing this… this feelings stuff… correctly. Nodding, I bring my eyes down to stare at the top button of his shirt, embarrassment flaring to life under my skin. All signs of that mischievous smile disappear, and his face goes serious, his eyes pinning me in place.

"I think…" he says, shifting his feet onto the floor in front of where he's sitting. He sits up and rolls his shoulders to release some of his tension. "That you're still doing amazing. That no matter how messy things are in your head, I can see you work through them. Where a weaker person would fail and crumble into a mess, you only succeed at working through it. Categorizing the feelings, the new experiences, while you work through it all—it's a wonder to watch."

"So, it's completely normal I forgot entirely about Sarah's murder, the murder of the other women because of the mess that's in my brain?" I ask, sarcasm lacing my voice as I wave my hands over my head, emphasizing where my brain resides.

"Yep," he says, popping the P at the end. "Sorry, but you're totally normal."

He stands up, walks over to where I'm sitting on the couch, and reaches down for my hands. I immediately give them to him, allowing him to pull me up off of the couch into a bear hug. Shoving my face into his chest, I bury my nose and inhale deeply. I let the smell of him wash over me in calming waves. I never knew the healing power of a scent until I met Cole or the healing power of a good hug, and fuck if he doesn't give the best ones. He tries to pull away, but I tighten my hold as if clinging on for dear life.

"Just five more minutes," I grumble into his chest, and am rewarded with a deep chuckle while he holds me tighter to his chest.

CHAPTER TWENTY
Tight Leash

I emerge from my bedroom, freshly showered, wearing a navy pantsuit, and still messing with my now pin-straight hair. Two fresh cups of coffee sit steaming next to where Cole is working on his laptop at the kitchen counter, and I stop halfway across the living room. I don't have any coffee here.

"I convinced Jeremy, with a hefty tip, to bring us a few cups of coffee," he says over his shoulder, seemingly knowing exactly what stopped my progression.

From his seat, he turns his laptop toward where I'm standing so I can see what's on the screen—an intake report filed Saturday afternoon from Fellmoor Psychiatric Center. The patient is a woman named Alicia Tomlin. She was voluntarily admitted for claiming she and others were kidnapped and then brainwashed into needing to eat the organs of all the "terrorists" in New York City. The blood drains from my head, leaving me dizzy. I struggle to focus enough to read the report a second time; the details are far too similar to our case to be a coincidence. Eyes closed, I take a moment to run through the details in the report, ensuring I'm not seeing similarities where there really aren't any.

"It's just too similar," Cole says, bringing me back from my thoughts. "Normally, when psych patients are admitted into the hospital and claim they've done violence to others like this, a police report is made. That prompts local PD to check the claims against any open cases that match what the patient claims to have done. Of course, this one will raise a few red flags once the interview with local law enforcement takes place, which is supposed to be this afternoon by some officers from our precinct." I don't point out that I already know the protocol and have been the interviewing officer on more than a few of those calls.

"Some officers." I snort a laugh. No fucking way. We have to be the ones to interview Alicia. I chug down my coffee and toss the cup in the trash by the counter. Cole grabs my arm to stop my progression.

"Hold it, Jess…" I let him pull me down into the chair next to him. "This report is confidential; we shouldn't even have it." He sheepishly looks away from me, and I wonder how he ended up with it. "I know some people in Fellmoor and received this one off the record."

Looking back at the report, I realize his having this is a clear breach of doctor-patient confidentiality. Someone would have to have one hell of a relationship with the doctor for them to put their livelihood on the line like this. It would have to be a personal relationship... most likely a strong personal relationship—for someone to risk all of that. I inhale sharply and swing accusatory eyes from Cole down to the name on the bottom of the report. I slowly read the name aloud.

"Dr. Valerie Suarez..." I exhale loudly. Goosebumps march down my arms, and I ponder what sort of personal relationship Cole could have with this woman. Am I even ready to find the answer to that question? My anger begins to poke to the surface. Has he been in a relationship with this doctor this whole time? Have I just been here making an ass out of myself? I let the pieces fall in place, my glare turning deadly. "You're dating her."

"Dated... in the past," he quietly corrects.

That explains why he won't make eye contact with me and the light pinkish coloring on his cheeks: he's embarrassed. Realistically, I know he's dated women before. I would have to be blind to think he hadn't. A man who looks like Cole has most definitely dated a time or two. So, I'm not sure why knowing the name of one of the women he dated has me feeling like I just swallowed a bag of cement. I cross my arms over my chest, staring him down, and do my best to clear the darkness starting to creep in from the edges of my vision. *Dated* is most definitely better than *dating*. I remind myself to breathe.

Eventually, I want to know Cole's past. One day, I want to learn all about his history. I want to learn about him: about his first kiss, his past relationships, and even his first love, but today is not that day. I shake my head clear of the fog threatening my brain and do my best to act like a sane person. I move the conversation in a different direction before he has a chance to explain anything about Dr. Valerie Suarez, who I'm already mentally preparing to hate.

"Okay, so if we aren't supposed to know about this, then how do we get ourselves involved? It's not like we can just waltz into Fellmoor to start interviewing Alicia Tomlin without a reason. I'm sure I don't have to remind you that I'm supposed to be on sabbatical," I say. The last word sounds a little angrier than I meant it to. He sits up straighter in the chair but otherwise gives no reaction to my angry comment.

"Well, I guess then it's a good thing Valerie isn't the

only person in Fellmoor I know."

He doesn't look at me while he admits that, which makes me internally groan. You have to be kidding me. His comment leads me to believe he just serial dated the entire female staff at the mental institution. Maybe he's not exactly who I thought he was, not that my past is shrouded in virginal white, but at least I kept it away from my job. He clears his throat, finally making eye contact with me.

"My younger sister is a patient there," he admits. Well, that was not what I was expecting to come out of his mouth, and it makes me feel guilty about my quick assumption of him. "Right, well, I guess I have to tell you a little bit of her story for that to make sense."

I nod while watching him fidget with his cup, smoothing his fingers around the rim in a nervous gesture, not unlike when I bared my soul to him in the diner. It hits me then that I *have* bared my soul to him. I've told him my dirty little secrets for better or worse, but this is the first deeply personal thing he's shared with me. His sister is in an institution for who knows what reason, and he trusts me enough to tell me. That starkly contrasts what I thought would be happening after I told him everything. Honestly, though, who am I to judge? Up until a month ago, I was a psychopath who probably should have been in there myself. I want to comfort him and let him know I, of all people, will not be judgmental, I will understand, and he has nothing to be embarrassed about. It almost makes me forget about Valerie... almost. I hesitate while I watch him compose himself before he tells me his story.

"My baby sister, Sherri, was admitted to Fellmoor about ten years ago. The case against her is still open; it's the reason I got into forensic psychology and profiling." He shifts on his stool to face me before he drops another bomb I was certainly not expecting. "Sherri killed her fiancée."

He carefully watches my face for a reaction, but gets none. I've spent my entire life training my face to fake a reaction. Thankfully, at this point in time, it works the same way to fake a non-reaction.

"She doesn't really remember the actual murder part, but what she does remember leading up to it is pretty gruesome." His eyes close and he lets out a shaky sigh. "Her fiancée at the time was mixed up in some illegal dealings. He was into heavy narcotics use; Sherri was trying to wait it out. She thought if she was patient enough with him, if she just showed him there was someone who cared enough to stick around, then he would come to his senses. Except it just got worse, and he started hitting her regularly. She hid it well from us, avoided family functions. Later, my sisters and I found out she even stopped going to work." He pauses briefly to roll his shoulders out. "This went on for about a year before we noticed how far back she pulled from the family. I think there was a four-month period we didn't even see her. She would call one of us every so often, but she was always too busy to make it to any dinners or get-togethers. We… I should have noticed." He shakes his head with clear regret and I place my hand on his forearm in an act to comfort him, earning a watery smile.

"The night she killed him, Chris came home pretty trashed, which led to a massive argument between them, and like all the times before, he started beating on her. This time, he was so rough with her that he broke her nose and cracked her eye socket. I guess something inside her finally snapped. She says she blacked out and the next thing she remembers was waking up in the hospital, handcuffed to a bed. She hasn't been the same Sherri since; she's distant and cold. Almost like she's another person entirely." He shakes himself out of the memory and meets my eyes. "Between her lawyer and her Doctor, Valerie Suarez, they were able to get her admitted to Fellmoor instead of prison."

Now I understand why he's been so understanding

with me and my situation. He knows what it's like to have a person switch into something or someone else. The way he stared at me like a lab mouse was now making more sense. He wasn't scrutinizing me like something he had to fix; it was hope reflected there. It was hope that he could somehow fix his little sister and I'm the key.

"Yeah, that's a good way to get us into Fellmoor," I say, swallowing down my personal feelings about his sister's doctor. If this will get us more information on our case and hopefully a step closer to figuring out who's responsible for all this, then I need to keep my own feelings on a tight leash.

CHAPTER TWENTY-ONE
Fellmoor Psychiatric Center

Fellmoor Psychiatric Center is just like all the other psychiatric centers I've had the unpleasant chance to visit. With its dull architecture and monochromatic colored walls, it feels like it slowly sucks your soul away by boring it to death.

At the admittance counter, I surrender my ID and weapon to the security guard; in return, she hands me a sign-in sheet to fill out. I glance over at Cole, who has already signed in, and watch him place his guest badge with his photo onto his shirt. He's the picture of calm. I turn my head back to the guard and she snaps my photo while I'm mid-turn. I frown at her while handing back the clipboard. My frustration begins to boil over as I take my ID back from the counter. In response, she graces me with the fakest smile I think I've ever seen, which says a lot since every smile I've ever smiled up until a month ago was fake. The photo on the sticker I snatch from her outstretched hand does nothing for the frustration. My cheeks look even rounder than they are, and my eyes appear to be floating in front of my face, making me look like a displaced spirit from some B-rated horror flick. Rolling my eyes, I stick it to my shirt despite how awful it is and offer her a fake smile in return. I'm not going to let her shitty attitude affect me. Cole's hand slides into mine, lacing our fingers together and my stomach does a few flips. The new smile that plasters itself to my face is anything but fake.

At the end of the hall is another guard. He briefly glances at our ID stickers but never makes eye contact with either of us before opening the door to escort us inside. Great security team. I bite my lip and fight back my snarky comment with a slight eye roll. The hallway leads further inside the facility before snaking to the right. We walk past rows of bedroom doors secured with large latches on the outside and metal bars in front of their small square windows. The walls are peppered with boring, nondescript pictures between each doorway. They are the only reminder that we are, in fact, in a psychiatric ward and not in a maximum-security prison.

Cole stops us in front of a door with a typed name tag

with his sister's name and gently knocks. After a moment, a woman's voice carries through, telling us to come in. Our lazy escort unlocks the large latch on the door, allowing us to open it and step inside while he takes a spot leaning against the wall next to it.

Inside, the room is small but comfortable in size. It contains a narrow twin-size bed with a small empty nightstand except for a plastic cup. On the opposite side of the room sits a small wooden dresser secured to the wall. In the far corner, in front of the only window, is a white plastic chair with a small matching table next to it, covered in magazines. My eyes skim over them and finally land on the figure standing beside the chair, watching us. She's beautiful, with high cheekbones, naturally golden skin, and the same moss green colored eyes as Cole. She looks like she belongs to a long-lost royal family and should be ordering a slew of servants about while they tend to her every whim. Of course, she's a bit thin for her height, but that's to be expected in a place like this. She watches me for a moment as I observe her before she eventually decides I'm not that interesting and turns back to vacantly staring out the window.

"Hi, Sherri," Cole says, walking up beside her and placing a gentle kiss on her cheek. She doesn't react and continues to stare out the window. "I'd like you to meet my..." He pauses, looking back at me. He's probably trying to decide whether it's best to introduce me in a personal capacity or a working one. I find myself holding my breath while he does. "Partner, Detective Jessica Fairling." In the end, he decides to stick to work.

He notices that I flinch at the formal introduction and offers an apologetic smile. Logically, I know why he introduced me that way: he wants to open the discussion to the murders, so he can ask her what she knows about Alicia. But if there's one thing I've learned through all of this, it's that feelings and emotions are rarely logical. Sherri finally turns away from the window to eye me warily. I can only assume she's had her fair share of police interviews and isn't looking for another one, even if her brother is the one who brought me in. I clear my throat, fidgeting under her stare.

"Hi, Sherri, it's nice to meet you." The small wave I offer is more than awkward. In response, she sighs and perches on the edge of the plastic chair. She motions for Cole and I to sit on the end of her bed.

"I know who you are," she says, before leveling me with an unfriendly gaze. "Since I'm considered to be one of the better-behaved patients in this God-forsaken hospital, I get special rewards like newspapers and shitty fashion magazines." She holds up her fingers in air quotes when she says 'special rewards.'

She pulls out yesterday's newspaper from under a few magazines and tosses it onto the table in front of us. Front and center, on the first page staring back, is a photo of me. The photo is old, from when I was in the police training academy. Below it is a small blurb about my relationship with Sarah, and my face scrunches in distaste. Further down the page is a photo of Sarah with her arm hanging over my shoulder. Sarah's eyes seem to sparkle, and she has an easy smile on her face; she's mid-conversation with someone out of camera's view. My face, however, is vacant. My eyes lack any sort of sparkle, and my emotionless face seems to scream out to everyone that there's something seriously wrong with me. I look up to find Sherri watching me and I quickly smooth my features, offering a friendly smile which she doesn't return.

"We're investigating the murder of my sister," I say, pointing to the photo of Sarah. "And, subsequently, the murder of four other women in New York City that we believe are linked." I glance over at Cole, who hasn't taken his eyes off the newspaper article. I guess I'm on my own with Sherri.

"What does that have to do with me?" she asks, crossing her arms over her chest and leaning back in the chair. "I was in here, so it obviously wasn't me... this time," she snarls, baring her teeth and looking absolutely feral as she does.

"Sherri!" Cole practically yells at her. "That's not something to joke about." She rolls her eyes at her big brother, then brings her attention back to me.

"Well, actually, it has nothing to do with you," I admit. The nervous energy bouncing around inside of me forces me to stand up and move around. "What can you tell me about Alicia Tomlin?"

Sherri gives nothing away, not even a twitch of recognition when I mention Alicia. Instead of responding, she stares at me, utterly still. I raise my thumb to my mouth to start chewing, but I awkwardly lower it, catching myself and thinking better of it. She tracks the motion with cold eyes.

"She's kind of a pussy," she finally says. Before I can stop myself, I snort a laugh at her candid reply. Cole shoots me a look that clearly says not to encourage his sister's shit behavior. Sherri, however, gives me a smile, pleased at my response to her comment. "Well, she is. She came in here with this bad ass story about tearing people limb from limb, leaving them all over New York City..." Her eyes widen. "Oh, shit! You think it was her?" She points back to the newspaper article. "You think she went all cannibalistic on your sister and those other women, don't you?"

"No. I don't think it was her... exactly," I say.

She raises an eyebrow like she's calling bullshit on that. I shift from foot to foot, feeling a bit nervous voicing my opinion on an open case to someone who is currently in a psychiatric ward for murdering her boyfriend. My initial response is not to share any information on the case. However, with a person like Sherri, or rather a person like I used to be, if I'm not offering up information that keeps her entertained, then she will just stop talking to me and we'll leave here with nothing.

"Alright, I think she may have been involved. We... think she may have been involved," I correct, waving a hand between myself and Cole since, technically, the rest of the department, including the chief, has no idea about Alicia. "This story of Alicia's is too close to what's happened to these women for us to dismiss it."

She just nods her head for a moment, appearing deep in thought as she rubs her chin with her fingers. A mischievous sparkle shines in her eyes when she looks back up at me.

"I want in."

"In?" I ask, giving her a puzzled look.

"Yeah, in on the case. I'll be your undercover spy here

in Fellmoor." She gives Cole a challenging look. "I'm bored as shit here, and I'm pretty good at faking shit so that people think I'm whoever I want them to think I am." Cole rolls his eyes at her, about to shoot down her offer. Before he can, I raise my hand to stop him.

"Alright, but no one can know what you're up to, not even the other detectives that come in to interview everyone later today," I say.

Cole gives me a dirty look; I know this is going to come with some sort of lecture later about this being against protocol. If only he knew all of my other against-protocol plans, then this one wouldn't sound so bad. Sherri's eyes go dark, and her smile turns to something I can only describe as lethal. It causes the hairs on my arms to raise, simultaneously sending goosebumps down them.

"I accept your terms, Detective," she agrees before standing up and offering me her hand to shake. I take her palm in my own and note that her skin is slightly colder than mine.

The remainder of our visit is uneventful. Sherri doesn't offer up much to Cole, despite his many questions about her progress, while, for the most part, she ignores my existence. Truth be told, I don't mind. Having Sherri's full attention was a little nerve-wracking, from her dead eyes to her scrutinizing stare that has a way of cutting right through to your bones. I wonder if that's why anyone I've ever interrogated in the past caved to me even when they wouldn't for anyone else.

I tune out their conversation, staring at the newspaper article, lost in the memories that dance around in my head, until I hear Sherri tell Cole that Valerie isn't in today. That part I manage to pick up on as I fight my lips not to curve up in a relieved smile.

CHAPTER TWENTY-TWO

Prey Always Fears a Predator

Strange dreams ruin any chance of a good night's sleep and leave me lying awake, tangled in a cold sweaty mess in my bedsheets again. I drag myself from bed in the darkness before dawn to find my way into the kitchen in the hopes a few cups of dark coffee will give me the illusion I slept at all. Since I'm technically still on leave for a few more days, I have no reason to be up this early, but there's apparently no rest for the wicked. I chuckle to myself; maybe once upon a time, I was the wicked, but now, I think I'm just the anxious.

Settling onto the couch for a quiet morning, my plan is to use my time today to research if there are any other crimes in the last twenty years similar to the current ones we're investigating. If I can locate others, and if we're lucky, that'll give us more evidence to work with. Maybe then I can somehow link them back to this same group of scientists and possibly track down any survivors to gather more information from them. It's a long shot that they would even talk to me, but anything will help at this point.

My phone rings, startling me enough to jolt up and spill scalding hot coffee down the front of myself. "Fuck!" I hiss, trying to peel the shirt from my burning skin while my phone continues its assault on my quiet space. When I finally answer it, I let the person on the other end know how I feel about this early morning attack the best way one can over a phone.

"What?" I bark out, voice dripping with irritation.

"Good morning, Detective Fairling." Chief Harding's gruff voice greets me on the other end.

"Oh, Chief Harding… good morning," I say, all the irritation leaking out of my voice when I realize who I just barked at.

"I need you to get in here," he pauses, before adding in practically a growl, "now." His tone has me flinching, clearly the effect he paused for.

"Yes, sir." I squeak out before realizing the line is dead. "Double fuck…" I half whisper to myself and rush back into my bedroom to get dressed.

In a small act of rebellion, I throw on something casual.

I am, after all, still on leave until next week. I shouldn't have to be business casual for this. Jeans with a plain black shirt is more than sufficient, I think. Of course, I wear my boots equipped with an ankle holster. Lately, it seems I don't go anywhere without my "mental support weapon," the ridiculousness of it has me chuckling out loud. It's not unusual for officers to carry an off-duty weapon, but I just never felt the need to, so I still find that part amusing. Just one more change in my everyday life that having emotions has made.

I climb the steps leading into the NYPD precinct, a heavy feeling pulling at my insides. I feel like a child who's been called to the principal's office for punishment. I don't like it. Inside, I find Chief Harding standing at his doorway while waving me into his office. Not wanting to piss him off any more than he already seems to be, I hurry inside and close the door behind me. A shudder works its way through me in anticipation of the shit storm that's about to rain down on me, most likely for my insubordination while on my forced sabbatical. He gestures for me to sit on the small leather loveseat in the back of his office. I gently sit on the edge of it, and he remains standing, leaning against the front of his desk. The idea he's having me sit down for this means it will take a while, which has my stomach in knots. The discomfort of him towering over me only adds to my anxiety, and my heart rate kicks up a few notches.

"I heard about your extracurricular activities," he says, raising an eyebrow in my direction.

He doesn't elaborate, which leaves me to assume he's referring to the visit to the psychiatric ward and not the activities of a more personal nature. I can't imagine Cole would have told him about those activities, but he may have told him about our visit to his sister in Fellmoor. Nevertheless, I feel my cheeks flush hot at the memory, and I wonder what the chief would have to say if he knew about the other activities. Suddenly, my mouth feels dry, and I find myself sinking deeper into the loveseat. I stare at the desk behind him to avoid the way he's looking at me. He grunts and my attention reluctantly returns to his face to find a deep frown.

"I thought I specifically told you not to go poking around about this case during your down time, which, I *thought*, you agreed to understanding." He pauses dramatically, shifting his weight and crossing his large arms over his chest. I sink down even further into the loveseat and ask it kindly to just swallow me. "Then, I hear from two detectives that your name shows up on the sign-in sheet only an hour before they arrived at Fellmoor to interview a suspect." His bushy eyebrow raises while he impatiently waits for my response. I swallow my saliva, knowing I don't have a good excuse for this one, so I'm unsure of how I should respond.

"I... I think there's been a misunderstanding," I say, my hands going up in a surrender motion. "We, Cole and I, went to Fellmoor yesterday to visit with his sister. She's a umm..." I pause. It isn't really my place to tell him about Cole's family situation, but honestly, I don't see another choice to get out of this. "His sister is admitted there." I finally manage to give him full eye contact from my slumped-over place on the loveseat.

"How convenient for you both," he says before pushing off from the desk and walking around it.

He grabs one of the files sitting on the corner of it and tosses it across his desk within my reach before he makes his way back to the front of his desk, retaking his initial position. Inside the folder, I find Alicia Tomlin's police statement, if you could call this a statement. There's zero information here about what I know she disclosed on arrival regarding her captivity, and no mention of brainwashing or cannibalism. The entire thing reeks of disinterest, and I shake my head furiously. How are we supposed to get anywhere with this shit?

He hums his agreement at the look of disgust on my face. "I can see you feel the same way I do about the bullshit leaking off that page," he says, frowning.

His heavy sigh brings my attention to the deep frown lines on his face that appear to be spreading. The black circles under his eyes are getting darker by the day from lack of a good night's sleep—I know the feeling. I hand him back his folder.

"Jessica, I need you back on this case," he admits. My body hums with excitement. "I know it was my idea to send you home for a week." He breaks eye contact with me, clearly feeling guilty over forcing me to take time off. I don't feel bad for him at all. "But this case has blown up and I need my best detective back on it." Butterflies take flight in my gut from his admission that he thinks I'm his best detective.

"I can officially come back today," I say, straightening my back and extracting myself from the loveseat's tight grip.

"Great, I left copies of all the new info we have on your desk," he says. I frown while he turns to face his desk. Shit, I must have missed more than I thought. "It's the file you just read… I left a copy of the file you just read on your desk," he admits. I let out a sigh of relief as his shoulders drop; he turns his exhausted stare back to me and offers a defeated smile. That's not good.

Exiting his office, I all but skip across the hall to my

own. Settling into my own space, I start placing the files on my desk for what feels like the hundredth time when Cole saunters in. He stops just inside the doorway; a look of surprise briefly flits across his face, and I offer him a smile.

"Good morning, Detective," he says, returning the smile without commenting on my early return.

"Morning," I say, before handing him the statement from Alicia Tomlin. "He took one look at this shit and decided it was best for me to return early."

I don't have to explain who, since only one person here can call those kinds of shots. Cole skims over the document and places it back on my desk with a sour look on his face.

"Yeah, I can't imagine why," he says, voice dripping with sarcasm.

"How do you feel about another visit with Sherri and, possibly, your doctor friend?" I do my best to keep the look of distaste from my face.

I don't like the idea, but, honestly, she's going to be the one with the most information on Alicia at this point. Maybe she can shed some light on the validity of Alicia's claims or let us know if she's just insane and it's all just a coincidence. He gives me a guarded look, and my name slips from his lips, his tone pleading. I raise my hands in front of me in a surrender motion to stop him.

"I get it. I'm not naïve enough to think I'm the first woman in your life, if that even is what I am. It's fine, really it is. I've never felt jealousy over another person before; sure, I've been jealous over other people's accomplishments and merits, but this is all new territory for me. So, I don't have the coping mechanisms for this. I'm working with what I've got," I admit. He frowns at me, and I let out a defeated sigh before offering him a disarming smile, hoping to shelf this discussion for another, much later, time. "Yet... I don't have the coping mechanisms yet," I add, hoping to diffuse the situation.

I can't let how I feel about Cole or anyone else get in the way of solving this case; this is way bigger than me, than us. He reaches across the desk, and his large hands swallow mine.

"Okay, but I want you to understand whatever happened between Valerie and I is very much in the past. In fact, whatever it was, was born from a place of fear and confusion. She and I weren't right." He gently squeezes my hands in his. "You can ask me anything about it. Furthermore, yes, that is what you are, a woman in my life. You are *the* woman in my life."

My cheeks burn at the resolution in his voice. *The woman.* The butterflies are back with a vengeance. It feels like they are devouring me from the inside and any minute I'll explode into thousands of them and float off.

"Okay," I say. My voice comes out in a whisper. I'm unsure whether I could keep my voice even enough to say anything more. But I also want to ask what happens if I just don't want to know.

After a few seconds of silence, he gets that he's not getting anything more out of me and releases my hands to stand up, pulling his phone from his pocket.

"I'll call Valerie and see if she can meet with us today," he offers.

He exits my office to make the call, and I raise my hands to rub my temples in the hope of releasing some of the tension I can feel building there. The tension begins to dull to a gentle ache in my skull as Cole returns with news.

"She's available at three today," he says, not looking at me.

I do my best to be agreeable with what was actually my plan in the first place and plaster what I hope is a passable smile onto my face.

"Great. We can grab something to eat first, then head over early to talk with Sherri. Maybe she's had a chance to get some information from Alicia in the meantime," I say. At least this way, I won't have to do this on an empty stomach.

****

Entering Fellmoor is much more palatable this time. The guard manning the entrance gives me a heads up when my photo is being taken, allowing me to at least have my head facing the correct direction. I don't need a glamor shot, but damn.

We are escorted down the hallway to Sherri's room. This time, her door is propped open, and inside, she's reading in the chair by the window. I take a closer look at what she's reading, a copy of *Beyond Good & Evil* by Friedrich Nietzsche. It's an interesting book to be reading in a psychiatric ward.

"Hi, Sherri." Cole calls out when we enter the room and I wave from my position behind him.

She raises her head, giving a nod, then goes right back to her book, completely disinterested in our presence. My next step transports back to a memory from college so vivid my back aches like it would from actually sitting in that damn blue plastic chair.

Professor Archer scans the lecture hall before he fixates his bright honey-colored eyes on me; my heart rate slightly accelerates with the thrill of being seen. I find myself excited by the idea that he will ask me to "perform" in front of the class, then tell me how good I am at it afterward, making me the envy of every student in this lecture hall. The thought sends a zing of electricity down my spine, and I shift slightly straighter in my cheap blue plastic chair in preparation.

"Jessica," he breathes my name, almost too low for the class to hear. He clears his throat and glances around at the full lecture hall, as if coming out of a trance. He has an inherent fear of me, but he's not in tune enough with himself to know why—prey always fears a predator. "Jessica, please give us the pleasure of sharing what you believe Mr. Nietzsche meant when he penned the famous quote 'Whoever fights monsters should see to it that in the process he does not become a monster'."

A slow unkind smile makes its way across my face. I was hoping it would be this quote he asked me to interpret. Clearing my own throat, I bring my hands to rest palm down on the top of the well-worn table I share with two other students in the hall.

"Well, professor..." My emerald gaze makes its way to him, and I let a little of my mask slip. Pleased by the slight widening of his eyes, I force the mask back into place, letting him think maybe he imagined it. "I think Mr. Nietzsche had it all wrong," I say. His eyebrows raise and he leans slightly forward. His interest in my answer is almost a physical nudge against my psyche as he forgets for a moment that I make him uncomfortable. I run my tongue across my bottom

lip, wetting it, and his eyes track the movement. "See, Nietzsche believed that in order to fight the monsters, you couldn't be a monster. But, in actuality, the only successful way to fight the monsters, to really make a difference, is to become that which you are fighting: a monster."

The brown-haired preppy jock next to me chuckles under his breath and Professor Archer extends his hand, palm up, inviting him to share with the class what he finds so amusing. Sitting up straighter in his chair, he faces the professor.

"I disagree with my fellow student," he says, before glancing at me out from the corner of his eye. "There's no way a person can gaze into that abyss, become the very monster he's fighting, and win. That's just not possible. Once you cross the line and become the monster yourself, then there's no reason to fight the monsters because it's what you are."

I feel the coldness seeping back into my gaze; I turn it onto my classmate and soak in the feeling of power as he fights the urge to move back from me.

"Bold of you to assume all monsters are of the same ilk," I hiss.

Just then, the classroom bell rings, letting us know we're out of time. Professor Archer claps his hands together, interrupting my stare down of my classmate.

"Well, class, it appears we are out of time, which is a

shame because I would love for us to continue this debate. Let's plan on that in our next class." I smile to myself and begin counting down the moments until then.

A shiver runs down my spine when I come back from the memory, and I find Cole giving me a questioning look. I nod to let him know I'm okay; he smiles before giving his attention back to Sherri.

CHAPTER TWENTY-THREE

Language of Monsters

Sherri marks her page, placing a scrap of paper into her book and puts it down on the windowsill next to her. She unfolds her legs and stretches in a way that reminds me of a large cat.

"I talked to Alicia last night in the cafeteria before she went all psycho, and the guards had to haul her to her room to strap her in for the night. Turns out she's one nosy little bitch," she says, standing up from the chair to come stand in front of me. I shift on my feet and fight my body's urge to give me some distance from her. Her answering smirk tells me she's aware of the effect. The irony in that isn't lost on me. "Apparently, whatever drugs they were using on the hostages weren't strong enough for our little Alicia. Looks like she was into some heavy usage before they scooped her up. So, whenever they shot the hostages up, she would lay real still and pretend to be passed out like the rest of them. When they were gone, she would go snooping around." The smirk on her face makes me think maybe she admires Alicia a little bit for that.

"Did she happen to mention what she found while snooping?" Cole prompts, after a few too many seconds of silence from Sherri.

"Yeah, actually she did," she snipes at him, rolling her eyes like the little sister she is. "A location: Red Hook, Brooklyn. Apparently, they posted up in some abandoned warehouse, but from her description of the inside, it's not abandoned at all: it's some makeshift lab." She stalks back to the window and peers out toward the dreary sky, threatening rain again. "She told me about some of the experiments they're doing there. They're implanting things in people's brains and injecting various substances into little kids trying to change their genetics or some shit."

My stomach tenses. Are they performing experiments on little kids? The group we read about was only interested in convicted murderers. Now, they're experimenting on children. My stomach drops as a vision of my nephew Aaron pops into my head; I quickly shake it to clear the image. Sherri turns back to us, a look of pure fury on her face.

"You better catch these fucks and serve them justice on a silver platter. Don't give them the mercy of some bullshit trial that takes five years to see the inside of a courtroom, then ten more years in a place like this awaiting some sort of decision. Actual justice." She pins me with a look I can only describe as knowing, like she can see something inside me that matches something inside her.

A chill works through me—my darkness answering her darkness. I realize she's asking me to become the monster, to become the thing that stares back from the abyss. The darkness I'm constantly pushing down inside threatens to poke its head up, not appreciating the tight leash it's been on since my emotions started showing through. I sharply inhale from the feeling of claws scratching in my skull, as if the monster is clawing to be set free. I offer her a slight nod that I don't think Cole sees.

"It doesn't work like that, Sherri, you know that. There are procedures in place that have to be followed and rules that need to be adhered to. We can't just go all vigilante out there; no one is judge, jury, and executioner here," Cole says, looking over to me for support.

I only offer him a blank stare. It's not that he isn't right.

There are procedures to be followed and rules to be adhered to; it's just, I'm not sure I'll be doing that. I offer him a watered-down smile, not wanting to have this argument in front of another person, but also not wanting to leave him alone in his righteous pursuit of upholding the law.

If Sarah was here, she would also tell me I need to uphold that procedure and follow the rules. She would say they're there for a reason, that they were created by people with empathy, morality, and far more experience than me. If she were here, I would've blindly followed her lead, trusting her guidance, as I always did. Everything she ever taught me served a greater purpose, whether to let me fly under the radar, keep my secret, or to do the "right" thing. But she's not here anymore, and I now know what it feels like to actually have feelings for other people. I feel things for her, for Cole. I can feel guilt, anger, and a whole lot of sadness. Don't get me wrong, I get that there's a moral code that's been passed through the social network of humanity. I really do, but I just don't give a shit about it anymore. In fact, I feel less inclined now that I have emotions to follow that moral code and stick to the rules.

What if everyone before us had it wrong? What if justice should instead be served by those who have been wronged or by those who are sticking up for those who have been wronged? The fiercest judges, the fiercest jury, and the God damned executioner all in one. Why should that right be given to seven people sitting in a courtroom who don't know the victims of the accused? People who have most likely never been wronged by having someone they love torn away from them in a brutal and heinous fashion. No, I don't think I'll follow the rules this time. I think it's time to color outside the lines, no matter what the consequences for me are. I haul in a deep breath and bring my focus back to Sherri.

"Thank you for finding out all this information for us; it's really helpful for our case. We're going to do everything within our power to make sure they're brought to justice," I say out loud, mentally adding on, the kind of justice one finds on their knees with a bullet ripping through the back of their skull.

Sherri opens her mouth as if to protest, and I settle into a cold determination. I feel the comfortable darkness slither up my spine before it peeks out from behind my eyes. I feel the dead space inside me that I've lived in my entire life until a few weeks ago. It's still there, inside. Buried just below these newly found emotions, it's waiting to be let out. At this moment, I welcome it and loosen the leash. I let it see the light of day for the first time since Sarah died and offer Sherri a glimpse of my darkness. I tell her, in a language she and I share, that I have no intention of letting these assholes walk away from me once I find them. I tell her in the language of monsters. Her mouth snaps shut as understanding crosses her face, and she nods slightly. She shuts that look down before Cole can even process that she and I are having a silent conversation about murder or that she now understands what I'm capable of.

"Well, it seems like you two have it under control then," Sherri says, smirking at her brother.

She takes her seat back in front of the window, grabs her book, and opens it to where she marked it. She's done with us. I raise my eyebrow at Cole in a silent question, and he gestures toward the door. I guess he knows she's done with us, too.

My stomach riots as Cole and I head down the hallway toward the administrative offices. My insides scream that I don't want to do this, and my brain tells me to just go home and let Cole handle this part on his own. He must sense my nervousness because I feel his big hand slip into my smaller, much sweatier hand, giving it a gentle squeeze and offering me some of his calm. The unease I feel from needing reassurance eats away at me. I've only ever been good at antagonizing people and I sure as hell have never needed to be reassured. A memory from one of the first serial killer cases I worked seeps in.

Slipping shoe covers on over my sneakers, I take my first steps through the back door into the kitchen. The undercurrent of violence lingers in the air, causing the hairs on the back of my neck to stand on end. I pause in the doorway to roll my shoulders in an effort to shield myself from some of the energy in here. Closing my eyes tightly, I take in a cleansing breath before proceeding further into the house. When I finally open them, it feels as if a lens slides across my vision. My greedy stare now coasts across the scene before me, focusing on the violence left in its wake and ignoring the technicians buzzing around, working the scene.

The kitchen walls to my right are heavily speckled in a splattering of blood that covers not only the wall but arches up to the ceiling, leaving a perfectly angular spray as only a severed carotid artery can make. A woman's body lies spread eagle on the kitchen floor, arms bound over her head by rope and secured to the handle of a drawer. The lack of bruising on her wrists tells me she was both tied and posed after death. I step closer to her body, my brain barely processing the technician hovering over her with white gloves and a mask over his face as he gently scrapes the underside of her fingernails.

To the left is a man's body, posed so he's sitting at the

kitchen table. Both his hands have been impaled and secured to the pine wood dining table with matching steak knives. The sheer force someone would have to put behind the knives to push them not only through a grown man's hands but into a pine table leaves me slightly breathless. His feet are tied to the legs of the chair with the same rope that the woman's hands are bound with. His ankles, rubbed raw with blood seeping down over his feet, tell me he was tied up and made to watch whatever happened to the other victim while he struggled to free himself.

Where the kitchen opens up to the living room is a large puddle of coagulated drying blood, enough blood to know whoever it belongs to is no longer alive, probably the woman in the kitchen. I slowly walk past the technicians, crouching to photograph the puddle, and then make my way to the second floor. I glance inside each room lining the hallway and make my way to the end. I finally enter the master bedroom, and a shock of energy assaults my senses. I involuntarily shutter.

"Detective Fairling," Chief Harding's gruff voice greets me. I walk farther into the room and up next to where he stands beside a king-sized bed covered in more blood. He gestures to a symbol drawn on the wall behind the bed.

"Just like the last one." I nod my acknowledgment toward the symbol that's been crudely painted on the wall above the

headboard in blood, most likely from one of the victims downstairs. "Mercury with a cross over it."

This particular killer uses the alchemical symbol for the spirit or life, Mercury, then puts a big X over the top of it, creatively showing he's extinguished life. We find them painted in blood at each crime scene. It's his calling card.

"I went ahead and called in a toxicology screening on the bodies downstairs. They're being bagged and taken to the morgue now by…" Officer Hayden Langston abruptly halts in the doorway and abandons the remainder of his sentence once he notices me. After a moment of staring, he clears his throat and turns his attention back to the chief. "Unless there's anything else you need from me, Chief Harding, I'll be following behind to watch the autopsies," he says while casting a nervous glance back to me, thinking I don't notice.

Hayden has had an aversion to me since our sophomore year philosophy class when we had a healthy debate on what Friedrich Nietzsche might have meant when he penned his famous quote on becoming a monster. I may have let my mask slip a little, showing him a taste of what it's like to have the abyss stare back. He's kept a healthy distance from me since. I lock eyes with him before he can turn away and smile sweetly while I offer him a little taste behind the mask again today. His body tenses, and I can tell he's fighting the primal urge to step back, as he's always done around me. He is fighting the urge to back out of the door and run far away from the danger that is me. Oh, little Hayden, if you only knew how much I enjoy your fear, you might not be so willing to show it to me.

Cole stands next to me in the middle of the hallway, rubbing gentle circles on the back of my hand with his thumb, bringing me back from my memories. His patience is admirable. I smile at him, hoping it shows him just a modicum of how much I appreciate it before we continue down the hallway to the administrative offices.

CHAPTER TWENTY-FOUR

Counterintelligence

The office door we stop in front of is slightly open and offers my first glimpse of Dr. Valerie Suarez. She sits at her desk, scowling while feverishly typing on her laptop, not yet noticing us. Her dark olive skin practically glows against the light pink blouse she's wearing, and the collar just reaches the nape of her neck. Her brown hair is so dark it almost appears black and is swept into an effortless bun secured by a pen high atop her head. I internally shrink when she mindlessly pushes her tortoiseshell cat eyeglasses up the bridge of her nose, looking like something out of a teenage boy's 'hot for teacher' daydream.

Before I can turn and tuck tail out of this place, Cole clears his throat and gently raps his knuckles on the door, slightly startling her. A warm smile spreads across her face when she realizes who's knocking, and she walks over to embrace him in a warm hug. When she releases him, she offers the same warm smile to me, and I do my best to return it, but I'm not sure mine reaches my eyes. Even still, she steps toward me and offers her hand to shake. I make sure to clasp it gently so I don't release any of my frustration at how pretty she is on it. Her dainty hand emanates warmth through my own as she places her left hand on top of our already clasped hands in a familiar manner, surprising me. I look into her startlingly blue eyes then quickly look away from the kindness I see in them. Unfortunately, from that look, I already know that there's no chance this woman is unkind and that there's no way I'm getting out of here still hating her. My shoulders sag when she releases my hand, offering us to sit in the chairs before her desk. She returns to her desk and folds her hands in front of her; she sits on the edge of her chair as her eyes shift back and forth between us.

"Cole, you didn't tell me how beautiful your new partner is," she says, giving him a sly smile before turning her attention back to me.

My cheeks flush at the compliment. I have to wonder if this woman has seen herself in a mirror lately or if she's just saying this to disarm me. Cole smiles at her, then clears his throat.

"Jessica, this is Dr Valerie Suarez," he says, nodding toward her. "Valerie, this is Detective Jessica Fairling."

"Oh no, you can call me Val. I hate being called Valerie," she says, straightening the front of her slacks with her hand. A nervous tick, maybe? She turns serious eyes on me and gets us back on track for why we're here in the first place. "Cole tells me you're the lead detective on the serial killings that have been all over the news lately, and that he's assisting with the profiling." I nod to confirm. "I'm guessing since you're here, he also shared the details on my latest patient, Alicia Tomlin."

She gives him a pointed look, silently chastising him for sharing the sensitive information. I shift in my seat, clasping my own hands in my lap as an uncomfortable admission, hoping to keep him out of any further trouble.

"Yes, I am. The chief feels we didn't get much information from the officers who came by and took her statement. Cole was kind enough to share the information with me, leading us to pay you a visit to discuss everything that was left out of the statement by my colleagues."

The look Cole gives me from his seat next to mine gives me a small amount of fortitude and allows me to sit up straighter in my seat. Really, it could just be from the fact that he's choosing to look at me sitting here in my plain shirt and jeans, instead of at Val with everything she has going on.

"Ah, yes, those two officers didn't even take notes," she says, shaking her head in disgust. She walks around to the back of her desk and places a folder in front of Cole and me. "Alicia suffers from paranoid delusions that caused her to do unspeakable things to people," she says, noticeably shuddering.

I can't help the chuckle that slips out while I offer a sad smile, having to blink away the image of my sister's cold dead eyes staring at the sky.

"Unspeakable—that's one way to put it," I muse, leaning forward over the folder to scan the documents inside.

It mostly contains notes from Val on what she thinks is wrong with Alicia, along with more of the same details I already saw on the initial report she shared with Cole.

"I'm sorry about your sister, Detective," Val says. I glance up at her and she pins me there with sympathetic eyes. "What a terrible thing. I commend you for staying on the case to see it through."

She lowers her lashes and again begins picking at some unseen lint on her pant leg. Definitely a nervous tick. I'm not sure how to respond to her sympathy, so I keep silent while I continue reading the notes on Alicia's condition.

The psychosis seems to be random since there are no previous psychotic episodes to note in Alicia's life, no abuse, and no bad behavior. She was, for all intents and purposes, a normal kid—good grades, played softball in middle school, and even was a high-school cheerleader. She graduated with a 3.5 GPA, enrolling in a local college to pursue a degree in business management. She was set to graduate within less than two months.

"Alicia wasn't adopted, was she?" I ask, closing the folder and sliding it back onto the desk.

"Mmm, no, I have a copy of a birth certificate right here," she says, turning her laptop toward us while opening a file containing the birth certificate showing as such. "Why?"

Turning her laptop away from us again, I glance at Cole, wondering if sharing information about an ongoing case is a good idea. He offers a slight nod, telling me he trusts Val. Of course he does; she sent him the private details on this patient, knowing they might help him with this case. So, I take a leap of faith and decide to trust her, too.

"Well, all the victims were adopted," I say, with a sigh. "Except Sarah, my sister. She's the only one who wasn't adopted, but I... I was." I swallow thickly while the heaviness of guilt settles in my gut. I feel the comforting weight of Cole's hand gently on my back just below my shoulder blades.

"Oh," she says. Her eyes slightly widen in understanding of my unsaid guilt. Great, two psychologists in the same room to study what makes me tick.

"We have a team working to get in touch with the previous management of the agencies, but sadly, we haven't been having much luck with that. It seems one agency closed about ten years ago, and their files have since been misplaced," Cole says, a clear look of distrust about that information.

"That sounds awfully convenient," Val agrees, drumming her fingers on the desk. "Do you think this is something Liam would have access to?" Cole shrugs in response.

"Who is Liam?" I ask, looking between them.

"My fiancée," Val says, a dreamy smile taking over her face. My eyes drop to her left hand, where I don't see a ring, and she huffs a small laugh while lifting her left hand in between us wiggling her fingers. "I don't wear jewelry to work; it is too dangerous with the patients."

I nod, and she picks up her phone to begin calling who I assume is Liam. I shoot Cole a surprised look. Why he didn't just tell me she was engaged to someone else? It's not like he didn't know I was uncomfortable with his and Val's history; that would have been a very simple way to ease my concern, yet he never mentioned it. He gives me an easy smile, giving no indication that he knows what I'm thinking. Which I'm sure is absolute bullshit. Lately, it feels like he always knows what I'm thinking.

Val hangs up from her call and smiles at us. "Liam is free for an early dinner. We can meet him in forty minutes at the diner down the road. It's close enough, so we can walk."

"Not to be rude…" I hedge, my eyes tracking their way from Cole before going back to Val. "But how is your fiancée going to help with a murder investigation?"

"Oh." Val laughs, and the sound reminds me of bells chiming. Great, one more thing that's beautiful about her. "Liam's in the CIA. He mostly works with missing persons cases, child trafficking, and the like." She stands, unable to hide the grin that spreads across her face as she talks about him.

"Oh." I manage to squeeze out. Yeah, that would do it. Cole and I both stand with her.

"Let me just run to the front desk really quick to let the nurses know that I'm going to be stepping out for an hour. I'll be right back." She rushes out the door and is down the hall before either of us can reply.

From the corner of my eye, I see Cole staring at me and I shift on my feet, finding myself uncomfortable under his careful watch. Without looking at him, I drop my shoulders in a defeated shrug.

"Fine," I huff. I give him my eyes and let out a dramatic sigh of defeat. "I suppose she's not so terrible after all."

He chuckles, amiably draping his arm around my shoulder and bringing me into a sideways embrace. The position allows me to get a lung full of the delicious scent of Cole, sandalwood and vanilla. I greedily soak it in. The scent instantly calms my nerves, and I let a smile peak out. It amazes me that the scent has such a strong effect on me, or maybe it's the man behind the scent.

"All right, you two, we're all good to head down to the diner." Val smiles at our nearness and beckons us to follow her outside into the warm New York evening.

The diner is only a short walk from the facility and, surprisingly, isn't empty inside, since it's still early for dinner. The hostess that seats us also sets us up with a pot of freshly brewed coffee. I take a tentative sip to find it's not burnt to death, a small miracle to come across at a diner in downtown New York. The chime over the door goes off, and Val's face transforms from a beautiful, confident woman to the bashful face of a teenage girl with her first crush. I watch with mild curiosity as her cheeks flush pink and her pupils slightly dilate while she fidgets with her hands in her lap. Liam must have been the reason for the door chime.

"Hey, it's Cole!" A masculine voice rings out behind us.

I hear the sound of a slap on a shoulder, and I turn to look at who I can only assume is Liam. He clasps Cole's shoulder with one hand and uses the other to shake his hand in a way I can only describe as manly. I'm surprised to see he's so tall, taller than Cole, and he also has a slightly more athletic build than Cole does. His face is all hard lines and deeply tanned, giving him a rugged outdoor appearance. Like the NYPD, the CIA puts all their recruits through rigorous training, but unlike the NYPD, they don't stop their training even after they become full-fledged agents and are assigned to their departments. Liam's cornflower blue eyes swing to me, and he offers a warm smile which I try to return.

"Hi, I'm Agent Liam Murphy," he says, his handshake firm but not overly tight.

"Detective Jessica Fairling," I say, dropping my hand back into my lap, still feeling the warmth in it from his.

I get a slight nod before he turns toward Val. He gives her a panty-dropping smile before leaning in for a kiss that leaves not only her, but also me, slightly breathless. The man clearly knows what he's doing. I avert my eyes while I clear my throat and grab the menu to have anything else to focus on as I feel my face flush pink. The waitress returns with a coffee mug for him and, without even glancing at the menu, he tells her he's ready to order. She scribbles all of our orders down and hurries her way back toward the kitchen, leaving the four of us alone to stare at each other in the small booth.

Liam's the first to break the silence. "So, Val tells me you're the lead detective working on the recent serial killings going on around town and that I might be able to offer some sort of assistance?"

My mouth opens to explain the case details, but I hesitate. It's ingrained in us as detectives to keep the details of open cases to ourselves and not share them with outsiders, especially not outsiders from federal offices. The last thing our department wants to do is to lose our cases to the feds. Liam's intelligent blue eyes bore into mine as he patiently waits for me to give him anything.

I release a sigh, deciding this is the best shot we have of getting the information we need to move forward and I offer the basics of the case to him. I make sure to hold back some details of the murders, knowing some of them are intentionally being kept private in case someone comes forth with information that hasn't been released; that way, we can vet them as serious. There are a lot of crazies around that, sadly, would like to be able to claim credit for things they didn't do, hoping for their fifteen minutes of fame or whatever notoriety it brings them.

CHAPTER TWENTY-FIVE

The Warehouse

"I've been looking into the shell company that leased the warehouse, but they've covered their tracks well. Unfortunately, I haven't been able to uncover who actually owns the company yet," Liam says, surprising me.

He shakes his head and absentmindedly stabs his hand through his already shaggy brown hair, giving the appearance he's just rolled out of bed. Which, for all I know, he has. He goes on to tell us he's already started digging in his spare time on the information Alicia shared about the warehouse. It looks like Cole wasn't the only one Val was spilling Alicia's secrets to. I look at her and see she's intentionally avoiding my gaze.

"Well, honestly, that's more information than what we had a few hours ago." I say, working to keep my voice even and contain the excitement I'm feeling for finally having some sort of new information on this damned case.

My excitement grows even more when I realize not only do we have more information, but we were even able to obtain it without having to find another victim. I remind myself just because this is where Alicia claims they were holding her, it might not be accurate information given her mental state. It's also not guaranteed that just because they were there, they still are. For all we know, they could have moved to another warehouse, another town. Hell, they could be in another country by now with all the media attention that's been on this case. I battle to keep my expectations low so as not to disappoint myself.

Liam pulls a notepad from his back pocket and scribbles down an address in the Red Hook warehouse district area. My heart rate kicks up when he lays it on the table next to my coffee cup. My fingers itch from their position in my lap to reach out and snatch the paper. I want to grab it, run to the car and head straight to the warehouse district. I feel Cole's hand come to rest on my knee; the gesture is meant to be calming but instead causes my breath to hitch and my heart to speed up at his nearness.

"Thank you, Liam," I say, doing my best to quickly recover from the unexpected reaction to Cole's hand. I smile as I rip the page from the notepad and tuck the paper safely away in my back pocket.

My mind wanders to all the outcomes that can result from raiding the warehouse, all of them ending with me happily closing this case. Everyone else at the table engages in small talk, unaware of my violent daydreams. I start paying attention to the conversation toward the end when Liam is discussing some of the more notable cases he's worked on, most of which I'm already familiar with, but a few I'm not. He has an impressive resume. I wasn't sure what to expect from a CIA agent, as I've never had dinner with one before, but his sharp intellect and easy demeanor have left me feeling comfortable in my decision to involve him. I can only hope Chief Harding will agree with my judgment call to share the case details with a fed. Maybe when I call him with the warehouse information, I can accidentally leave out where I got it. It's not exactly lying, just a slight omission of information.

As it turns out, not only is Val ridiculously likable, but so is Liam, working for the CIA, hunting down human traffickers by day and rogue serial killers in his spare time at night. What's not to like? And, I have to admit to myself, the more time I spend with them, the less I can find myself hating her. She's just too nice. In a way, she reminds me a little bit of Sarah. It's the altruistic way she offers everything she has in order to help us. It elicits a pang of longing for my sister so sharp I have to give up on finishing the remainder of my dinner.

A call comes in from one of the nurses at Fellmoor and prompts Liam and Val to leave the diner first. Cole and I use the alone time to hash out a plan for how we're going to proceed with the warehouse information. Naturally, I want to go directly to the warehouse and end this. My logic is that the longer we wait, the more damage these people can do and the higher the risk of them being able to snatch up more victims. Also, the higher the flight risk will become. Cole wants to carefully plan a raid like you would see in the movies. Sometimes his cunning mind and vast knowledge of criminal cases make it easy for me to forget he isn't actually a detective in the department. Then, we get into a debate like this, and I'm reminded all too well that even though he's here consulting with me, we are from totally different professional worlds.

We conclude that the best way to move forward requires some compromise from both of us. We decide to call the chief and have him send over backup units to the warehouse district while Cole and I head over to scope it out before they arrive. Then, when backup arrives, we'll proceed to gain entrance to the warehouse. With any luck, these assholes will be inside, and we can finally close this case. It's not exactly how I want to do it, but maybe I can take one or two out if I play my cards right—a small concession. My stomach tightens with anticipation, as this could be the end of the two-year-long search. Could it be this simple? I take a shuddering breath. I guess we're going to find out.

Cole's first to break the silence on our walk back to Fellmoor, where the car waits. "Jess, you have to promise me you won't go inside this warehouse until we have some sort of backup." I shoot him a sideways glance, not stopping my brisk pace as we walk to the ward. "I'm serious. I feel like I know you by now, and I know what this case means to you," he says, tone lighter and almost pleading as he tenderly grazes his hand across my own. I recognize the gesture for what it is, a ploy to get me to soften to him, and as much as I want to deny it, I have to admit it does work.

"Yeah, okay. I promise we'll wait. The only thing that'll cause me to go inside before backup arrives is if we see or hear probable cause to enter the warehouse." I tilt my head slightly to look into his concerned eyes and offer him a sad smile, shamelessly using the oath I've taken to protect and serve against him. He has to understand I can't just ignore it if I see someone being harmed or other probable cause from outside the warehouse. I can almost see the gears churning in his mind. I can see he wants so badly to try to protect me from this. He wants to protect me from whatever he believes we're going to find, but I can tell he also understands it's my duty to get involved in things like this.

After watching me for a few more moments, he finally offers a sharp nod, letting me know he's reluctantly approving my plan. Guilt for manipulating the situation settles in my gut, tightening it even more. At this rate, my insides probably look like a pretzel.

I agree to let Cole drive the unmarked patrol car so I can call the chief. I start by sharing what we've learned from Liam, quickly glazing over who Liam is in the hopes of not getting my ass chewed. I then go over our plan for the warehouse and make sure to emphasize that we will wait for backup to come before going inside.

"Fairling," Chief Harding grunts on the other end of the phone, "I'm not sure I want you two heading to that warehouse without backup *first*. We have no idea who these people are and by the time backup arrives, it's going to be dark. There's a possibility they have more people we don't know about; we have no idea what they're capable of."

I want to tell him that *he* has no idea who these people are, but swallow it down, knowing that would just open a whole other line of questioning. He is right; it is going to be dark soon, which is all the more reason why we need to get going quickly.

"I know that," I snap before thinking. I pause, realizing my mistake. I need him with me on this. Sucking in a breath, I quickly alter my tactic to a more agreeable one. "That's exactly why Cole and I will use whatever daylight we have left while we wait in the car, scoping things out from a distance and gathering intel until backup arrives."

I'm going to this warehouse whether he agrees with the plan. It'll just make my life a whole lot easier if he's on my side with this. He grunts his frustration again; this time it's almost a growl, letting me know he's going to give me what I want.

"Fine, but I want your asses to remain in the car until I arrive with backup." Oh shit, he's coming? "Tell me you understand. I need you to tell me you aren't going to do anything stupid," he all but yells through the receiver.

He's never been this controlling with me. Usually, he lets me handle my cases however I see fit. He's never shown this level of concern before.

"Yes, sir." I respond in my most neutral voice, doing my best to tamp down the frustration of being treated like a rookie. I don't even bother adding on the caveat of entering the building if I have probable cause. He may be my superior, but even he can't ask me to break my oath.

I fill Cole in on the other side of the conversation after the chief, in his normal fashion, abruptly ends the call. I tell Cole that he agreed to dispatch backup immediately, along with himself, apparently. He, of course, agrees with the chief's strict order to wait until he arrives. We are silent the remainder of the drive to the warehouse, and my mind races over and over how I can manage to finish this case the way I know I have to without anyone interfering.

Cole pulls the car into a secluded parking area a few lots down from our target; he eases the car behind a pile of old pallets under an overgrown tree, giving us some coverage from the warehouse entrance. He puts the car in park, and I rifle around in the center console until I pull out a pair of binoculars to start scouting the area from my passenger seat vantage point. The warehouse has two large rolling doors, which, of course, are closed, hiding whatever's going on inside from view. To the right of the rolling doors is a loading dock where two sprinter-style vans are parked in front of a small foot door. There's no company sign outside the building. I suppose that isn't entirely out of the realm of normality, considering most of these warehouses are being used by large companies for product overflow storage and are not accessed by the general public.

Cole rolls down the windows before shutting the vehicle off, and a slight breeze works its way in from the nearby bay, making it just barely tolerable to sit inside the vehicle. I slouch down in my seat, resigning myself to get comfortable while waiting for backup to arrive when a van pulls up. Its back and side windows are spray-painted black, making it impossible to see inside. The driver's side door swings open, and a man exits, glancing around nervously. He slams the door behind himself and walks to the back of the van, and opens the doors, giving us a clear view of the cargo area.

Looking through my binoculars, I can see inside the van. Makeshift rails hang from the roof with shackles attached every few feet, and the cargo area's floor is covered with cardboard that looks stained with dark spots. The front cabin of the van is separated by a mesh grate, like what you might see in a delivery truck. My breathing picks up as I watch him pick up a long chain with what appears to be handcuffs on the end of it, unshackling it from the floorboard and he drapes it over his shoulders like an insidious snake.

My mind immediately recoils in horror. I watch him

close up the van and make his way to the foot door next to the loading dock, squashing any doubt we could possibly be in the wrong place. The hairs on my neck stand up on end; there's no way I can sit here waiting the remaining forty minutes for backup to arrive. That's enough time for these assholes to completely clear whatever hostages and equipment they have out of this warehouse. We can't let that happen.

CHAPTER TWENTY-SIX

Undercover

"Jessica!" Cole whisper shouts my name, roughly grabbing my forearm and dragging me back into my seat. "You are *not* going into that warehouse until backup is here."

The stare I pin him with is dark enough to make him loosen his grip on my forearm, and I pull it out of his grasp.

"Listen to me, Cole." I struggle to make my voice come out calm, with all the nervous energy rolling around inside me. I turn my body to face him. "I have to know what's inside that warehouse. I need to see if there are any more victims inside." I tilt my head back, looking up at the car's ceiling and haul in a deep breath. I need to calm my nerves so that what I have to say comes out less frantic than how I actually feel. "I took an oath to protect innocent lives, to do whatever is in my ability to keep people safe, when, and if, I'm able. This is one of those situations that I am able to. This is my job, my life, and if that's a problem for you, well, I suggest you recuse yourself from both this case and my life to go back to the safe confines of a classroom."

I flinch as soon as it's out of my mouth, knowing how much of an asshole I just came off as to someone who has only ever been kind to me and looked out for my best interests. Regret settles in my belly, causing me to open my mouth to apologize, but before I can, Cole raises a hand to stop me.

"I get that, Jess, I really do," he says, pleading with his eyes for me to understand. "But this is different. You're related to one of the victims, making this very personal to you. Not only that, but you're able to feel things now that you couldn't feel before. That's the recipe for the perfect storm, for something to go catastrophically wrong." He sighs, looking up at me through his lashes. "If you go in there, I'm going with you." It is not exactly what I was expecting him to finish that lecture with, but I'll take it.

"Fine," I grit out.

Judging by the surprised look on his face, I think he was expecting an argument. I also see fear swirling around behind his eyes before he's able to smooth his features and nod in agreement. He's not comfortable with this. We exit our respective sides of the car, and he comes around to join me on the passenger side as we crouch down out of view of the rolling doors.

"My guess is, since the doors and loading bays are on this side, the other side will have the windows where we can hopefully see whatever's going on inside," I say.

Before he has a chance to respond, I take off in a light jog to the back of the building. I hear his shoes on the gravel as he follows closely behind. Crouching behind some rotting cable reels and pallets stacked against the back of the building, we're able to partially conceal ourselves from the windows that line the wall. One window in the row is slightly cracked open and I point at it, showing him where I intend to go next, and he nods his response. Creeping over to the window, I listen just below the sill for any indication that someone's on the other side of it. I hear muffled voices filtering out of the small crack in the window; they sound far enough away that I pop my head over the ledge and can finally see what's happening inside.

The room directly in front of the window has high ceilings and mostly empty floor space except for a few dark-stained mattresses piled in one corner. The warehouse appears to be divided into two different rooms. From where I stand, I can see a dingy yellow light coming from the doorway leading farther inside to what appears to be a much larger room than the one the window's attached to. Through the doorway, all I can see is a bunch of medical equipment stacked against the far wall of the other room. The man I saw enter from the loading dock door paces past it while in a discussion with someone out of view. Judging by his tense posture and angry gestures, they don't appear to agree on whatever they're discussing. That could work in my favor. If I want to get inside the warehouse without being noticed, having them distracted by each other is ideal.

I gently push on the window to test if it's nailed in place and keep my attention pinned on the man through the dingy glass. The window creaks before giving in and noisily sliding up the rusted track. I pause for a moment in case the noise attracts his attention. Lucky for me, he's too enthralled in his conversation and doesn't seem to notice the sound. My heart kicks up speed, the sound like thunder in my ears. I brush off bits of metal shavings and rust that's fallen into the window track, making room to climb through before checking back on the man. My eyes dart back to him in the other room, and he's pointing to something further inside that I can't see, causing his arms to bulge and showing me exactly what

I'll be up against if this turns into a hand-to-hand scenario. "They can't… Why would… Fucking idiots…" Snippets of his conversation float over to me, not making much sense without the missing parts and leaving me in the dark about their argument. I have to get closer.

I return to my task of pushing the window further up in its track so I can shimmy my way inside, hoping they keep yelling at each other and don't notice the racket I'm making. The man in the doorway lets out a rough laugh, causing me to stop my progression with the window. I look up in time to see him storm off through the other room and hear a door slam shut just moments later, giving me the opportunity to get inside the warehouse while there's no one within eyesight. Before I swing myself up and into the tight window, I quickly turn back to Cole and point inside, letting him in on my plan. A frown etches its way across his lips as he finally understands he isn't able to stop me from going inside before backup arrives.

Pushing on the window one more time, I'm able to get it to move another inch, giving myself just enough room if I flatten myself completely on the way in. I take a moment to clear my head, coming to terms with the fact Cole can't make it through this window, and I'm going in alone without any sort of backup. I let out a heavy breath and manage to wiggle my way through the small opening; my hips only get caught momentarily because of my belt buckle. I land as quietly as I can on my hands and knees before crawling my way over to crouch behind an old barrel in the far corner. From my new position, I have a different view into the second room than I had at the window. I can now see there are four more men in the next room, standing in a small circle, pointing animatedly to something in the corner. The way they're huddled together blocks whatever they're discussing. I scan the room I'm in for anywhere closer to the doorway, anywhere that I can conceal myself and get a better view. There's a decently sized pile of wooden planks and debris closer to the door. It's tall enough that if I lay down on my stomach, it should cover me from view; the only issue is getting over there without being noticed. I almost jump out of my skin when the door to the other room slams open on its hinges and the man who was in the doorway storms in, yelling at the others in a language I don't understand. The timing is perfect, and I use the distraction to quietly make my way behind the pile of debris and settle with the cold concrete floor against my belly.

From my new vantage point, I see what they were blocking: two small bodies, tied to wooden chairs by a rope around their ankles, their hands zip-tied in front of them, and black hoods covering their heads. I watch them shake like leaves with fear, huddling as close as they can to one another, and my mind recoils. The men finally stop yelling and come back into view before each one of them bends down, picking up a piece of the medical equipment stacked up against the wall behind the two prisoners.

From this distance, I can't make out exactly what all the items are. Some of them are covered with towels, and the smaller items are being stuffed into duffel bags. A shuffling sound brings my attention from where my eyes are tracking two men walking to the front door and onto the other three men as they start yelling at each other, causing the two small bodies in the chairs to whimper. The delicate sounds remind me of a scared child and cause my mind to go to my nephew, Aaron. A horrible dark thought snakes its way into my skull, and the darkness inside of me stirs to life. What if they go after Aaron?

For a brief moment, the tension in my gut has me feeling like I might vomit, which would definitely give away my hiding spot. Squeezing my eyes shut to block out what I'm seeing, I work to calm my nerves with a deep breath while I wait for the nausea to pass. Once I'm certain I'm not going to lose the contents of my stomach on the warehouse floor, I open them in time to see four of the five men step outside the door, carrying a large box covered with a sheet. Unfortunately, my position behind the debris doesn't allow me to see the entirety of the other room, and I have no idea how much stuff they have left to move. With any luck, they'll take their time with the large box they just took outside and won't come back right away, because I need some luck for the shit I'm about to pull.

I push off the floor, yank the pistol from my ankle holster, and silently flip the safety off before I flatten myself against the wall next to me. The adrenaline hits me like a freight train, and my breath leaves my mouth in heavy pants. I catch sight of Cole watching me through the window. His face is more serious than I've ever seen as he glances toward the other room and nods to let me know it's clear. From his position outside, he can see through to where the other door is located. Hopefully, he can yell through the window whenever the others come back and at least give me a few second heads up when they come back. Taking a deep breath, I step out from behind my cover and turn my body, leveling my gun at the back of the man's head as he stands, facing the two victims.

"Freeze, you piece of shit," I say, voice coming out calm and even, which surprises me considering those are two things I'm not feeling at this moment. "NYPD, backup is on the way. I have a gun aimed at your head, so stay right where you are."

I take a slow step into the room and glance back at the open door while the man puts his hands above his head. Seeing no one in the doorway, I glance behind me toward the window where Cole is but no longer see him there. I have a moment to wonder if he's all right before the man in front of me spins around and runs toward the door. My arm immediately shoots out, and I grab his shirt collar hard enough to knock him off balance onto his ass. From his new position on the floor, he grabs for my left leg, but I sidestep faster than he can grab. I kick him in the ribs with my right boot hard enough that I hear a loud snapping. He makes a wailing sound, clutching his side, and folds himself into the fetal position in front of me. The scene brings a cold smile to my face; a few broken ribs will be the least of his worries by the time I'm done with him.

After hearing my introduction as NYPD, the two prisoners, that I now see are two teenage girls, have managed to get themselves up from their chairs to remove the ropes and hoods, but not the zip ties from their wrists. I glance down at the man still curled in on himself on the floor and decide I don't trust him to stay that way long enough for me to cut them free. Instead, I motion with my head for them to go to the back room I was hiding in. That'll at least give them some protection if the others come in through the door until I can get back to them. Grabbing the man on the floor by his shirt, I manage to pull him up to his feet and then back him up with my gun into his injured ribs until he falls down on one of the chairs. I use the ropes lying on the floor to tie his hands behind his back and secure his ankles to the chair legs.

Darkness begins to creep in on the edges of my mind, making it difficult to think of anything other than violence. I hear the sound of squealing tires outside as I unsuccessfully try to fight my way back from it. My mind is still dark as I watch a violent tremor begin in the hands of the man in front of me, no doubt from the stark realization that his comrades just left him alone to a terrible fate.

CHAPTER TWENTY-SEVEN

Something Cold

The man's eyes frantically dart around before they settle on the two girls, now in the other room, which pisses me off. I lean forward, blocking his view of them to rip off a strip of his shirt and use it as a make-shift blindfold for his eyes.

"You can't save them!" he yells, thrashing his head back and forth, trying to remove the cloth unsuccessfully. I turn to make sure they are okay in the other room and aren't getting curious enough to come back over to him. "Just like you couldn't save your sister!"

My head whips around, and my focus hones in on him as my vision begins to blur. Something cold slithers through my veins, and a violent shiver wracks its way through me. My teeth clench, making my jaw pop, and I start to feel myself slipping into a familiar dark place inside me—a place I haven't been since I started to have emotions and feelings.

I brush the barrel of my gun across his temple as I reposition it from the side of his head to the flat space in between his eyes. A small whimpering sound slips from his mouth, almost too low for me to hear.

"I'm going to ask you this once," I spit out, before I pause to roll my shoulders in an attempt to alleviate some of the tightness building in them. "Where. Are. They. Going?"

I make sure to pause between each word, giving each one time to sink in, letting him know how serious I am, in case the gun I'm currently pushing against his skull wasn't already. A shaky intake of breath behind me lets me know Cole's entered the room. For a fleeting moment, a small kernel of panic has me wondering what this must look like to him. I wonder what he's thinking, seeing me with a man tied to a chair, a strip of his own tattered shirt covering his eyes as a blindfold, while I hold a gun to the tender space between his eyes. Can he see the inky black of my soul peeking out behind my eyes?

"Help me." The man in front of me whines as his head swings around, voice pleading after hearing someone else enter the room.

"No one is going to help you," I say, gently sliding the

barrel of my gun back around to his temple. A tender caress of cold steel to remind him I'm the one in charge. "I suggest you tell me what I want to know... and quickly, I only have so much patience left in me."

The gentle trickling sound of his urine, as it makes its way out of his pant leg onto the cement floor below, hits my ears a moment before the acrid scent of it fills my nostrils. Disgust knots my gut, and something buried deep in my brain starts fighting me. It screams that this is wrong; I'm wrong to do this to another human being. I try to take a deep breath and push that voice back down, but I'm almost overwhelmed by the scent of the man's fear. Instead, the breath comes in as more of a gasp. How much longer can I do this?

"Answer me!" I scream my frustration at him, causing his body to jolt hard enough that if he weren't tied to the chair, he would have fallen out of it.

"I don't know," he whimpers, barely loud enough for anyone to hear. "I honestly don't know. Joseph set the whole thing up; he was the only one who knew where the plane was going." He sobs, trying to take in enough breath and causing himself to hiccup. "I swear to you, I don't know." His voice rises to a panic before his head goes slack on his shoulders, then lolls to the side. He's unconscious, a blessing for us both.

My breath shudders and I feel Cole gently pull my arm down. He moves the barrel of my gun from the man's temple, and I let my arm hang loosely at my side, still holding it. I let him pull me into his chest, and I greedily breathe in the scent of him, calming myself. I let some of the warmth return to my body and take a small step back from the ledge I'm teetering on.

"He has nothing else to tell us," he says into my hair.

My shoulders slump with the knowledge that he's right. This man has nothing else for us, which makes him useless. My arms wrap around Cole, holding him tightly, wanting nothing more than for this to be all over and just a distant memory. A faint sobbing from the other room causes me to pull back. The girls in the other room need him right now. They need the softness he can offer. I have no softness to offer them. Right now, I'm nothing but hard edges and sharp corners. Cole stares down at me with eyes full of sympathy, looking at me in a way that tells me that he knows what I have to do next. His eyes give me silent permission to fulfill my promise to Sarah, the promise that I would kill every last person who hurt her.

"It's okay," I say to him.

It's not okay.

"It's not the first," I admit, and I know it won't be the

last.

I squeeze his hands and do my best to offer some semblance of a smile. A deep frown etches across his face at my admission; I give him a gentle nod toward the other room, where the girls are sobbing a little louder now, knowing this is not the place to have this talk. My eyes plead with him to get them out of here before I do this. He says nothing as he retreats to the other room and a calmness filters through me when I hear him telling them it's all going to be okay. He gently coaxes them through the warehouse while he tells them they just need to hold out a little longer until the ambulance can arrive and get them seen to. I soak up his words as if they were meant for me. I imagine he's telling me it's all going to be okay and I just need to hold out a little longer until this is all over.

I turn back to face the unconscious man tied in the chair as they walk behind me toward the warehouse exit. The door grinds open, and after a few moments, I hear it bang shut, and I finally turn back to look around, seeing no one else with me. Still, I wait, wanting them to be farther away before I do this. I do not want to traumatize them more, even if I'm saving them and people like them from the assholes who would hurt them.

The piece of shit tied in front of me lets out a gentle

whimper and rolls his head to the side, letting me know he's no longer unconscious. I kick his booted foot, causing him to jump in the chair and strain against the rope he's secured with.

"Couldn't make this easy on us both and stay unconscious, could you," I say before sighing heavily. I raise my weapon to his temple again. "I hope you've made peace with your actions and come to terms with the special place in hell you're going to find yourself in."

I haul in a steadying breath and reach back inside myself. This time, I invite the darkness to return to the surface. I beg for it to come out of hiding, to envelop me in its cold embrace and turn me into a monster. It's more than happy to oblige.

"Oh God, please. Oh God, please. Oh God…" he begins chanting, and I chuckle at the absurdity.

"I don't think it's Him you need to be bargaining with right now," I spit, disgust lacing my words.

Using both hands to steady the gun against his temple, I widen my stance and slightly turn my body to the side, preparing for the recoil from my weapon. I release everything from my lungs to calm my galloping heartbeat and train my focus on the vein jumping wildly in his neck. My finger tightens, coaxing the weapon to let loose its round with a deafening noise.

I don't bother to flinch as I numbly watch the bullet rip through his skull, tearing through flesh and bone before exiting cleanly on the other side. My focus stays trained on the vein in the side of his neck while it needlessly continues to pump for a few long seconds afterward. Blood slowly trickles through the hole the bullet left in his head, leaking down to join the puddle of his piss on the concrete floor below. Time seems to stand still while I stand frozen in place, watching the blood pool.

By the time the darkness releases its hold on me again, my fingers are numb from gripping my gun so tightly. I hear sirens and voices coming from outside the warehouse. I stare down at the gun in my hand, then over to the dead man with a head shot, still blindfolded and tied to a chair. The reality of what I've just done hits me like a ton of bricks. Fuck. This looks… well, it looks like exactly what it is—murder.

"Detective, are we clear?" Chief Harding calls out from behind me.

I turn my head to see him huddling low behind the door frame for protection from whatever threat inside this room has his detective standing with service weapon in hand. Our eyes meet and he shoots me a look that tells me to hurry up with a response. My head turns back to the dead man in front of me.

"Clear…" I say, the word leaving my mouth as barely a whisper. I clear my throat and try again. "Clear."

The word somehow comes out calm and even the second time, despite me feeling neither of those things, as I lie to him. He doesn't know the biggest threat is still in here. My shoulders sag with the knowledge that I failed to fulfill the promise I made to Sarah—the promise where I told her I would kill every single one of the men who hurt her and the other victims. I wonder if she'll forgive me for getting caught before I could fulfill it. No matter what happens, I don't regret my choice because I know in my heart of hearts, if there was ever a good enough reason to give up my life, it would have been to stop these fuckers. I just have to live with the regret that I was only able to get one of them.

Chief Harding stands stiffly beside me, service weapon in hand, hanging slack at his side. He takes in a deep breath and surveys the scene. His eyes stop to examine the dead man, leaking blood and brain matter from the back of his head that's tied to a chair with a crudely fashioned blindfold over his eyes. After he's had his fill of that, his eyes shift to me. He tilts his head to the side, staring at his detective, who's standing within arm's length of the dead body, service weapon in hand, covered in blowback from the killing shot. Not that he isn't sharp, but not a lot is left for the imagination; it's clear what went down here.

I can only hope he'll leave Cole out of it; he doesn't deserve to go down for something I chose to do. I bend down, slowly placing my gun on the cement floor. I lace my hands behind my head and spread my feet shoulder-width apart, knowing what's going to happen next. I spare a glance at him while I wait to be cuffed and put out of my misery. My breathing comes in rapid succession, and my head spins while I do my best not to pass out. He turns his entire body so he's facing me, holsters his weapon, and lets out a deep sigh.

"Put your arms down and help me with this sack of shit," he says, turning back to the body.

I watch slack-jawed when he pulls the blindfold off the man and leans down to begin untying his legs from the chair. What the fuck is he doing?

CHAPTER TWENTY-EIGHT

Two Become Three

Outside the warehouse, a pair of first responders sit with the two girls. They are now wrapped in large blankets and have been given something warm to drink. Chief Harding nods to the responders as we walk past them, making our way to where Cole is leaning against the chief's car and talking to a couple of officers. His gaze shifts from where the girls are being tended to up to meet mine. He doesn't look the least bit surprised that I'm not in handcuffs being hauled off to prison right now.

"Cole," Chief Harding says, nodding to him and waving the officers away, leaving the three of us alone.

"Chief Harding," Cole responds, turning his body to face us. "I was just telling those officers about what happened inside the warehouse. How that man was about to snap my neck until Detective Fairling intervened, shooting him in the head. If it wasn't for her, I'd be dead now."

Cole's eyes land on mine, and I know they must be bulging from their sockets. The chief nods at Cole while he places his large, warm hand on my shoulder and gives it a comforting squeeze.

"Why don't you take Detective Fairling back to the station while I finish up here. I'll meet you there shortly to take both of your official statements."

Not trusting my voice enough to speak, I just nod my head in agreement before I stumble toward the car Cole and I left parked in the next lot over. As I slide into the passenger seat of the car, my body begins to shake from the excess adrenaline I didn't burn through, and my teeth begin to chatter. I do my best to focus on my breathing while Cole gets into the driver's seat and starts the car. I shake out my arms and the shaking finally begins to subside. I'm left with a bone deep exhaustion and I let myself slump in the seat while we sit in the deafening silence of the car.

"Why did you do that?" I ask, squeezing my eyes shut so tight it causes colors to dance behind the lids. "Why did you both do that?" I open my eyes and watch Cole. He's staring straight ahead to where a police car containing the victims is pulling out of the parking lot and onto the road.

"Because, Jess, you've helped me to understand that in order to fight the monsters, you have to become a monster yourself." He turns toward me, making full eye contact, and I fidget slightly at the intensity of it. "But I know that you will find your way back. I know it because you're the strongest person I've ever met, and your moral compass shines brighter than any star in the sky."

With that, he faces forward, puts the car in gear, and drives us back to the station, leaving me to wonder if I really am as strong as he thinks.

Inside the station, Cole and I make our way to the Chief's office and wait for him to return to take our statements. I plop myself heavily in one of the chairs in front of his desk and Cole goes to get us some coffee from the break room, if that's what you can call the brownish sludge that comes out of that place. From my seat in the center of the office, I let my eyes wander the room until they settle on a large bookshelf that sits behind his desk, overflowing with books and messy, stacked up papers. In the midst of the chaos is a collage photo frame with four photos in it. I get up and make my way around his desk to get a closer look. For all the times I've sat in this office, I've somehow never noticed this frame before. Inside the collage frame are photos of Chief Harding; they appear to be from before he became the chief of detectives.

The first photo is him in his uniform with his arm around another man's shoulders. They both look young with vibrant smiles, and the shadows that now haunt his eyes are not present yet. The second photo is him, with the same man, standing next to a barbecue grill at a cookout. Both men are in T-shirts and shorts, toasting one another with hot dogs instead of drinks, sporting goofy grins. A smile sneaks across my face at the thought of Chief Harding so young and carefree. The third photo is, again, of him and the other man holding awards while at some formal- looking ceremony. They're wearing their full-dress uniforms for the event, standing arm in arm with two heavily made-up women in shimmering cocktail dresses, both men grinning ear to ear. The fourth and last photo almost takes my breath away. It's Chief Harding, standing in front of a casket holding a folded flag, the kind you get when your partner dies in the line of duty. As I lean closer to look at his face in the photo, I can see those shadows I'm so used to by now behind his eyes. I recognize that look for what it is, the haunted one that comes along with this job, the one you get when you see some shit you were never supposed to see.

My heart catches in my throat when Cole opens the door, startling me before he offers an apologetic smile and places the sorry excuse for coffee on the desk in front of where I was sitting. I take one last look at the photo frame and make a mental note to ask Chief Harding about these photos before I take my seat next to Cole. He watches me as I drink down the swill that passes for coffee in this precinct, probably trying to gauge where my crazy level is after this evening's events. I know, once Chief Harding gets here, we'll have to talk about what I've done. The last thing I want to do is have that conversation twice.

"I don't know who that is," I say, nodding toward to collage frame, hoping to steer whatever conversation we're going to have before the chief arrives in a different direction. Cole watches me momentarily before turning his head toward the frame and nodding.

"That was his partner, Marcus," he says, with a sad smile that causes tears to well up in my eyes, obscuring my vision.

My tears are not for Marcus, or even for Chief Harding. As sad as it is that his partner is dead, my tears are for me. They're because I don't know how I survived so long the way I was, never noticing or caring about anything outside myself.

Before I can get too deep into my pity party, Chief Harding swings the door open wide, then shuts it quickly. He sweeps around the desk, then takes a heavy seat in his chair, turning toward us and pulling out a notepad.

"Let's get this down on paper quickly, so we can go deal with the two girls from the crime scene. I've given strict orders no one is to question them but us," he says, giving Cole a look I can't even begin to decipher.

For the next half hour, I sit in a trance of some sort while they go over the details of the best way to explain what went down in the warehouse. They leave out the most damning part… the cold-blooded murder. The murder I committed, the murder I swore to my dead sister I would commit, that I carried through with, and they both helped me cover up. My attention finally comes back toward the end of the conversation.

"… the perp had his hands around my throat and was threatening to kill me. Detective Fairling did the only thing she could do in that situation; she saved my life by shooting him in the head," Cole finishes spinning whatever bullshit story they've just concocted as the chief scribes it down on a notepad.

I stare at the two men, my partner and my commanding officer. My emotions well inside as I realize these two men are giving me exactly what I need. Each one is loving me the best way they know how. Chief Harding, as my protector and teacher. Cole, as the only man who truly knows my darkest secrets and somehow sees a light inside me, anyway. Never in my wildest dreams could I have imagined what that could feel like to have people who truly care about you and unconditionally accept you. A smile splits across my face, and a feeling of calm courses through me. It makes my head feel a little tingly, and my chest feels warm.

"Cole caught the perp off guard, elbowing him in the ribs and causing him to release his hold just enough so he could duck down and give me a clear shot," I add.

I look over at the Chief as he makes the amendment to the statement while nodding his agreement. That addition not only explains why I didn't hesitate to shoot someone who was holding a hostage so close, but it also explains the broken ribs I gave him when I kicked him on the ground before tying him to the chair. Cole places his hand on my forearm and gives me a reassuring smile that I return. We're in this together now, the three of us. We've all wordlessly agreed to see this case to its end, and that's exactly what we're going to do. The Chief finishes scribbling down his account of things after he arrived at the warehouse while Cole and I sign off on our part of the report before we exit his office to interrogate the witnesses from the scene.

Outside the Chief's office, the bullpen is full of officers

who've just returned from the warehouse as they unpack their tactical gear that they gratefully didn't have a need for tonight. As soon as we get a few steps away from the doorway, they begin to clap and chant my name, like I'm some sort of hero. I pause briefly before raising my hands, offering them a bow and plaster a big smile on my face. I take a moment to wonder if they'd be cheering for me if they knew the truth about what happened in that warehouse. I conclude that, since most of these officers have been the ones to respond to the calls when each of the victim's bodies were called in, they would. People's morals are funny that way.

By the time we arrive in the interrogation room, both girls have been given sandwiches from the sub shop next door and coffees from the break room. They are wrapped in blankets and sit huddled so close in their chairs that they're touching from shoulder to ankle while they both eat their meals. Cole and I take the seats opposite them at the table while Chief Harding watches from the back corner, leaning against the door frame. We go over the basic questions, finding out what they remember about their captors and if they remember anything about what was done to them. Lucky for them, these girls were only picked up two days ago and didn't endure any testing or experimenting. Most of their time was spent sedated in a dank, quiet room with bags on their heads until they were moved to the warehouse where we found them; the worst thing they endured was hunger. They were also completely unaware of what went on in the other room and had nothing to add to our statement on what happened with the shooting.

The vise that had been squeezing around my chest lets up, allowing me to breathe a little easier. Of course, a small part of me hoped they would be able to offer us more information about their captors, but a bigger part of me held out hope that nothing horrific was done to them during their captivity. The best piece of information they had for us is that they were both from the same adoption agency. They were old enough to remember their time in the orphanage before being placed with their new families, along with its name and location. We leave the girls in the interrogation room with instructions for a couple of officers to contact their families so they can go safely home.

CHAPTER TWENTY-NINE
The Connection

Inside Chief Harding's office, I lay the case files across his messy desk and stack the adoption papers for each victim on top of their respective folders to show him what we've discovered. I step back and pull my hair at the roots before running my hands the rest of the way through the messy strands, hoping the bite of pain will focus my mind and I can come up with something, anything, since the first adoption agency is a dead end. Having closed down years ago, we could only collect an incomplete employee list with a few personnel files. Unfortunately, there wasn't anything useful in the files, nor was there anything that could tie the two agencies together.

Cole releases a heavy sigh from the seat next to where I'm standing, and my exhausted eyes make the journey from his crossed ankles up to the look of defeat in his own exhausted eyes. I hate that look and want to do whatever it takes to wipe it from his face. Unfortunately for me, the one thing I can think of to get us moving forward again and possibly offer us something fresh on the case is also the one thing that's going to get me in even deeper shit with Chief Harding.

"Okay," I say, before pausing to swallow the pooling saliva in my mouth. I turn to face Chief Harding, who's staring down at the documents in frustration before I admit another sin. "I may have done a thing we aren't supposed to do." I cringe as he looks up at me, a single bushy eyebrow lifting at my confession.

"Another thing?" Sarcasm drips from his words and he tilts his head to the side, waiting for me to continue. I ignore the jab.

"I may have met with an agent from the CIA to get the warehouse information." I grimace a little and chance a look at his face, finding a deep scowl. "I didn't ask for their involvement in the case. I know that's not my place. But the reality is, these guys all have heavy European accents, and the chance of them leaving the country now they know we're on to them is really high." I sit heavily in the chair next to Cole, while both their eyes track me. "We need help, help that has a bigger reach than we do."

Chief Harding sits in silence, taking in what I've just

confessed and my insides to riot with anxiety. I mentally go over all the reasons he should and could fire me right now. After what feels like an eternity, he closes his fist tightly on the desk and drops his shoulders in defeat.

"Okay, I get it. In any other circumstance, I'd be mad as hell," he says, shooting me a pointed look, making sure I understand how lucky I am. "But in this case, I have to agree with you. I just wish you would have cleared it with me *before* you did that."

He enunciates the word before, reminding me he's my superior, then looks at Cole, who nods back to him. It's starting to feel like they have their own inside language and I'm on the outside, stuck trying to translate it.

"We can reach back out to Liam and ask him to get officially involved in this case," Cole says, directly to the chief. The look I offer him is unfriendly. Since when does he get to suggest things like that?

"Do it," Chief Harding responds, sighing heavily. I give him a surprised look. That was far too easy to convince him of, especially when the suggestion didn't come from one of his detectives. "Just make sure you're involved every step of the way. I want to make sure this shit is seen to its end."

Then, surprising me even further, he gives me a knowing look. The look all but gives me permission to finish off the rest of my revenge. And just like that, I forget everything about the weirdness of whatever relationship has blossomed between him and Cole. Of course, I'm painfully aware adding the CIA into this case is dangerous for me; it brings in extra pairs of eyes that won't be as understanding of my previous condition. Not that I know him all that well, but I have a feeling Liam won't just ignore the death of a perpetrator, let alone four of them, murderers or not.

I'm left questioning if I can accept that, if I can accept the help that I know we desperately need, even though it could mean I may no longer get to be the judge, jury, and executioner to the remaining murderers. I come to the conclusion that I don't have much choice. My decision to see this to the bitter end comes with the very real possibility that I might have to sacrifice my own freedom or even my life, and I accept those terms. I nod my head, to no one in particular, and Cole sends a text off to Liam, making plans for us to meet with him tomorrow morning. Then, we collect every scrap of paper we have on these cases before we all go home.

I'm not surprised when sleep eludes me. I stare at my bedroom ceiling and listen to the sound of the seconds tick by from the clock on my kitchen wall. After all, how am I supposed to sleep when the backs of my eye-lids are painted the same red color of the blood that pooled under the man I murdered not twenty-four hours ago?

****

The diner is busy with the early morning rush when Cole and I take up residence in a booth in the back corner. I ask the waitress for a fresh pot of coffee and to be left alone once our companion arrives. She gives me a wary look before I place a fifty-dollar bill on the table next to my badge. Her eyes widen as she picks up the bill before sliding it into the pocket of her apron and nodding her understanding.

"Of course, Detective. My name is Ally. If you need anything, just holler," she offers before withdrawing herself and making her way to her next table, leaving us what privacy can be afforded in the back of a busy diner on a weekday as we wait for Liam.

He arrives a few minutes later and sets down his own folders of paperwork to share with us. He tells us that in our time apart, he's been looking into both of the adoption agencies. When I ask him how he knew about the second agency, he just gives me an incredulous look, like I shouldn't doubt his reach in the CIA. Of course, I know they have access to just about everything we do, which is normally very frustrating, but in this case, I suppose it saves us time. I briefly wonder how Chief

Harding would feel about that. Once he shares his latest information, we quickly go over the files Cole and I brought with us. I can only surmise, from Liam's lack of reaction, the information is nothing he doesn't already know. He's been thorough in his research, his reach affording him more information than we could dig up. The missing information gave him a link between the agencies, an overlap in both a family and an adoption agent.

"There have been four children adopted out to this particular family that have committed suicide. Four out of eight children in total," he says, placing four documents on the table in front of us. Skimming them, I see that two of the deaths happened at home, prompting a police report to be filed. The remaining two happened in a psychiatric facility, therefore not requiring a police report but only a death certificate, so no investigation. "The adoption agent for all eight of these children was the same person."

He points to a name on one of the police reports. My eyes widen. It can't be a coincidence that the same person is adopting out children to the same family from two different agencies, nor can it be a coincidence that four of them have committed suicide.

"Great, that sounds like a good lead for us to check up

on," I say, stuffing the files into my bag and standing to leave.

"Sit back down, Jess," Liam says at the end of a heavy sigh. My excitement fizzles as I sit back down to wait for him to tell me why we shouldn't be running to this person's house and arresting them on the spot. "That agent is dead. Heart attack a month ago."

"Yeah, because that doesn't sound suspicious," I say, my voice dripping with sarcasm. I arch an eyebrow before asking, "And the family?" Even though I know I don't need to. I somehow already know they'll also be unavailable. He nods, reading the look on my face.

"Fake name, fake address, no paper trails."

"Fuck!" I yell, causing other patrons of the diner to turn and give me nasty looks. I give them an apologetic wave and my face flushes pink. I wait to continue until they've all turned back to their own tables. "So, now what? How do we trace ghosts?" My voice comes out barely louder than a whisper.

"Well, remember how I told you I was tracing the shell corporation that rented out the warehouse in Red Hook?" He asks. I nod as a shiver passes over me, remembering all too well the warehouse and what I did inside it. "I finally got a name to attach to it."

My heart rate kicks up. Finally, something is going our

way.

"It pays to have informants in the banking business who owe you a few favors," he says with a cocky smirk, pleased at his own resourcefulness.

"I can only imagine," I say, laughing humorlessly.

"Anyway, this particular individual isn't the best at covering his trail and happens to have a private plane with documented flight plans to depart from a small airstrip about two hours North of here tonight at eleven," Liam says, his look turning lethal and causing goosebumps to make their way up my arms. "What do you say we give them a nice send-off?"

The answering smile that slips across my face is anything but warm, and Liam's eyes widen. My excitement causes me to forget for a moment that he doesn't know about me, about my previous mental state, or lack of mental state. I push the darkness inside me back down, but not before an idea begins to form, a stupid idea that could cost me everything but, in the end, would afford me the time I so desperately need to finish this. If we time it right, Cole and I can slip out without Liam and his agents, and I can finish this whole nightmare before anyone else has a chance to show up.

"I'll bring the champagne," I say, slipping back from the cold ledge I was just teetering on and adding a little warmth to my features with a smile.

"Perfect. I'll get everything set up on my end, and I'll be in touch when we have a plan together." His eyes linger on mine for a few more moments before he stands to shake my hand, then Cole's and leaves us alone in the diner.

As soon as Liam is out of sight, Cole turns his body toward mine and crowds me into the corner of the booth, making my pulse jump into my throat from his closeness. I have a brief moment to wonder what he's going to do this close to me in a crowded downtown diner before his low voice brings me back to reality.

"You better not be thinking what I think you are," he hisses.

His green eyes scrutinize my face as if he can see into my head and pluck out what's inside. His look tells me there's no sense lying to him because, somehow, he already knows exactly what I'm planning. I inhale sharply and give him my most innocent look.

"What would that be, Cole?" I ask. A shadow takes over his features, and his eyes leave my face.

"Fuck." He quietly curses and backs up from me. He shakes his head, probably realizing he's not going to be able to talk me out of this. "Let's go. We need to get back to Chief Harding to let him know we're planning on fucking over the CIA and hope he's on board with it."

A cold smile takes over my face and I feel the darkness begin pawing at the inside of my ribs. My partner knows me so well.

CHAPTER THIRTY

Dirt and Ash

We make the short walk back to the police station in silence, and my mind runs through all the reasons Cole should sit this out. After all, he's only supposed to be here to consult with me. It's not his job to put his life on the line to see this case through to the end. With only a block to go before we reach the station, I gently grab hold of his forearm to slow his progression, making him to stop. For a brief moment, I get lost in his moss-green eyes, staring down at me with concern and worry. It causes a part of me to pause and ask myself if I even want to go through with this plan. I shake those thoughts free; I have no option except to finish this, but he does.

"Cole, I need to know you're on board with this," I say, my hands lifting to stop him when he opens his mouth to respond. "Before you say anything, let me finish." His mouth snaps shut as he shifts on his feet and gives me his full attention. The seriousness of the situation dampens the normal effect his attention would have on me. "This is something that can completely destroy your career and also, most likely, get you thrown into prison or, worse, dead. I can't ask you to do this. In fact, I think I'm asking you *not* to do this. This is my vendetta, and no one else needs to be involved. I don't want to be responsible for destroying your life because of it."

I'm not even sure if I truly want him to agree with me. In the last few weeks, I've become so used to having him by my side that I can no longer imagine what it was like without him there. All my life, I've only ever been a lone wolf in both my personal life and career. That path served me well until my world went tits up with emotions and feelings and the man standing in front of me. I don't ever want to be alone again, but to save him, I will. He clasps my hand in his and pushes out a small, frustrated sigh.

"Jess…" he says, shaking his head and giving me a boyish smile that causes my insides to flip flop around like a fish out of water, as only he can do. "I would have thought what happened with the warehouse would have already answered this for you. I'm in this with you one hundred percent. You will not be finishing this without me by your side."

He squeezes my hands in his, sealing his fate with this vow. I take a deep breath, releasing the tension I was holding in my chest from expecting him to walk away and leave me to my fate. A million thoughts run through my head in this moment, a million things I want to say but don't know how. All I manage to squeak out is a meager "okay." Lame, I know. Turning back toward the precinct, I manage one step before halting in my tracks. Standing at the bottom of the stairs, patiently waiting for us to arrive, is Victor, the man from the marina.

"Shit," I breathe out, throwing a panicked look at Cole.

"What is it?" he asks, following my line of sight to the old man before giving me an alarmed look.

"That man there," I say, nodding toward Victor. "He's the one who's been sending me the letters and told me where to go when we went to my biological parents. That's Victor."

Cole's lips form an O of slight shock as he stares the old man down.

"What's he doing at the station?" he asks once he recovers, still eying Victor as he patiently waits for us to come over.

"I have no idea." I shake my head and continue the rest of the way to the precinct steps.

"Hi, Jessica." The way Victor says my name fondly

sounds as if we have some sort of personal connection. We don't.

"Detective Fairling," I say, my voice coming out unfriendly as I correct him. If my correction offends him at all, he doesn't show it. Instead, he offers his hand to Cole.

"Hi, I'm Dr. Victor Yates," he says, as Cole shakes his hand, giving him a distrusting look to go with it.

"What're you doing here, Victor?" I ask, crossing my arms and giving him another unwelcoming stare.

"I saw the news about the victims you recovered in the warehouse district, and I came to help. I brought some paperwork on the earlier trials that were performed that I think can help with reversing the effects on any of the survivors."

He offers a small notebook for my inspection, which I snatch from him and shove inside my bag, hiding it from view. I take a step back from him and quickly go over my options in my head while his beady eyes watch me from behind gold-framed glasses. He stands a step above me, wearing his beige windbreaker, like he did when he met me at the marina, where he cryptically gave me the breadcrumbs to find out about my parents. I may not like Victor, but he does have information I need. If he can help correct the wrongs that have been done to any future victims we find, and I can keep him close, then maybe I need to let him help us. Even if I don't exactly trust him.

"Okay, but we need to come up with some sort of cover for you," I say. His eyebrows raise in confusion. "I'm not ready for you to be locked away where I can't use the information you have while we're still looking for your partners."

"Ex-partners," he corrects, and I wave my hand at him in dismissal. I'm still certain he needs to answer for these crimes just as much as the rest of them.

"We should keep it as close to the truth as possible, just leave out the fact you're as guilty as the others." The look I give him begs for him to challenge me on that, but he doesn't. Maybe he's not so dumb after all. "You knew my biological parents. I found you when we went to Washington to gather more information on them. You studied genetics, have worked in labs and developed theories about this stuff. You want to help by offering up your previous expertise in the field." He nods, agreeing to the lie. "Okay then." I turn to Cole, who nods, also agreeing with the idea. "Great, now everyone's on the same page, let's go talk to Chief Harding," I say before turning to walk up the stairs into the station, trusting they're following me.

Victor sits inside the break room, where we set him up with a cup of coffee, while Cole and I meet with Chief Harding to go over our plans for later. He's surprisingly amenable to excluding the CIA from our plans, and it eases my anxiety about the entire thing. We all agree there's no option to take backup with us to the hangar, knowing that if I want to finish this the way I want to finish this, then Cole and I will have to go it alone.

I fumble through our fabricated story about Victor, leaving the details vague. The look Chief Harding gives me screams that he knows I'm full of shit. For some reason, he doesn't call me out on it and lets me keep up the charade. He also agrees with my plan to deliver Victor to Val at Fellmoor so he can work with Alicia and see if he truly can reverse whatever has been done with her genetics.

With his blessing, Cole and I walk Victor over to Fellmoor and Cole texts Val to let her know we're delivering some help for her shortly in the form of a scientist. As luck would have it, her schedule's open for the afternoon. I spend the rest of the walk reviewing the details of the concocted story with Victor, while stressing the importance of keeping it vague. Maybe I pepper in a few threats to his freedom, which I have no intention of letting him keep, no matter how much help he is to Val or the victims. I only let up when the deep scowl on his face solidifies that he understands I'm not someone to be fucked with.

Val meets us in the lobby and leads us back to her office, where she gestures for us to take the two seats in front of her desk and another to the right for Victor. After a tense moment, where everyone in the room just stares at each other expectantly, I start the conversation with introductions.

"Dr. Valerie Suarez, this is Dr. Victor Yates; he knew my biological parents. He studied and worked in the genetics field before his retirement. He's been following the cases via the media and believes he may be able to help Alicia. He believes he can possibly find a way to correct the modifications that were done to her genes by the experiments," I say, plastering a fake-as-shit smile on my face and doing my best to sell the lie to her.

"It's nice to meet you, Dr. Yates. I'm excited to learn what your expertise can contribute. This is a perplexing case that will be making medical history if you can do what you say." She smiles as she shakes Victor's hand. Her face doesn't show any inkling of knowing my story is complete bullshit, and I feel a pang of guilt about lying to her.

"You can call me Victor," he says, offering her a kind

smile that I want to smack off his face.

As far as I'm concerned, this man's not kind and he's as guilty as the others. I bare my teeth slightly, which no one seems to notice. Another wave of guilt flows over me about not disclosing his nature to Val before leaving him in her care. Logically, I know I can't risk it; it's a secret I have to keep for the moment. Besides, I doubt he can get into too much trouble inside a heavily guarded psychiatric facility. Cole stands up and places a hand on my shoulder, bringing me back from my musings.

"Thank you, Val. We have to run. We may have some movement on this case and need to get back to the station," he says, causing me to wonder when the hell he became so good at this.

Back outside, the sunlight soaks into my skin and I greedily haul in a deep breath of fresh air. If I don't get away with what I'm planning, I'm going to need the memories of these simple pleasures to get me by in the dark box they'll surely lock me in for the rest of my life. A heavy sigh escapes my lips and I turn my face to Cole as he patiently watches me.

"Are you certain this is what we want to do, Jess? It's not too late to change your mind. We can still go in as planned, with Liam and his unit."

Before I respond, I weigh that option, turning it over on

my tongue and feeling how it tastes. I could break my promise to Sarah to see this through to completion. I could let someone else deal with them, let the long arm of justice take over and place them in prison before they're offered a fair trial amongst seven of their peers. The only people who would be disappointed with me would be my dead sister and maybe Cole's sister, who's locked in a psychiatric ward. Honestly, with all the drugs they give her, would she even remember? Would she just be convinced our conversation was a figment of her imagination? Cole's valiant speech in the car outside the warehouse replays in my head, reminding me my integrity is what keeps me from slipping into the darkness and never returning. I shake my head, deciding that option tastes like dirt and ash.

"No, that's not an option. I'll see this through to the end, no matter what that looks like."

He reads through the lines and nods his understanding as we return to the station to collect our gear for tonight. Chief Harding is waiting when we arrive to usher us into the armory where the flak jackets and weapons are stored.

"Jessica," he says, handing over a jacket with a closed-lipped smile. "Cole." He nods, passing another to him. "I don't think I need to tell you to watch your asses." We both shake our heads no. "There's an unmarked silver Ford Mustang parked out back; it's typically used by vice when they go undercover." I give him a questioning look. "I think you're going to need something a little less conspicuous than a police cruiser."

I let out a small laugh. Nervousness coils around in my belly, something I'm not used to feeling before going out in the field. He steps between us and places one hand on my shoulder, the other on Cole's.

"I spoke with your CIA agent Liam a little while ago, let him know who I was and asked him to share his intel with me. He intends to head to the airstrip at nine-thirty tonight, hoping to use the element of surprise by showing up early. I assured him you would arrive at that time in a separate car from them to help make the final arrests. He agreed that was best."

"Thank you, Chief," I say.

I look into his eyes and see concern shining bright. He squeezes our shoulders one more time and walks out the door without another word, leaving us to finish securing ourselves in our vests and me to arm myself with the cache of weapons hanging on the far wall of the room.

CHAPTER THIRTY-ONE

Runway

I bounce on my toes in an effort to force the weight of the weapons and flak jacket to settle. The clock reads ten past five, and the airstrip is approximately two hours from the station. We need to get going if we're going to beat Liam and his agents there. Cole and I slip out the door into a surprisingly empty station and weave around the vacant desks, making our way out to the back parking lot. Somehow, we manage not to cross paths with any officers on our way; even the parking lot is vacant of its usual bustle of swarming people. There's only one person outside on a smoke break and talking on his cellphone. He pays no attention to us as we hop into the unmarked silver Mustang. Before I ease us out onto the road that will take us north to the airstrip, I take a moment to silently thank Chief Harding. I'm not sure how he did it, but I'm certain it was him that orchestrated our unnoticed departure from the station.

The drive north passes in record time, both Cole and I too deep in our thoughts for chit chat. In the final twenty minutes, I find myself gripping the steering wheel too tight and have to make a conscious effort to loosen my grip. My stomach is in a knot, and my breathing is shallow. I fight the telltale signs of anxiety from taking over my body. A wild laugh escapes as I think how the times when I need to be calm and clear-headed are the times my body doesn't want to cooperate. My mind wants to race around all the scenarios that may or may not happen instead of focusing on the present situation. I fail to see how it's helpful.

"How are you doing?" Cole asks, breaking the silence.

Concern drips from his voice. It shouldn't surprise me, since I'm currently gripping the steering wheel until my knuckles are white and laughing at nothing.

"I'm…" I pause and rein in my instant reaction to say fine, because I'm anything but fine. "Nervous…" I finally grit out, unhappy I have this feeling in my arsenal of new emotions. "I'm nervous and I hate it."

It's his turn to laugh, the masculine sound going straight through me and causing my already tense abdominal muscles to flutter. Thanks a lot, hormones.

This is *not* the time for that.

"I'm nervous, too. It's a normal human reaction. What I meant was, how are you doing with the plan?" Oh, of course, that's what he meant. I mentally smack myself for being too far inside my own head to realize. "Do you still want to go through with this, or do you want to wait for Liam? It's not too late to change your mind. We can stop here and wait until they arrive."

He sounds hopeful that I may have changed my mind on the drive. I haven't. I blow out a breath and nod rapidly without taking my eyes from the road in front of us.

"No, I'm in this until the end. My mind was made up when I sat at my sister's funeral, watching my eight-year-old nephew give a eulogy for a mother that'll never get to watch him graduate high school or go to college or get married." Tears begin to blur my vision, threatening to fall, and I don't have time for that. I blow out a heavy breath. "There's nothing that will stop me from finishing this."

"Alright," he agrees, fidgeting with his jacket and pulling the straps tight around his chest. "What exactly is the plan, then?"

"From what I saw on the map Liam showed us, there's a small, abandoned parking area about a mile down the road from the airstrip. We should park there. The tint on this car is dark enough that no one can see inside, and I doubt anyone will think much of it being there. Chief Harding was smart, having us take this car." I say, and Cole hums his approval. "The sun will be fully down in the next few minutes; we can use the cover of darkness to hide while we make our way through the cornfield next to the airstrip. I didn't see anything else on the map other than the small hangar and the strip, so my guess is there won't be much to conceal us once we exit the cover of the field. We'll have to be ready to move on them pretty much on arrival." I glance over at Cole. He looks nervous but nods his understanding. "From there, since I'm the one who is armed to the teeth, you should hang back behind me as backup. Just because none of them were armed in the warehouse in Red Hook, doesn't mean they'll make that mistake twice, especially after their buddy turned up dead." Bringing Cole with me wasn't the best idea. "Maybe you…" I don't get to finish my thought before he shoots me a murderous glare from his spot in the passenger seat.

"Don't even finish that sentence," he spits out, practically growling. "I've been by your side for all of this. By now I think you and I both know I won't be leaving it."

He continues to glare at me, challenging me to argue. Not going to lie, that murderous glare is doing things to me, things it shouldn't be doing right now. The conviction behind his eyes when he's passionate about something is a huge turn on for me.

"Okay. That's my plan, then."

I decide not to push the poor guy's buttons and make him even more anxious than he already is. He lets out a sigh before shaking out his hands in front of him, releasing the coiled-up energy he was gathering to fight with me in case I told him he shouldn't come to the airstrip.

"Alright then. We park in the abandoned lot, use the darkness to conceal our arrival through the cornfield, then you point a gun at them and yell some stuff while I have your back."

Now that he says it that way, I think maybe I should give him one of my weapons in case he really does need to have my back.

"Have you ever shot a gun before?" I ask, giving him a sideways glance.

"Yeah, once or twice in college. I know the basics: point the end that goes boom toward the bad guy and never take the safety off unless you intend to shoot it," he says, voice clipped, and I can't tell if he's being sarcastic or just nervous, so I let it go.

"Pretty much. I'll give you my personal weapon so you aren't completely unprotected. The plan will be not to have you take the safety off, but better safe than sorry," I say, knowing I can manage with one less gun. I packed a total of four on my body for this excursion.

"Okay," he agrees, pushing himself back in his seat and stretching his legs as much as he can in the footwell of the Mustang.

The abandoned parking lot creeps up on the left side of the road, and I turn into it, putting us all the way into the back corner. The spaces here are slightly hidden by the tall, unkempt cornfield. I shut the engine off and take a few deep breaths in the absolute pitch-black darkness of the cabin, thanks to the dark window tint. I wait for my pulse to slow down and my eyes to adjust until I can see the dim light from the nearby streetlamps filter in through the windshield. I start to see outlines of things through the windshield and reach up to turn off the cabin light so we can open the doors without lights blasting from the car.

Outside, we both walk around to the trunk, where I remove the gun from my ankle holster. I pull the clip out to check that it's full, even though I already know it is. I snap it back in place and pull the slide back to put a bullet in the chamber. I slide the safety back on before I hand it to Cole. He nods his understanding about where the safety is, then tucks the gun into the waistband of his jeans, under his belt. Then, I double-check the 9mm on my hip, making sure there's a bullet in the chamber, before I check the other two strapped under my arms on my flak jacket. Call me cautious, but I want to make sure we're both walking away from this airstrip alive tonight. Once I have all my weapons secured, we start the trek through the tall corn plants to the airstrip and hope it does its job of concealing our approach.

The airstrip isn't large at all; the small strip of tarmac is only a few hundred feet long. It would not give me the warm and fuzzies to be on a plane that's expected to take off from it. Not to mention, the lighting on the runway is almost non-existent. Dim yellow box lights pepper their way down the runway, not offering much in the way of visibility for the pilot. How anyone is comfortable taking off from here is beyond me. To the left is a small hangar that looks as if it could accommodate one small plane and a few pieces of luggage at best, the map Liam showed us made it look larger. Further left of that is a small dilapidated building that looks like it's no longer in use. Judging by the chunks of roof that are missing, it's most likely condemned—a shady airfield for shady scientists.

Pointing to the small plane on the runway, I nod my head toward it, making sure Cole sees where we're heading. A few lights shine from inside the plane, giving us a better view of the people standing around it. From this distance, I can't really see what they're doing, just that they're there and moving around. Ducking down to almost a crouch, we make our way around the backside of the hangar for cover.

"Since everyone is on the right side of the plane, along with most of the lighting, I think we should approach from the left side," I whisper to Cole, and he gives a thumbs up with a nod.

We quietly make our way to the other side of the hangar, where we can see around the building to try to get a better view. Unfortunately, the lighting is too dim to see much, and we are still a bit far from them, as well as on the opposite side of the plane. I assume the figures are all men, based on the stockiness of their builds and height. Excitement bubbles inside me as I count four of them, which is the exact number of people I'm looking for. I feel a spike of adrenaline hit my system, making my heart rate kick up in speed and pound loudly in my ears. This is so close to being over with.

A wave of lightheadedness washes over me from the pressure of the darkness pushing against my ribs. It claws and pushes to be released, to be let loose on the remaining people responsible for the death of my sister. I take a deep breath while I do my best to ignore the feeling and attempt to calm my heart rate. I signal to Cole that we're moving forward. Mercifully, no one notices the two shadows creeping out of the cornfield and up to the plane's tail.

As we get closer, I hear the men arguing loudly but I can't make out what they're saying. I strain my ears to listen, willing my heartbeat to calm down and quit its deafening pounding in my ears. It's no use; either we're still too far from them or they're speaking in a foreign language. No matter, the darkness and I don't care what they're yelling about. We just want to watch them bleed out on the tarmac beneath us. The thought of their warm, sticky blood leaking from their skulls makes my heart pound harder in my ears until it's all I can hear.

CHAPTER THIRTY-TWO

Monster in the dark

"Freeze, you pieces of shit!" I scream, my voice giving way at the end while I round the side of the plane to stand in front of them. They finally stop their incessant arguing as they each turn to stare at me. "Put your hands in the air where I can see them!"

They all raise their hands in the air, and I take a mental count of them: four men, eight hands in the air. Absolute perfection.

"Get on your knees," I order, my voice coming out in a frighteningly calm tone. They all obey and drop to their knees. The cold surge of power their submission brings helps to calm my nerves, and I can finally hear over my heartbeat again. In the quiet, I now understand this is what my bloodthirsty black soul has been dreaming of since this began. This is what the darkness inside has been clawing at me for. It desires this moment, when I get to put all of these fucks in hell where they belong.

"You can arrest us, but you and I both know we will not be charged with anything!" The man kneeling at the end of the right side of the line yells out at me. "You're just wasting everyone's time," he adds to the end of it. His voice is too calm, and it makes my inner monster twitch as my attention turns to him.

"Arrest you?" I ask. A cold smile slides across my lips, and I let the darkness seep into my eyes. "Who said anything about arresting you?"

I train the barrel of my 9mm at his head. The click of the safety turning off sends a thrill down my spine, and the pure fear in his eyes gives me a jolt of energy. The euphoric feeling of power coupled with the relief of no longer having to fight to keep the monster that lives inside me, that lately has done nothing but claw and bite at me to let it out, in check, is an addictive feeling. I can already tell this one time isn't going to be enough; we haven't even begun, and I already want more. I snarl at the man when he has the audacity to smirk at me, even with my gun pointed at his head. I make the decision that he will die last, after he watches me slaughter his friends. I slowly swing the barrel of my gun toward the man next to him, his sharp intake of breath like a live wire to my heart. Slowly, I move the barrel to the next man, whose eyes are fixed on the ground.

"Look at me, you piece of shit!" I scream.

His eyes snap to mine, letting me see his fear. An almost sensual caress slides through me, and I let that feeling do its best to fill the empty void that's forever in my heart to the brim. I turn my gun to the last and final man in the line. My eyes widen, and my gun wavers from the tremor that begins in my hand as I realize that I've fucked up. The tremor moves up from my hand into my arm as I realize the catastrophic mistake I've made, now understanding the smirk from the first man. The last and final man in the line isn't the fourth scientist. He's the fucking pilot.

My mind misfires as I stare at the man on his knees, emitting more fear than any of the other men while kneeling in a puddle of his own piss. The man on the other end of the line clears his throat, bringing my brain back, and I turn to look at him while he stands, brushing off his knees.

"Stand up!" he shouts at the other men who follow his order. I turn the gun on him, and he raises a hand in front of his face. "Before you get brave again, little mouse, you may want to turn around to see all the reasons you need to put that gun down."

His calm voice sends me into a spiral of panic, and I blink rapidly. Fear clutches my heart in a tight embrace before I slowly turn. My arm lowers to hang loosely beside me, barely gripping the gun. I already know what I'm going to find before I look. I look anyway to find the fourth scientist holding my own gun against Cole's temple.

My poor heart sputters to a stop, forcing me to let out a harsh breath of air and clutch my chest, willing the stupid thing to start beating again. It thumps slowly once. Twice. A third thump causes my body to violently shake from the left-over adrenaline it pumps through me. I drop the gun to the tarmac and raise my hands in front of me to show the man I'm unarmed. He shakes his head and begins walking forward with my gun still pressed against Cole's temple.

"I'm sorry, Jess. He came up from..." Cole doesn't get to finish his sentence because the man cracks the barrel of the gun against his mouth.

I watch as Cole's blood splatters on the ground in front of him, and it takes everything in me not to run to him. My inner darkness begs me to fight that man with bare hands and sharp teeth to get him away from Cole. It wants to devour him from the inside out.

"It's okay," I say, my voice barely above a whisper. "It's

going to be okay." I lie to Cole, as I turn back to the man who's clearly in charge. "What's your price?" I ask. He just smirks at me, causing my anger to simmer back to the surface. "What's your fucking price?!" I scream, my voice shaking with fear and anger.

"Him," he says, nodding toward Cole, and I flinch. "He's our ticket off this tarmac. He comes with us then when the CIA arrives, which they will in about…" He glances at his watch. "Twenty-five minutes, you'll keep them from interfering with our departure because if you don't…" He trails off, letting my imagination run rampant with dark thoughts.

How the fuck does he know about the CIA coming? My eyes dart back to the man who's holding Cole in time to see him push Cole up the boarding stairs and onto the plane. A feeling of utter helplessness washes over me while my eyes well with tears and my brain goes over every different scenario with its outcome. None of them end with Cole and I leaving here whole. He keeps Cole in front of his body, shielding himself from any shot I could take while keeping the barrel of the gun against Cole's temple. There's no way I could hope to take anyone out before he could shoot Cole through the head. This is so fucked—I am so fucked. Of all the things I thought of happening, I never once considered that they could take

Cole. How arrogant of me.

"What do you want with him besides your safe passage?" I ask, tearing my eyes away from Cole.

"He's my ticket to you doing what I say." The man gives me a cold smile, showing me I'm not the only monster on this tarmac. "I want nothing more with him, but I'm pretty sure I can find a use for him once we get where we're going."

He flicks his eyes to the man holding Cole, and the man pulls him the remainder of the way up the stairs inside the plane, where I can no longer see them. My limbs burn and itch with the need to run up the stairs after them. I fold my arms around my middle, holding myself together while the other men follow them onto the plane.

"You will not follow us, or I'll do unspeakable things to him, making the previous trials look like child's play," the man threatens as he takes his first steps onto the stairs, offering me his back, and showing me he knows exactly how fucked I am. He stops at the top of the stairs, turning toward me. "It was a shame we ended up killing your poor sister and not you. A clerical error by the man who spoke to her, believing her lies that she was you when she met with him." It feels as if my eyes are going to bulge out of their sockets. I try to piece together when the fuck they would have been able to speak to Sarah. "You can rest easy knowing he was dealt with for that mistake." His smile makes my stomach churn, and bile burns the back of my throat. "But now we know about you and that the expression was passed down to you by your parents. He did us a favor by not killing you. You can rest assured we won't be killing you, little mouse. You're far too useful to us."

My mouth drops open. Oh, fuck, they know about me. A cold chill up my spine causes me to tremble in place. Shit, that must be what Sarah was doing talking to them, trying to find a cure for me. The tears well up in my eyes, threatening to spill over again as I start to process that Sarah died because they thought she was me. I push the revelation deep down inside where I can come back to it for dissection later.

"We'll be in touch when we're ready for you, Jessica."

He closes the plane door as the pilot turns the plane toward the open runway and begins to take off. I stand on the tarmac, watching the plane's ascent into the eastern sky. Tears stream down my face as the tiny plane turns to the northeast, heading somewhere overseas with the one thing good to me in this world—the one thing I can honestly say I love in this world.

Love. What a strange thought.

I remain standing on the tarmac, staring into the sky until the lights of the small aircraft dim and become barely visible. A scream that's barely human rips out of me as I collapse onto my hands and knees on the tarmac. The darkness nudges me from inside, the pain forcing me to focus on my breathing.

Big breath in, big breath out. I hold it until my lungs scream for air, and I finally have the strength to stand.

I haul another big breath in and hold it in until my lungs scream in pain. I feel the tears stop falling and begin to dry on my cheeks.

"Detective!"

Someone yells behind me, but it barely registers, and I stare back up to the empty sky where I was last able to see the plane that just ripped my still beating heart from my chest.

I take another big breath in, and I hold it until my lungs ache, until my body stops shaking from adrenaline. I keep holding it until my heart stops pounding inside my ears, making it so I can hear again.

"Detective Fairling!"

The voice gets louder as they get closer, but I continue staring at the spot in the sky, continue feeling the cold darkness creeping into every cell in my body.

One more deep breath in and I hold it until I start to

see black spots creep in on the outside of my vision. I keep holding it until I can feel nothing but that cold dark place inside me, begging me to climb inside, and make a home. And that's what I do. I step into the void inside, into the darkness, letting it consume whatever tattered shreds are left of me. I wrap myself in it and surrender myself wholly to the monster that hunts other monsters with no code other than its own.

"For fuck's sake, Jessica!"

I finally turn to see Liam jogging across the small tarmac toward me with his weapon in hand, wearing a windbreaker over a flak jacket, much like mine, except instead of having NYPD on the chest, his has CIA. I stare at him blankly. Some tiny part of my brain tingles with the knowledge that there's some emotion I should be exhibiting, like it knows there's something I should be feeling other than the cripplingly cold darkness at this moment. I just can't seem to bring myself to give a shit. He makes his way to my side, staring up at the sky where I was looking just a moment ago.

"Where's Cole?" he asks, looking down into my face.

I slowly bring my eyes from before me to lock with his own. He must see the answer in them because he inhales sharply and immediately calls his other agents over. He speaks quickly to them, telling them to contact the office in Germany to make sure they have people on the ground in Munich when the plane arrives. The agents scatter to do what he's bid them, leaving him and me alone again on the tarmac, where I stare back into the empty sky.

"Why were you here so early?" he hisses, drawing my eyes back to his.

"They knew you were coming; they were trying to leave early," I say. My voice comes out calm and doesn't sound like my own. He stops his furious texting to look over at me briefly before returning to typing. "We need to get Cole back," I say, turning to start the trek through the cornfield, and back to the car.

Without Sarah, without Cole, there's no reason to leash the monster inside me. I have no guiding star to show me the end of the abyss and no shining light to show me which way is up from down.

There's nothing but darkness and, finally, in that moment, I let it consume me.

To be continued...

Acknowledgments

Thank you to everyone who supported me while I wrote this book. To those of you who believed that I could do it, and even those of you who didn't, well, I've done it, so I guess you were wrong.

A special thank you to my dad, the first person I call whenever I need advice. He always has the answers. Without him, I never would have started writing at such a young age. I love you dearly.

Thank you to my partner, my love, my person, my dear husband. Jon, you are better than any book husband could ever hope to be. I can't wait to grow old with you.

And finally, a very special thank you to my entire Bean Scene Street Team, you ladies are amazing and I love each and every one of you. Thank you for believing in me so fiercely, my little penguins.

About the Author

Amber De Torfino is a thriller author, with a love for all things true crime and mystery. Amber's passion for storytelling began at a young age, fueled by her curiosity and love of reading. When not weaving intricate tales, Amber can be found drinking copious amounts of coffee or with her head buried in a book. She uses her spare time to teach other aspiring authors about the process of writing, editing, and publishing their own works.

She lives and continues to write in North Carolina, with her amazingly supportive husband Jon and their mischievous black cat, Sammy. Amber loves hearing from her readers, you can connect with her on her website www.amberdetorfino.com, where you can join her newsletter for exclusive content, updates on upcoming releases, and find all of her social media outlets.

Printed in the USA
CPSIA information can be obtained
at www.ICGtesting.com
CBHW011950090924
14302CB00002B/2

9 798991 187602